The Sinking of Souls

Jean Paetkau

Contact
e: jeanworks@yahoo.ca
t: Snufflewort
i: Snufflewort_
f: facebook.com/Snufflewort

The Breakwater Mystery Series:

Blood on the Breakwater
The Sinking of Souls

Dedication

This story is dedicated to all cancer warriors.
We are strong. We are beautiful.
We are love.

And to the readers who took a chance on
Blood on the Breakwater and made it a bestseller.

Also, to those who lost their lives in the
1904 sinking of the *S.S. Clallam*
off the coast of Victoria.

And love always,
Jason
Laura
Andrea
Haley
&
Jacob

Chapter 1

It was with some regret that Helene plunged her ebony paddle through the unruffled surface of the Salish Sea, sending an echo of circles in all directions like an early warning system of her approach. She disliked having to disturb the pristine aquatic environment through which her sleek kayak glided. However, she knew that an intruder, no matter how stealthy, always left a trace. Even a nautical breeze altered the world when it made landfall, tickling castaway leaves into somersaults. But there was no wind to ripple the water into white waves that Saturday morning, as though the air currents had worked too hard at the office all week and needed a day to rest.

Helene had been taking a break during her solo morning paddling trip, resting her arms as she captured a few photographs of the Trial Islands from the vantage of her fibreglass vessel. She knew that the absence of strong waves was a rare occasion for this particular ocean bay. And the calm conditions made handling her camera while trying not to drop her paddle that much easier.

Looming tall over the bow of her kayak, the lighthouse rooted in the southern island's rocky terrain made a natural subject for photography. The vertical lines of the whitewashed edifice were a blanched silhouette against a cornflower blue sky—the structure as steadfast in its stillness as a woman waiting for her lover to return from the sea. However, the human eye was naturally drawn to the building's scarlet cupola, its contrasting colour meant to warn mariners of danger during the daytime when the sun muted the brightness of the lighthouse beam. While observing the oceanscape, Helene experienced a shudder of sadness for the lives lost at sea. Or perhaps it just was that she needed to get moving to keep the October chill at bay.

Helene knew this would probably be one of her last kayaking trips until spring; the West Coast winter rains and winds would soon arrive in earnest. She was going to miss the serenity and autonomy of paddling the craft, an activity she had only recently come to appreciate and eventually enjoy. Her interest in kayaking had started out as a sort of medicinal therapy, the sleek craft an antidote to her lifelong fear of water.

The terror she had experienced for decades at the prospect of travelling by a small boat was something for which she assumed there was no cure. The unfathomable depths of the ocean contained creatures and crevasses too numerous to catalogue and Helene found security in knowledge and understanding. That's partly why she had become a journalist: to break down a complicated issue into manageable, comprehensible parts. She also wanted to hold people accountable for their actions, like corrupt politicians and abusers of women and children. She even once helped catch a killer. And there was no denying that the ocean was a mass murderer who was never going to face trial.

However, the previous spring, after Helene had chosen to dive into the Pacific Ocean to escape a killer, she had undergone a frigid baptism that had delivered her from chronic fear. The fact that she had come so close to drowning but survived had somehow loosened the shackles of her watery terror, perhaps proving that imagination can be more menacing than the tangible.

And after freeing herself from her phobia, Helene wanted to make sure it didn't return. To this effect, she bought herself a sea kayak, attended a few safety lessons and began going out on the water at least once a month. This self-imposed regimen was modelled on immunotherapy, something she was offered after experiencing anaphylaxis in response to a wasp sting. The treatment involved desensitization to a life-threatening allergen by receiving weekly microdoses for many months. Ultimately, regular exposure to the allergen could prevent a serious reaction from reoccurring, but if too much time passed without exposure, the risk of anaphylaxis would increase again. Similarly, Helene assumed if she stayed away from boats for an extended period, the absence of familiarity might make space for her fear to grow once more, like an abandoned vessel on a seashore becoming a lair for pestilent rats.

Drawing her paddle through the water to position herself at the apex of the larger of the two islands, Helene took in the view from east to west. On her left, she could make out the faint outline of the snowcapped slopes of Mount Rainier across the Salish Sea. In the opposite direction, there was a vista of the rolling hills of Metchosin, a community that lay just outside the reach of the suburban contagion of Greater Victoria. Between these two points stretched the undulating American coastline, a visual reminder of the immutable bond between Canada and the U.S. In fact, the commonalities of coastal communities like Victoria, Seattle and even Portland was often considered stronger and more natural than any affinity to other Canadian cities, such as business-minded Calgary in the neighbouring prairie province of Alberta. The unconventional culture of the Pacific Northwest was in fact a sort of convention; the coastal lifestyles of restless people who had followed the sunset and their dreams until the land fell into the ocean.

The lighthouse itself was a symbol of the dependent relationship between the two countries, built to keep mariners safe no matter which flag their vessels flew. But the calm waters Helene was enjoying that morning belied the treacherous conditions a storm could create around the Trial Islands. There was a legacy of deadly shipwrecks in the 19th century, a caution to sailors who dared disregard the dangers of local riptides and reefs. Helene had not been brave enough to kayak in the area until she honed her skills over the summer. Even then, she always brought along her GPS tracker and kept her cellphone handy in a waterproof bag.

Of course, the downside of staying in touch with people on land was that they could also reach her. When the ringing of her cell phone shattered the meditative mood of her watery sojourn, Helene glanced down with chagrin to see her producer's name on the screen. Although she had lived on Vancouver Island for more than a decade, she was a very poor example of counterculture values as she couldn't escape work, even on a Saturday. Taking in the transcendent panoramic view one last time before answering the phone, she experienced a passing envy of the resident orcas surfacing somewhere in the endless sea, creatures whose only boss was the changing seasons.

"It's the weekend," Helene stated bluntly. She had known her producer for too many years to play the part of the obsequious employee.

"I know, and I'm sorry," responded Riya Patel, sounding more excited than apologetic. Helene knew that the head of Vancouver Island Radio must have a good reason for the interruption, not so much from respect for the journalist's need to relax but out of resistance to paying overtime.

"It's about a shipwreck," Riya continued in an uncharacteristically oblique manner, causing Helene to assume it was a metaphor for a newsroom emergency. She was wrong.

"There's a news conference about a shipwreck, well a book about a shipwreck! And it's in your neighbourhood so I thought you might want to pop in and check it out."

Helene didn't know if kayaking had exhausted her mind as well as her arms, but she needed more information.

"A shipwreck? Did it just happen?" The journalist glanced around as though expecting to see a tanker tilting into the water like a sequel to *Titanic*. However, the scene around her remained defiantly tranquil.

"Of course not. If it was breaking news, I would be calling Vancouver to get them to fly a reporter and camera over."

Helene decided to ignore the implied insult that serious journalists worked out of the mainland bureau. Admittedly, if a reporter wanted to get ahead in the media business, relocating to the island was not considered a strategic career move.

"It's about a disaster from more than a century ago, and a book that was written about it. By my favourite Victoria author, A.J. Beck."

Although Helene enjoyed a good page-turner, she failed to understand why anyone would be holding a press conference about a book. What kind of urgency could be connected to an author who died more than half a century ago?

"It's at Craigdarroch Castle. The press conference. This afternoon. I love A.J. Beck and I would obviously go myself, but I buggered my ankle," explained Riya.

"How did you do that?" Helene had never known her producer to exert herself at anything more than speed walking to the coffee machine, her unruly curls bouncing in sympathetic agitation.

"Pickleball! Thought I would give it a try since we keep doing stories about how damn popular it is. Turns out to be bloody dangerous too."

The thought of her boss dashing across a gym floor in baggy sweatpants and a faded Vancouver Island Radio T-shirt was so jarring, she almost dropped her paddle into the water. For some reason Helene also imagined Riya wearing a cherry red John McEnroe headband.

"I can hear you sneering," Riya muttered over the phone line.

"Not at all," replied Helene, trying to hold back a chuckle. "That's great. I mean, not that you hurt yourself, but that you're getting exercise." Helene thought she better change the subject before she said something that would require changing jobs.

"I'll make you a deal. It's Saturday, and I was planning to spend the afternoon with my kids. So, I'll go to the press conference at Craigdarroch Castle, if you really need me to, but only if my kids can come along. They've always wanted to see it."

"Your kids have an appreciation for late 19th century Canadian architecture?"

"More like they've never been in a place that looks like a real haunted house."

"That makes more sense," said Riya. "All right, it's a bit irregular, but I suppose since it's the weekend, I can let it slide. Just make sure you are the one asking questions about the shipwreck, not your kids."

Ending the call and putting the phone back into her waterproof bag, Helene drew her paddle swiftly through the water. She thought it would be fun to have her kids see her working, and it might inspire a little more respect for the radio news that currently elicited a chorus of groans when she turned it on during breakfast. Oscar was sure to be excited to hear about a local shipwreck and Cleo might be interested in the stories of those who lived in the so-called castle as she had been enjoying neo-Gothic vampire books recently.

As the late morning sun glinted off the wet blade of her paddle, drops of water reflected a prism of colour before being subsumed into a sapphire ocean once more. Helene was grateful she had been able to explore the serene shores of Ross Bay before spending the rest of the day indoors. Admittedly, it was unorthodox to drag her kids along to a work event, but the press conference wouldn't last very long. And after all, what could possibly go wrong?

Chapter 2

After passing through the angular front entrance of Craigdarroch Castle, Helene gazed upwards to admire the ornate and vertiginous stairway. The structure was crafted from a deep amber wood, creating a climbing spiral that was equal parts splendid and functional. The elegant undercarriage of each flight bore a dozen carved rectangles, ensuring the wealthy occupants never had to lay their eyes on an unadorned surface. The winding structure provided access to all four floors of the stately home which was practically a skyscraper by turn-of-the-century Victoria architectural standards. In a way, the white oak stairway embodied the restless dissatisfaction of the rich, not content to simply build their mansion on the highest land in the city, they had to extend their reach just that much further. Perhaps their vain attempts to reach Heaven was why God had visited such a plague of troubles on the Dunsmuir family.

The journalist had arrived at the castle museum for the press conference a few minutes early in order to give her children a short tour. They first peeked into the library on the ground floor, a smaller but cozy room in a home built by a wealthy coal baron more than a hundred years ago. One of the richest and most influential Canadian men at the time, Robert Dunsmuir died the year before the extravagant building was completed in 1890. He never had the chance to live in the luxurious mansion or sit in the well-appointed library to turn the pages of Charles Dickens' *Bleak House* by gilded candlelight.

Taking in the opulent chairs and stained-glass windows, Helene's teenage daughter Cleo seemed uncharacteristically overawed. The 14-year-old usually had an irreverent comment for every situation, but for once she simply gazed in ruminating silence, roaming from one ostentatious room to another. In contrast, Helene's son Oscar stayed close by her side, tightly gripping her hand. It was as though he was trying to restrain himself among the perilously expensive and breakable objects. The ornamented dwelling would have made an advent calendar of destruction for the violent characters from his favourite video game. Helene gave his sweaty palm a reassuring squeeze, recognizing the trepidation and self-control with which he moved across the creaking floors.

Cleo found her voice on the second floor when they were taking in one of the bedrooms of the Dunsmuir daughters. Positioned between a bed too small for 21st century sleepers and a fireplace too large for current climate change concerns, a mannequin stood in a light mint green dress trimmed by a fussy lace collar.

"Are you serious?" Cleo's voice contained both disgust and incredulity.

"What? You don't think Olivia Rodrigo would approve?" Helene inquired. The mother took great comfort in the fact that her daughter's favourite singer seemed more interested in being angry than being in love. It was an attitude she thought more women should adopt.

"If living in this mansion meant wearing that dress, you can count me out," Cleo stated flatly. And then another object caught her interest. "Was that used for scaring off vampires?"

Helene followed the direction of her daughter's gaze to spy a metallic contraption laying on the top of a dresser. At first it appeared to be a cross between a charm bracelet and a Swiss Army Knife, but a more studied examination revealed that the antique was composed of a hefty brooch to which a variety of items were fastened by thin chains.

"It's called a chatelaine." An enthusiastic museum docent had come up from behind. "It was a sort of tool kit for a Victorian woman. They could attach watches, sewing tools, perfumes or even a small knife. It was worn on the front of a dress. Very practical, but it was a status symbol too."

"So, bling," said Cleo thoughtfully, "but useful. I like it."

"Yes, exactly. Nineteenth century bling!" replied the docent, pleased to be making a connection with one of the younger visitors to the castle.

Smiling at the docent as she followed her daughter toward the stairs, Helene was grateful that her children always spoke to adults with confidence. Although perhaps it was a result of spending too much time with their mother instead of their peers. As a single parent, driving her kids to the homes of classmates after work was rarely something she had the time or energy to do.

When the trio arrived on the third floor, they gathered in the roped-off area of the Dunsmuir family's entertainment room. The cavernous chamber was dominated by a massive billiard table on which a half dozen balls were neatly arranged; it was as though the tableau was simply awaiting the return of players who were enjoying refreshments in the drawing room. An informational plaque explained that in the late 19th century, billiards was considered an appropriate distraction for upper-class women, but only if played at home to avoid the risk of gambling in public houses. To the left of the billiard table, sheet music was propped up on a piano stand, awaiting the perusal of a socialite trained to perform for potential suitors. There were other sources of diversion in the elegant space including a black phonograph and a telescope impotently aimed at a shuttered window. Helene thought there was something quite melancholy about turning a room designed for amusement into a permanently cheerless diorama.

"What's that?" Oscar asked in a hushed voice, pointing at a wooden antique resting on the seat of a silk couch. The letters of the alphabet had been inscribed onto a kidney-shaped board in a Baroque font.

It was only because Helene had watched the occasional 1980s horror movie that she was able to identify the object of her son's attention.

"That's a Ouija board."

"A wedgie board?" Oscar frowned in confusion while Cleo looked on in amusement.

"Ouija. People used it to talk to ghosts. Spirits. They would ask questions and the pointer spelled out a reply on the board. I know it seems odd, but at the time this home was built, that kind of thing was very popular. Something to do when you hung out with friends." Helene was not surprised her son was drawn to a communication tool used by clairvoyants. On previous occasions, Oscar had described having conversations with people who were no longer alive.

"Does that mean there are ghosts in the house?" Oscar asked as he glanced around the room.

"If there are, let's just hope they don't have to do their haunting in those itchy dresses," interjected Cleo.

Releasing a short chuckle, Helene mused, "Corsets aside, I wouldn't spend too much time feeling sorry for the women who lived in this house. My understanding is that the Dunsmuir daughters pretty much had free reign of the place. No men actually lived here besides their nephew Robert for a few months after he was orphaned."

Failing to be distracted by his mother's historical anecdotes, Oscar asked, "Are the ghosts happy?"

Helene was spared having to give her son a straight answer about the moods of the resident spirits by a booming voice calling down the staircase. Thankfully, the summoning to the press conference sounded more like the voice of a punctual god than a disembodied phantom.

As they made their way up to the fourth floor, the family paused on a generous landing which boasted a panoramic view of Victoria and beyond. Moving up next to a pane of glass, Helene briefly glanced down at the castle parking lot. Not normally afraid of heights, she experienced a brief dizzy spell at the sight of the uninterrupted drop. Scolding herself for entertaining morbid thoughts on such a beautiful day, she trailed her children up the stairs.

Arriving at the top floor of the house, Helene was impressed by the number of local reporters who had shown up. She guessed the appeal of writing a great weekend headline was stronger than the lure of sunshine on a Saturday. There were more than a dozen employees of local print and radio milling around, exchanging friendly pleasantries while their TV colleagues were busy trying to set up cameras for the best shot.

The press conference was being held in the rooms that had been used for balls and large social events during the reign of Queen Victoria. Three gowned mannequins with impossibly petite waists were clustered in a corner next to an antique upright piano. It wasn't difficult for Helene to imagine dancers sweeping across the now listing wooden floors, embroidered hems swaying to a popular waltz by candlelight. But she had learned on a previous tour that the voluminous space had also been used for more studious ventures. Decades after the Dunsmuir family fortunes had dwindled and the castle had been sold off, the building had been turned into a university. The dance hall had been converted to the Victoria College library, with notebooks to be scribbled in, rather than debutantes' dance cards. It was as though the room had repented its frivolous ways and converted to a scholastic existence.

Knowing that the press conference was about to begin, Helene shepherded her children past a second smaller stairway in the corner of the ballroom, presumably used by the Dunsmuir servants to ferry food from the kitchens. She claimed three chairs near the back and pulled out a pad and pen. The Dunsmuir house had not been wired for press conference audio feeds, so, to satisfy the radio format, she would have to do a quick one-on-one interview with a digital recorder once the presentation was done. She still had no real sense of the reason for the press conference, her producer's hints at a maritime disaster were intriguing but not particularly illuminating.

Along one wall of the musty room, a few people lingered who were clearly not journalists, lacking any paper or mini recorders for interviewing. A twitchy young man was wearing a thin but expensive looking down vest, designed for the rugged climates of restaurant patios. Helene decided he must be someone's assistant. Next to him stood a tall woman who appeared to be in her early 30s. Despite, or perhaps because of her short hair and drab straw-coloured sweater, she possessed a monkish aura, like someone who had given up material possessions to dedicate their life to a higher cause. A bit incongruous to the rest of the group, a matronly woman wore a 1960s floral button-down shirt and pleated slacks that appeared cheap and synthetic. She nervously clutched at a tattered paper like it was an amulet that must never be mislaid.

Helene wished she could whisper her quirky musings to her longtime friend Alex Chang, a journalist who worked for a local paper. Alex would have her own biting observations of the crowd, perceiving a neurosis from a relentlessly tapping leg or a frayed shirt cuff. However, the writer was on her honeymoon in Berlin, having married a detective Helene had introduced her to less than a year ago.

Contentedly uncoupled for the most part, Helene admittedly felt a little left out of the new marital arrangement. She had unconsciously assumed Alex would also always be single, her friend having only ever indulged in fleeting affairs with equally non-committal women since the two journalists had met more than a dozen years ago. And although Alex and Detective Karolina Kalinowski had fallen rapidly and deeply in love in a matter of months, Helene believed her friend had mostly agreed to the formal marriage to protest against the recent global rise in anti-queer sentiment. Whether it came to wearing an elegant Grace Kelly ensemble or defying bigots, her friend Alex liked to make a statement. And she had certainly done that when promenading down a lush garden path in a sleek white silk dress that made no allowance for breathing. Detective Kalinowski had sported a chocolate brown velvet suit tailored to show off her curves and any firearms she was packing.

Recollections of the bright summer wedding at the Abkhazi Garden in Victoria faded as the sound of shuffling at the front of the historic yet slightly dreary room indicated that the press conference was about to begin. Seeing that Oscar was intently playing his muted video game and confirming that Cleo was lost in the pages of her novel, Helene then focused her attention on the individuals standing near the microphone. Examining the faces more closely, she almost dropped her favourite pen at the jarring realization that the tall man enthusiastically grinning and even occasionally waving at the audience of journalists was none other than the tech guru Roddy Beck.

The dramatic increase in the clamour of conversation indicated that Helene's colleagues had also recognized the wealthy entrepreneur. Any remaining regrets among the reporters for giving up a leisurely Saturday afternoon for work had been vanquished as there was now a palpable excitement in the crowd. Helene could only wonder what Roddy Beck, a ruthless businessman who had recently developed a real estate app, was going to say about a book featuring a historic shipwreck. But of course, he was the great-grandson of the writer A.J. Beck, a woman who defied the corsets and other social dictates so reverently immortalized at Craigdarroch Castle.

January 8, 1904
Morning

When I first envisioned my escape from the jewelled cage that was my marriage, a boat had not been a method of contemplation. A dusty carriage, perhaps, rumbling down unfamiliar streets, or a soot-stained train even, thundering across an expansive prairie. However, when furtively examining a map by candlelight in my dressing room, it was the destination which ultimately dictated my means of transport. Vancouver Island, off the west coast of Canada, seemed almost a kingdom unto itself, with an ocean for borders. The Pacific waters would act the part of a yawning moat between myself and the one who would undoubtedly make a pursuit. And so, I settled on a ship as the vessel of my salvation, providing safe passage through a maritime portal to a new life.

I knew that I must draw as little attention as possible to my person while making the journey, and this would require an act of alchemy on my appearance. This was done easily enough by purchasing threadbare trousers and a shapeless coat at a market in the dockyards of Seattle. I was loath to give up my patent leather boots, as they were sturdy as well as comfortable, but a lowly deckhand might be arrested for theft if caught traipsing in the footwear of the upper classes. I did make a solemn promise to myself that I would visit a cobbler soon after finding shelter in the new country I wished to make my home. The final and most vital element of my costume was a frayed cap of checkered design. After first inspecting the item for any evidence of lice, I then affixed it to my head, knowing it must stay in place until the ship made landfall.

When I approached the S.S. Clallam docked in the Seattle harbour, it was a hive of activity. The crew was busy attending to last minute tasks before leaving port, rushing purposefully from one deck to another. In a more stately manner, the upper-class passengers made their way up the gangway followed by servants hoisting steamer trunks. The less wealthy travellers carried their own bags, but their burdens did nothing to diminish the excitement on their faces for the journey ahead.

The black-bottomed passenger ferry boasted two outdoor decks and a lower level with a line of windows out of which a head occasionally bobbed. I noted that the vessel was also equipped with a half-dozen lifeboats, a reassuring measure despite the short trip to Victoria via Port Townsend.

When the time of departure drew near, it was no great challenge to strike up a conversation with a sailor whose scruples were easily overcome by a flash of silver. I introduced myself as Bert, and he instructed me to grab a wooden crate and carry it up the gangway. I was only grateful the weight of my burden did not expose my lack of experience at any sort of menial labour. It was a reminder to keep my manicured hands out of sight as they would betray my rank as much as my knowledge of letters.

Although I was eager to go below deck and away from the crew's scrutiny, I did pause at the ship's railing to take in a curious scene. As a herd of sheep was being led along the dock to the gangway, the animal at the fore of the bleating throng unexpectedly froze in its tracks and refused to move. No amount of goading, even from the end of a switch, could alter the stubborn resolution of the moody mutton. When the vessel pulled away near 10 o'clock, the creature was left behind, apparently a landlubber in fleece. A few minutes passed before I heard one of the shiphands mutter that the defiance of this "bellwether" sheep, trained to lead the herd onboard, did not bode well for the voyage.

Determined not to let the inauspicious actions of the beast dampen my good spirits, I tried to shake off the memory, like sea spray from a lamb's wool coat. I ascribed any continued tightness in my chest to the long strips of cotton sheets with which I had bound my chest, to keep my breasts and fair sex a secret.

Chapter 3

"I want to thank all of you for coming here today, despite the vague invitation you received. But have no doubt, your nose for a good story will be amply rewarded."

Roddy Beck imparted a beneficent smile on the crowd that brought back Helene's childhood memories of a Mennonite pastor delivering promises of salvation from an austere wooden pulpit. And yet there was something perhaps more Catholic and papish in the blind reverence society offered up to dazzling tech geniuses like Beck. As someone who enjoyed the elite lifestyle of owning multiple sprawling homes in exclusive locations while maintaining a figure and face even better-manicured than their prairie-sized lawns, Beck embodied the aspirations of those who wanted their rewards in this life, not the next. And vanity had certainly been stricken from the list of venial sins.

Beck brushed back his lush salt-and-pepper hair with one hand, causing a pricey-looking wristwatch to catch a beam of sunlight from a window. He then launched once more into his prepared address.

"As you know, my family has a long and storied connection to the city of Victoria. This includes my uncle who died last year after a sudden heart attack at his home in Moss Bay. And his death was a great loss not only to me, but to the community he loved and served. He was a regular volunteer at the local library and he always helped out at holiday parades. My own parents died when I was young, and in many ways my uncle stepped in to teach me how to be a man and to lead a good life." Beck briefly paused as though to honour his uncle's memory with silence and then took a long drink from a glass of water. As the crowd seemed to hold their collective breath for him to begin speaking again, Helene thought the man was gifted at stagecraft as well as digital engineering.

"What some of you probably don't know is that the untimely death of my uncle has made me the guardian of my great-grandmother's legacy, including her home in James Bay. And I have spent the past year sorting through her house, trying to better organize the literary treasure she left behind." Somehow, despite his reverent tones, Helene suspected the wealthy man had paid assistants to go through any dusty crates.

"As Victoria's most celebrated writer, A.J. Beck penned hundreds of stories about life in the early 20th century. She wrote moving descriptions of how industrialization affected the men and women on this island—and transformed Victoria from a sleepy coastal town to a popular place to live and visit. She also had a deep affection for Craigdarroch Castle which was the site of a military hospital during the First World War. Her favourite nephew was badly injured in France, and he received both care and kindness from the staff. My great-grandmother would sometimes visit the patients and regale them with stories of island adventures, a boost to their morale which had been battered along with their bodies." Beck shared a magnanimous smile with the crowd, as though he could take some credit for his ancestor's compassion.

"Furthermore, unlike most writers of her time, my great-grandmother noted the destructive impact all this change was having on Indigenous Peoples. She was never able to get these stories published due to the racist attitudes of her time. However, I did recently discover a collection of them, along with a never-before-published full manuscript."

Beck took another dramatic pause, giving time for murmurs of astonishment to be shared among the audience. If she needed any more proof of the power of his charisma, Helene noted that both her children had put down their distractions and were waiting for Beck to continue.

"The story left behind by my great-grandmother recounts the ill-fated final journey of the *S.S. Clallam*. It is a little remembered maritime disaster that unfolded off the tip of Vancouver Island in January 1904. The tale is one of both wasteful death and secret survival. And the most astonishing revelation from the pages left behind is that my literary ancestor was a passenger on the doomed vessel!"

Astonished gasps escaped from many audience members, although Helene doubted they had ever heard of the *S.S. Clallam* before. As someone who had avoided travel by boat for most of her adult life, Helene was also disinclined toward stories featuring shipwrecks, whether in Hollywood films or history books. But like everyone else gathered on the top floor of Craigdarroch Castle, she wanted to know more.

"How do you know it's authentic?" The slightly nasal voice of rival radio reporter Gary Graham seemed to break the spell under which the room had been cast. Helene smiled at the predictable attempt to steal the spotlight by one of the few members of the local media for whom she had virtually no respect. Graham would have put his own great-grandmother on a sinking ship if it would have boosted his radio ratings. And his morning show was quite popular, proving the timeless appeal of scandals and half-truths.

But if Graham had hoped to unsettle Roddy Beck with the interruption, he was disappointed. The tech guru had taken the question in stride, almost seeming to welcome it. "That's the perfect segue for me to invite Professor Zofia Bosko to come up."

Stepping to the side of the podium, he made a beckoning motion toward the woman in the dull brown sweater who was standing amongst the collection of stray individuals at the far wall. From her hesitant walk to her rigid frown Helene assumed this woman disliked attention as much as Beck craved it.

Wincing as she leaned into the microphone, the professor said, "I am very pleased to be here today, and I want to thank Roddy for inviting me to be part of his discovery." If her mousy looks were anything to go by, the woman should have had a nervous and thin voice; weak in timbre as the speaker was timid in appearance. However, each word the academic spoke rang out like an individual sonorous bell, rich and complex, a dulcet chord rather than a single note. It was a voice, Helene noted, that would have been fabulous on the radio.

"Ever since childhood, I was entranced by the writings of A.J. Beck. Her gift for transporting the reader back to early 20th century Victoria. Her dedication to sharing the stories of bold women that would otherwise have been forgotten by history." The academic spoke with increasing passion as she delved into what were obviously familiar themes. "I am currently writing my own short treatise on her contribution to Canadian literature. A concise but hopefully definitive work on the genius of A.J. Beck." Zofia looked up at the crowd proudly, as though announcing the birth of a child in the coming months. When no spontaneous applause erupted, the academic carried on.

"I can therefore say with humble confidence, that I am one of, if not *the*, leading expert on the writings of A.J. Beck. That was, of course, why Roddy contacted me after uncovering what he believed was an unpublished novel." At this point the professor really was beaming like a proud new parent. She turned to Beck and nodded, which he took as a cue to reach into a box resting on one of the antique tables where he retrieved a ream of paper.

There was a stuttering of camera flashes as Roddy held out what appeared to be the newly discovered manuscript and artifact. The cream pages of the thick stack had curled edges and were held together by a faded blue ribbon.

24

Zofia had to raise her voice to be heard over the commotion in the room. "After spending almost a year studying this manuscript, comparing the lexicon and phrasing to the existing writings of A.J. Beck, even testing the paper for authenticity, I can, with near absolute certitude, state we have uncovered a new work by the late, great writer. And it is no exaggeration to say that this is one of the most exciting literary discoveries in the history of Canadian academia!"

Like island cougars stalking their prey, the journalists couldn't be restrained any longer, and they verbally pounced on Beck and Zofia with questions about the manuscript's provenance and contents. And as the demands for answers grew louder and more aggressive, Helene experienced a growing discomfort that her children were witness to the chaotic scene. When an angry voice rose above all the others, Helene knew it was time to get her children out of the room.

"LIAR! YOU ARE A LIAR! Claiming to care about history at the same time as destroying it for profit!" The woman in the floral blouse who had also been standing against the wall had stepped forward and was now shaking her fist in the direction of Roddy Beck.

Reaching for her phone, Helene gave thanks that her sister had recently moved to Victoria. As a single mother who was not used to depending on others, Helene hesitated only a moment before typing the request for help.

```
Can you pick up the kids?
Craigdarroch Castle
Please!
```

Helene did not have to wait long for a reply. Her sister Lela didn't turn off her phone even when sleeping, lest she miss a message on her dating app.

**just finished awesome yoga class
be there in 5**

Telling Oscar and Cleo to pack up their things, Helene stuffed her notepad and pen into her backpack. For their part, the children seemed disappointed to be leaving just as things were getting exciting.

Helene had hoped to keep their exit inconspicuous, escorting her own children out of a press conference was not how she wanted to be remembered as a journalist, but it was impossible to access the stairway without walking directly past the older woman who had only taken a brief pause from her tirade.

"You promised my husband and me that our home would be preserved by developers. You claimed they would simply build condos around it. That was in the agreement we signed. But two weeks after we moved out, our cherished home was a hole in the ground. And what's more, I know you couldn't have done this without the help of city councillors. You probably paid them off!"

The former homeowner was now waving the tattered paper in the air, possibly offering it as proof of her accusations.

As a journalist, Helene longed to stay in the room to discover if there was any truth to these allegations, but her protective instinct as a mother won out. Urging her children gently past the aggrieved individual and several castle staff members wearing black linen vests looking unsure about whether to intervene, Helene was relieved when they finally began their descent on the wide stairway. However, the woman's furious words echoed against the walls of the winding chamber, chasing them like an angry spirit who refused to be forgotten.

Tumbling out the castle's curved front door, Helene and her children blinked in the bright sunlight. The air seemed especially fresh after the slightly musty interior of the mansion. Just as they were getting their bearings outside, an elegant woman wearing a long camel-haired coat and matching suede boots rushed by and entered the building. Too well dressed to be a member of the press, a tech geek or even an academic, she appeared more like a modern descendant of the Dunsmuir family, showing up 120 years too late to claim the castle.

In an attempt to distract her children from what they had witnessed upstairs, Helene purposefully sang the wrong words to a pop song they both liked, and she managed to inspire a duet of protests. About five minutes passed before Lela pulled up in her cherry red SUV, the music from her own teenage years blasting from the open windows.

"Just have to pee. Drank a massive smoothie before yoga this morning. Love that wheatgrass!"

Wearing lavender leggings and a tight white tank top, her sister jumped out of the car and ran into the gift shop. The children got settled into the vehicle while waiting for their auntie to return from the bathroom. Another five minutes passed before Lela reappeared, lipstick freshly applied.

"Just drop them off at home. Cleo will figure out some dinner if they get hungry before I'm done here," instructed Helene, impatient to get back into the castle.

"Not a chance! Auntie Lela is taking them out for burgers and fries!"

Cleo looked at her mother and rolled her eyes. Helene just shrugged in response. Sometimes Lela embraced her part as the 'fun auntie' with the enthusiasm of a vaudeville actor, perhaps trying to make up for the years when she had lived in another province.

"OK but remember their allergies. Oscar needs a bun with no butter. And their EpiPens are in their backpacks."

Like their mother, both children had life-threatening allergies, Cleo to nuts and Oscar to dairy and bananas. Helene had recently shown her sister the method for injecting them with epinephrine in the case of anaphylaxis, but she wasn't entirely certain how well her carefree sibling would cope in an emergency. However, she knew that Cleo could handle almost any situation; living with anaphylaxis had made her kids grow up quickly.

Watching the crimson car take a tight corner in the castle parking lot at high speed, Helene tried to shake off feelings of apprehension. She had to work on trusting other people to take care of her children.

As she pulled out her phone to check the time, Helene wondered how events were unfolding indoors. Had the speakers gotten back on track, enlightening her colleagues with more intriguing details about the newly discovered manuscript? Or had the woman in the floral blouse derailed the press conference entirely with her accusations of unethical, if not illegal, behaviour by Roddy Beck? Either way, she didn't want to miss out on a moment more of a possibly memorable headline.

However, Helene needn't have worried about failing to be present for the day's biggest event. As she turned back toward the stone archway that sheltered the main entrance, a throaty scream erupted from the sky above. This was shortly followed by the horrendous thump of a heavy object slamming into the ground.

Tentatively peering around a classically carved column, Helene spied a body sprawled on the castle driveway from which blood was spreading. The smashed face of a designer wristwatch was all the confirmation she needed that Roddy Beck's time for making deals, honourable or not, had run out. Craigdarroch Castle had just added a new spirit to its collection.

28

Chapter 4

"What was the woman yelling about?"

"How Beck had let developers destroy her home."

"This was connected to the shipwreck story?"

"Not as far as I could tell."

"And where exactly did he fall from?"

"The police said it was the balcony outside the top landing. It's just above where the press conference was held, a small rotunda with stained glass windows and a narrow sort of deck. Not really meant for standing on." Helene was trying to paint a full picture of how events had unfolded at Craigdarroch Castle for her producer, but this was challenging considering her own absence from the final moments indoors.

Riya was sitting behind her office desk; her ankle was in a brace and propped up on a chair. Helene had asked how she was recovering, but the question was ignored as her boss demanded more details of the press conference that had ended in a death. The producer's own physical injury had done nothing to weaken her intellectual appetite for breaking news.

It was a Sunday morning in an otherwise empty office, even the normally relentlessly chattering radios and TVs had been turned off by the cleaners. Riya had insisted they meet to discuss the next phase in covering one of the most high-profile fatalities to have occurred in Victoria. The news of Roddy Beck's untimely demise was on the front cover of Canadian financial magazines and American celebrity gossip rags.

"But what about the shipwreck story? Where did Roddy Beck claim to have found the manuscript?"

"In the basement of his great-grandmother's house. In some crates no one had bothered to open for almost a hundred years." Helene had already shared this information with Riya, but either the excitement or the painkillers meant her producer needed to rehash the details.

"It was about the *S.S. Clallam*," Helene continued, "a ship I've never heard of. But I looked it up online and it was one of the deadliest maritime disasters in the area. It happened in 1904, in January, when it was sailing from Seattle to Victoria."

Riya held up her hand to indicate she needed a moment to think. Helene used the pause to check if there were any text messages from her children at home. But Oscar and Cleo seemed to be managing fine on their own.

"So, the way I see it, there are two stories we need to cover. First, the death of Roddy Beck and, second, the discovery of the manuscript. They're connected, obviously, but also each big enough to merit their own coverage." Riya adjusted her ankle slightly, wincing in pain as she asked, "Do you feel up to working on both, or should I ask for some backup from Vancouver?"

"No, I should be good," Helene said as casually as she could manage. "And since, as you say, the two are connected, it will save a lot of time not having to keep another reporter up to speed."

"OK, well if something changes, let me know." Riya replied without putting up a fight. This caused Helene to wonder if she might have been played, the producer only mentioning Vancouver to make her work harder. Either way, the last thing she wanted was someone from the mainland putting their byline on her story. As Riya had said, the two stories were both really big, and in the cutthroat world of media layoffs, she couldn't overlook a chance to boost her profile.

Helene was about to start sketching out her ideas for Monday's coverage: getting the latest information on Beck's death from the police, writing a short online profile on A.J. Beck to match the radio coverage. However, before she could explain her strategies to Riya, the newsroom's front door buzzer went off.

"Who the hell would be coming here on a Sunday?" Riya asked in a tone that bordered on outrage. Since her producer seemed a little off her game and every movement appeared to cause her pain, Helene opted to stand up and check the video screen in the corner of the room herself. The door security feature had been installed six months earlier when attacks on reporters and newsrooms had started to rise across Canada. All the station decals had also been removed from vehicles, an unsettling, if necessary, response to violent incidents.

Peering at the screen closely, recognition slowly dawning, Helene exclaimed, "It's the woman from the press conference. The professor. The one who's working with Roddy Beck on the book. *Was* working, I suppose, now that he's dead."

"What the hell are you waiting for?" demanded Riya, whose increasingly cranky mood had found a new target. Helene did not need to be told twice to leave the office; her producer's painkillers were definitely wearing off.

Grabbing her coat and backpack from her desk, Helene headed out the front door to find out why and how Professor Zofia Bosko had tracked her down.

However, a few minutes later, Helene was wondering whether inviting the academic to have a chat at a local cafe was the right decision. She was struggling to follow everything Bosko was saying over the din emanating from the espresso maker. But she knew that if she wanted someone to relax and share information, the scent of coffee and chocolate was more conducive to conversation than the dingy smell of printer ink and old carpet wafting through the newsroom.

Helene had ordered a plate of french fries, since it was almost lunchtime and the cafe made the string variety she preferred. Zofia declined to order any food and waved away Helene's offer to share the fries with a slightly nauseated look.

"I heard your piece on the radio this morning about Roddy being killed at the castle and then I realized you must have been one of the reporters who came to the press conference," said Bosko.

"Yes, I was there," responded Helene, not wanting to point out that she had actually been outside when the death had occurred. She had missed seeing important preceding events inside the castle, while of the tragedy itself, she had seen too much. With this thought, the image of the shattered and bloodied wristwatch briefly returned.

"Do you mind if we back things up a little," asked Helene, wanting to take control of the conversation. "How did you first get involved with Roddy Beck and the discovery of the manuscript?"

"As I said at the press conference, I am probably the leading expert on A.J. Beck. I've spent the last ten years reading and analyzing her writing, including a first edition of *An Island Lost*. I've also studied all the primary documents connected to her life. Everything from reviews in *The Daily Colonist* to her favourite recipe for scones. Not that she baked. That would have gone against her persona as an emancipated woman."

Helene sensed that Zofia could talk at length about the life and times of A.J. Beck in the early 20th century, but for as much as she appreciated the resonant pitch and timbre of the academic's voice, she didn't want to spend her entire Sunday on work. So, when the academic took a sip of coffee, she used the opportunity to bring the conversation around to more modern events.

"And so, Roddy approached you, knowing your reputation?"

"Yes, that's right," smiled Zofia, "And I can't tell you how excited I was to hear about the possibility of a previously unknown manuscript. I knew that if it turned out to be authentic, the ramifications could be profound." Zofia gazed off into the distance with unfocused eyes. "What would it add to the oeuvre of her work? How would it shift her standing as one of Canada's preeminent writers? What would we learn about the lives of protofeminist women inhabiting a society still very much rooted in colonialism?"

With growing exasperation, Helene realized that talking to the academic was very much like trying to keep a toddler on task. Zofia kept drifting off into abstract contemplations when the journalist needed a clear timeline and description of events. She decided skipping forward might help.

"Once you had authenticated the manuscript, what was the plan?"

"To publish, obviously. We wanted to share this new work by such a beloved writer with the world. And there was even talk of translations. Very few people know A.J. Beck has a strong following in Germany. There is a large fan club based out of Munich, of all places. My personal hope was that this novel would have brought people back to truly great literature. These days most bookstores only seem interested in selling biographies of movie stars. The more disreputable, the better."

"What can you tell me about the book, beyond that it features a shipwreck?" Helene asked, her curiosity piqued.

"I would really love to, but unfortunately, I signed a confidentiality clause which restricts me from revealing further details until Roddy publishes the book. Of course, as an academic dedicated to sharing knowledge, this went against my principles. But that was the price of being involved in the project. Now that Roddy's dead, I'm not sure what will happen."

Helene couldn't help but notice the affection in Bosko's voice when she repeatedly spoke the name "Roddy." It made her wonder how close the tech genius and the academic had become through their shared passion project.

"But if you can't tell me more about the book, and everything seems to be on hold, then why did you want to speak to me today?"

Zofia looked at Helene as though the journalist was a pupil who was failing to live up to expectations.

"Because he was murdered. And I want you to catch the killer."

Glad that she didn't have a mouthful of coffee to spit out in surprise, Helene decided she needed to get the facts straight before considering any allegations of murder. Taking out her notebook, she asked Bosko to describe how the press conference had unfolded after the woman in the floral blouse had started shouting.

Zofia said that Beck had tried to assure the woman who had caused the disturbance that he would speak to her after the event was finished, but she wouldn't be placated. As she continued to spout accusations, Beck eventually gave up and told the journalists he would send out a detailed press release about the A.J. Beck book later that day. At that point everyone began to disperse from the top floor of the mansion, although a few journalists did attempt to interview the woman who had caused the disturbance. However, once Beck had left the space, she seemed to have lost the fuel for her vitriol. Zofia specifically recalled the sight of the woman making her way down the expansive stairwell, now looking deflated and quite elderly. Despite the woman's accusations, Zofia was adamant Roddy would never be involved in any shady deals. The academic seemed to believe that people who cared about great literature were incapable of unethical behaviour. As a journalist, Helene had no such illusions.

What Zofia could not recall was exactly where Beck had disappeared to after the press conference was cut short. She had given a few brief interviews to journalists, but again was limited by the confidentiality agreement. She thought around ten minutes had passed from the time the microphones had been turned off until the wretched scream echoed from outside the building's north-facing wall. Then there was a crush of bodies as the few people remaining on the fourth floor tried to make their way downstairs as quickly as possible.

Wanting to get ahead of the crowd, Zofia had used the servant's staircase, passing by the kitchens and the family smoking room in the attached wing of the house. Using this means of descent, she managed to reach the body before the rest of the crowd had exited the building. Helene did vaguely recall the academic running up and kneeling next to Roddy's body. What she hadn't realized was that Zofia had discovered a piece of paper clasped in her friend's lifeless fingers before surreptitiously grabbing it and tucking it away.

While the coffee shop conversations blithely continued around them, Zofia held out a blood-stained paper, indicating that Helene should take it.

Before accepting the offering, Helene asked, "But why are you giving this paper to me and not the police? It might help with the investigation into Roddy's death." After working with Detective Kalinowski to solve a murder connected to the art world, she appreciated the need for preserving the chain of evidence.

"Police?" Zofia gave Helene a withering glare. "I was taught not to trust the police. My mother escaped from Soviet-controlled Poland and she knew the milicja were as corrupt as the leaders giving orders from the Kremlin. They say it is better in Canada, but I don't believe it. Look how they treated the First Nations people. No, journalists were the only ones brave enough to speak the truth under

Communist oppression. And this hasn't changed. They will tell the real story, no matter the cost."

Although flattered by the academic's high opinion of journalists, Helene knew that these days many of her colleagues were more concerned about hanging onto their jobs than holding people in power to account. But she decided this overestimation of the media's moral uprightness might work to her immediate advantage.

Reaching forward she claimed the proffered paper, gingerly pulled back sides made stiff with blood and read the scrawled message.

Meet me on the fourth floor landing
after the press conference
or I will tell her everything.

Chapter 5

The crisp autumn sun which had made the ocean glisten during Helene's Saturday kayaking venture had been usurped by a wash of grey cloud by Sunday evening. And when Helene peered out her bedroom window the following morning, it was to the sight of wooden James Bay houses shrouded in a ponderous, melancholy fog. It was as though her neighbourhood was a Victorian widow who had donned mourning weeds overnight, and she wondered if the impressive influence of Roddy Beck, in death and as in life, extended to the weather.

It was only after she had made her way upstairs that Helene remembered her children were off from school. Their teachers had a professional development day, which Helene hoped was code for drinking beer in bathrobes. She had taught social studies in her early 30s at a small high school in California before deciding journalism would be a more fulfilling career, and she maintained infinite respect for the combination of inspired theatrics and beatific patience teachers employed to keep two dozen teenagers interested in topics like the Industrial Revolution.

As far as her own children were concerned, she knew they were going to use the break from schoolwork to hone their proficiency in video games and scanning social media. Despite being slightly frustrated at the sight of Oscar and Cleo staring into screens at 7 a.m., Helene appreciated not having to pack lunches and drive them to school. She decided to instead enjoy the extra time before work to walk the breakwater, a routine which had been neglected during the summer months of kayaking. Although the dense fog had smothered the sunrise, Helene still brought along her camera as a companion, more out of habit than any hope of capturing a stunning composition.

Making her way along the wide oceanside path, Helene could only see about 50 feet ahead. To the south, the Washington State coastline was masked by clouds scaffolding from the leaden sky to the languid ocean. Along the sidewalk ahead, lampposts cast eerie, bright spheres, like stage spotlights in a grim Dickensian play. When she finally arrived at the start of the breakwater, the narrow track faded into the fog, as if the water droplets had dissolved the edifice of granite and concrete.

In the end, Helene was glad to have brought along her camera. Although there was no sunrise to infuse clouds with vivid shades of rose like a sky painted by Monet, stark shadows created gloomy tableaus that were equally captivating. The ribs of the breakwater railings cast dark stripes along the path until they converged into the mist like a portal to another kingdom which only opened under sunless skies.

Walking at a moderate pace, it took Helene about 15 minutes to reach the end of the breakwater, a square platform dominated by a lighthouse flashing a crimson warning to mariners. Switching her camera to black and white, Helene took a few shots of the harbour pilot's boat heading out to guide a tanker into safe harbour; their navigational skills would be put to the test in such low visibility.

Handling her camera with bare hands, her fingers quickly grew stiff from the cold, bringing back memories of her frigid plunge into these same waters the previous spring. She had been trying to escape a killer whose body had not been retrieved by the Coast Guard. Helene imagined the bones were now resting on the ocean floor, never to be properly buried or mourned. Thankfully, her unsettling recollections of struggling to reach the water's surface for air were cut short by a text message notification.

```
New council meeting on housing
Thursday 10:30
Reax to accusations at press
conference?
Get digging
```

Embracing the distraction, Helene replied immediately, typing on her phone with numb fingers.

```
No Problem
Will drop by city hall today
See who will talk
Also check for police update
Murder? Accident?
```

During their discussion at the cafe on Sunday, Zofia had done her best to persuade Helene that Beck's death was suspicious. But the journalist was going to need more than a scrap of paper containing an ambiguous message to be convinced a crime had taken place at the castle. Raised by academics in Alberta, Helene knew that entire university careers could be built on a unique interpretation of one medieval text. Journalists, on the other hand, needed more than the divine musings of a 16th century monk drunk on honey mead before letting an article go to print. Having at least two sources for a story was one way to prevent ending up in court facing charges of libel.

Less than an hour later, after ensuring her children had enough food to survive for the day, Helene drove down Victoria's Government Street at low speed. The narrow road, which became pedestrian-only at noon, was like the spine of the downtown core. The busiest stores and most popular pubs lined the route, attracting both locals and tourists in search of everything from Cowichan sweaters to island-distilled gin. The buildings were brick and Colonial in

39

style, allowing visitors to enjoy a European atmosphere without the bother of a transatlantic flight.

In contrast, Victoria City Hall, which was near the end of the trendy shopping district, was an unattractive memorial to the curves and stucco characteristic of the 1960s. The front courtyard held a fountain composed of a circular base surrounding three towering, bronze-flecked sculptures reminiscent of Stonehenge. Although probably much celebrated in an era of miniskirts and lava lamps, the fixtures now looked dated and grubby. Numerous proposals had been put forward to beautify the entire rotunda and to make it more inviting to the community. Helene thought what the space needed was not so much a redesign as a makeover courtesy of a bulldozer. But leveling the place was far more efficient than anything city council could dream up.

Having parked her car, Helene stood in front of City Hall, unsure how to begin her investigation into any questionable activities connected to housing developments. Opportunity struck when she spotted a city councillor heading toward the front doors.

"Good morning, Rupert," Helene said cheerfully, cringing at her own false bonhomie.

Not slowing his pace, the municipal official gave her an annoyed sidelong glance, but then recognizing the journalist, came to a halt. As much as reporters needed politicians to agree to interviews for their stories, politicians needed journalists to keep their names in the headlines. Councillors whose faces were familiar to voters tended to be returned to office in the next election.

In his mid-30s, Rupert Davies was one of the younger members of council. He possessed a thatch of dark hair untouched by grey, and a beard, which he kept stylishly trimmed. He also walked with a cane, an implement which could either be an aid or a weapon. Possessing a charisma that made him popular with both older and more youthful voters, he was generally unflustered by questions from the media.

Helene knew she couldn't maintain the attention of the busy and popular councillor for very long, so she pulled out her mini-recorder and cut to the chase.

"I understand a meeting on approvals for new homes was announced at the last minute. Is this in response to concerns raised at the press conference on Saturday? The one where Roddy Beck died?"

"First of all, let me express my condolences to the Beck family. Such a devastating loss, especially after the death of his uncle last year. I am personally going to ensure the flag is lowered to half-mast this week to honour the contributions of such an important community leader."

Davies spoke in elegant phrases that seemed geared to a crowd rather than a singular journalist. Helene suspected the councillor was hoping to find himself quoted in the afternoon newscast.

"I do, however, take issue with your use of the words 'last minute.' Unexpected business has come up, so we will gather to discuss it in a timely manner. That is often the work of council."

Helene was impressed by the politician's ability to find fault with her phrasing as a way to avoid talking about the issue at hand. The journalist was not put off by this classic technique in media manipulation.

"But do you think it's possible that some housing projects have been rushed? And rules have been overlooked or broken? And what about the allegations of corruption on council?"

In replying, Davies made no attempt to mask his exasperation. "As you are well aware, we are in the midst of a housing crisis. New rental stock is desperately needed to meet growing demands. However, I have made it clear in my work as councillor, that the needs and wishes of the current residents must be considered. It is not fair to change

41

the nature of a community without the input of that community." Raising his cane to provide extra emphasis to his final declaration, Davies then made noises about not wanting to be late for a meeting.

Watching the tail of the councillor's long wool coat billow in the breeze of the front door, not unlike a king's cape, Helene suspected she had just witnessed an early election speech for a run at the mayor's office.

She couldn't help but feel frustrated by the exchange. In terms of offering clarity around issues connected to dodgy housing approvals or how Beck might have been involved, the councillor's answers were as obfuscating as the fog that had engulfed the breakwater that morning.

As if to provide the journalist some encouragement in uncovering the truth, a brilliant beam of sunlight momentarily broke through the cloud cover and illuminated the refuse marring the City Hall square like blemishes on the face of a town famous for its beauty.

Chapter 6

"I called ahead and made an appointment. I just don't remember the name of the person I talked to."

Helene knew she was telling a lie. The receptionist knew she was telling a lie. But thankfully, social conventions disallowed the young woman in a cream sweater and plaid skirt from challenging the journalist.

Helene had not bothered to try to arrange an interview before driving to the headquarters of RoddTek Inc., located near the airport in Sidney. After the loss of their CEO, any media request would have been turned down over the phone, so Helene showed up in person as it was always harder for people to say no face-to-face. And now that she had spoken an untruth, she decided to dig in. Half-measures were not the way to get things done.

"I had arranged to speak with Roddy Beck's assistant. Or, former assistant, I guess. My boss wants me to write an article about your boss and I need some background on the apps he created. Not really my area of expertise. More used to covering stories about bike lanes and baby orcas." Offering a guileless smile, Helene sensed she might be overdoing the part of a small-town reporter who is out of her depth. In response to the journalist's entreaty, the receptionist merely raised her eyebrows and picked up a blue phone receiver.

Ten minutes earlier, when Helene had turned off the highway and driven up to the monolith of blue reflective glass, she was impressed by the titanic dimensions of the corporate headquarters needed to run something as nonmaterial as an app. Used to working in newsrooms that no longer even offered free coffee to staff, she found the largesse of the operation impressive if not disheartening.

The appetite for accurate news coverage had been replaced by an addiction to downloading the latest shopping apps.

"Ameer says he can give you five minutes," the receptionist eventually conceded after replacing the phone receiver. She handed Helene a guest pass and led her to a row of elevators.

A short vertical journey in the mirrored compartment brought her to an impressive hallway of offices. The door that was her destination opened with a barely audible swoosh, revealing a room lined with a plush beige carpet that swallowed the sound of footsteps. Behind an imposing walnut desk stood the young man Helene had seen loitering at the edge of the press conference. He was now wearing a thin, baby blue sweater vest that managed to look both casual and very expensive, but his ruffled dark hair stuck out in odd directions, belying any attempt to appear untroubled by recent events. The nameplate on the desk read *Roddy Beck, CEO,* so the assistant must be minding the throne while the corporate jockeying ensued.

"Ameer," the young man introduced himself while standing up, motioning for Helene to take a seat on a wide couch. Sinking several inches into the soft leather cushions, the journalist immediately regretted her decision. She now felt at a serious disadvantage in terms of height, it was hard to grill someone with questions when they were looming over you. From the thick carpet to the matching beige walls, the room seemed designed to soothe. Perhaps to keep employees and prospective business partners off guard.

"Thank you for seeing me," said Helene before placing her backpack on the couch next to her. "I have a few questions that I was hoping you could answer."

"I'll help, if I can," replied Ameer affably. He then pulled the chair around the desk and sat down across from Helene. Even though he was no longer on his feet, the journalist still had to look up to meet his gaze.

"I'm doing a short biography for the radio about Roddy. And I need to have a better understanding of his contributions to the world of technology. I believe the real estate app, HomeHitch, was his latest venture. What exactly did it do?"

Ameer sat back in his chair, as though relieved the journalist was not going to ask more difficult questions. Describing the function of the company's cash cow was comfortable territory for the assistant. What he didn't realize was the journalist also had ways of soothing people into dropping their defences.

"As you know, there simply isn't enough housing on the island for all the people who want to live here. The rental vacancy rate is incredibly low and homelessness is on the rise. And as I am sure you are also aware, there is a vast population of baby boomers living in large houses in neighbourhoods like Moss Bay, often alone. These folks are getting to the time in their lives when they may want to downsize, even move into a retirement home. Now as the city pushes to remove red tape and zoning restrictions to speed up the construction of new housing, developers are hungry to find single family lots that could be turned into duplexes or even sixplexes. That's where we come in. We want to take the stress out of connecting homeowners with developers. To do that, we created an app where people can enter the details of their property, and then the property developers can go through the listings and find a good match for their project. It's a win-win for everyone."

"It didn't sound like a win-win for the woman who spoke up at the press conference," said Helene while smiling like she had complimented his aftershave.

In response, Ameer sat upright in his chair. He seemed suddenly aware that there was an intruder in the room. Like a rodent that had been discovered chewing on wires. For Helene's part, making people uncomfortable meant she was doing her job. She also knew that Ameer couldn't immediately throw her out of the building, not without looking like he was guilty of something worth investigating.

"We intend to speak with Mrs. Fernandez and follow up on her concerns," declared Ameer, not realizing he had given Helene the name of the woman in question. The journalist tucked away the nugget of knowledge for future research while the assistant continued his retort. "However, as you can imagine, Roddy's death has created more pressing issues. Like, who will fill in until a new CEO is appointed? And, anyway, I thought you were here to talk about his legacy. Not unfounded allegations made by a lonely senior citizen probably just looking for attention."

"So, tell me about the app. Did Roddy create it himself or did he have support of a wider team? How much of a genius was he?"

Helene's intention was to mollify the assistant with a bit of flattery for his dead boss, however, her words seemed to have the opposite effect. He immediately got up and started pacing the carpeted room.

"We are a team here at RoddTek. One person may have an innovative idea, but many individuals will contribute to its creation. That was Roddy's philosophy."

Helene was tempted to point out that Roddy was the only one whose face was featured on the front of magazines after the launch of an app, and she couldn't recall any mention of a "team" in magazine articles. But before she could speak again, the office door swung open and the elegant woman in the camel coat who had shown up late to the castle press conference walked in. Standing with her back to Helene, her blonde hair reached just past her shoulders, silky and unruffled. She was the kind of woman who made other women hate themselves.

"What are you doing in this office?" she asked Ameer point-blank.

"I'm trying to keep things going," he replied. "The company doesn't just stop because Roddy is dead."

"Well, that's my job now, as he left everything to me." The woman announced smugly.

Ameer looked at her in disbelief. "But that's not possible. That's not what Roddy promised. And anyway, you're divorced!"

Helene finally made the connection between the beautiful woman and the wealthy entrepreneur, recalling a lavish wedding on a private beach in Hawaii in the 1990s.

"Yes, but the papers had not yet been signed. So, it all still comes to me. Including whatever happens with that ridiculous old story he uncovered. As if Roddy cared about books! His idea of reading was the *Golfing News*."

"But I've been a key player in this company for over a decade!"

"And I'm the one who put in the initial funding. Just after Roddy left university."

It was exciting for Helene to have a courtside seat to the corporate squabble; usually she had to make do with sanitized press releases. But her focus on the hostile exchange meant that she didn't immediately realize her phone was ringing. Scrambling to reject the call, Helene had not been fast enough and when she looked back up, the glamorous visitor was glaring in her direction.

"Who the hell are you?"

"Helene Unger, Vancouver Island Radio."

"Jesus Christ, you're with the press?"

Helene smiled and decided to push her luck. "Yes, I am. And in the wake of your husband's death, would you like to make a statement?"

The woman simply scowled at Helene and then turned back to Ameer. "I'll talk to you later."

As abruptly as she had arrived, the woman exited the room, leaving a trail of expensive perfume in her wake.

"I should probably go too," said Helene, knowing she had witnessed more than she was supposed to.

Not yet recovered from the encounter with Roddy's almost-ex-wife and her announcement, Ameer just nodded in response.

Pushing open the heavy office door, Helene couldn't help but wonder what it would be like to be wealthy and dead, having family and colleagues fight over your fortune like they are facing homelessness. The one advantage of being a single mother is any future funeral would only be attended by honest mourners.

January 8, 1904
Midday

It is without regret that I shed possessions, wealth and high status in the process of wholly recasting my life. However, the silver pocketwatch which had been given to me by my late father was one of the few articles I did not discard along with my unfortunate marriage.

The cherished and lovingly engraved timepiece indicated it was just before noon when the S.S. Clallam made a hard landfall in Port Townsend. The coastal settlement was where the vessel would clear customs and deliver the sheep before setting off for its final destination of Victoria.

Although I had resolved to spend the passage out of sight, concealed in the dimly lit goods room, I could sense, if not observe, the impressive speed of the modern steamship as it passed over the depths of the waters coursing between Washington and Vancouver Island. Before departing from my oppressive home, I had researched the vessel's abbreviated history, how it had been launched a mere eight months earlier by the Puget Sound Navigation Company. Possessing an engine fuelled by coal and a Douglas Fir frame, the ship boasted dozens of staterooms, the kind I would have inhabited before I had exchanged my carpet bag for a burlap sack. Aspiring to begin my life anew, I felt a kinship with the youthful vessel. I half-wished my husband could have seen me, garbed in the manner of a street urchin, tucked up in the warm bowels of the groaning vessel, like a character from the Henry James novels he so loved to malign.

If my husband did have his way, the writing of fiction would be made unlawful. He perceives it to be a frivolous and even dangerous distraction for a serious mind. It is only his beloved newspaper that deserves the attention of readers and to this cause he has devoted his life and ultimately aspired to dedicate mine.

When we were newly married, I believed my husband appreciated my keen mind and breadth of knowledge on all manner of subjects, nourished by my own father from a young age. However, not much time passed before I understood his true feelings on female intelligence. On the occasion of almost every dinner party we attended, he would at some moment unfurl his ugly prejudice against my sex. How our minds were meant for planning menus and staying abreast of the latest trends in fashion. It was quite to my astonishment that in the same breath he delivered these condescending notions, he would whisper his love for me, as though the arrows of his insults were not piercing my breast.

I therefore had to mask my utter bewilderment when, one evening in late March, my husband approached me with a request to review his latest article. The subject matter was of the planned renovations and repair of a local theatre that had been devastated by a fire. He knew, of course, this was a cause about which I was most passionate, a focus for my otherwise idle existence. He explained that his editor was keeping to bed with a high fever and there was no other body available for the assignment. With a quick retort caught in my throat, I demurely accepted the task, so eager was I to exercise my own intellect. I could hardly contain my incredulity when the article was eventually published, and with the changes I had recommended.

In the months that followed, a draft of an article would simply appear on my letter-writing desk. I assumed this manner of exchange enabled my husband to maintain his dignity, not having to deign to ask for a woman's assistance at a task he professed was only suited to men. This must be how he unearthed my novella, which I had hurriedly left tucked under stray papers rather than locked in a drawer when a friend came calling without an appointment. It was a tale of a kitchen maid in possession of both a grand beauty and high intelligence which would inevitably manifest great difficulties for someone born to a low station in life. I will never forget the scene of my husband bursting into the library where I had been enjoying a solitary afternoon tea, reading my words aloud in a mocking tone before thrusting the pages one by one into the fire. As I watched the singular copy of my story ignite and transform into cinder, I did resolve to similarly incinerate my marriage.

The idea of making a life separate from my husband had been one I dared to only seriously entertain after receiving a small inheritance from a favourite spinster aunt. The relation had never taken to my husband, and I presume the bequest was meant to sow seeds of independence, if not outright rebellion. For the past year, my husband had made several attempts to claim possession of the funds, but the Married Women's Property Act protected my interest. The legal doctrine restricted the use of such gifts to pay a husband's debts, and I suspected my own spouse of acquiring many, mostly in gambling houses.

Before embarking on my escape, I had resolved that it was safer to adopt the costume of a deckhand and stow away on board the S.S. Clallam rather than to buy a ticket, even under a pseudonym. My husband had a network of newspaper contacts across the country, and I presumed his ego would not rest until he tracked me down like wild game.

As I drew my coat closer for warmth and adjusted my position on a wooden plank, I was determined to appreciate the crude comforts of the ship storage room, despite the perilously shifting cargo. I was savouring a bid for freedom, a pleasure I could not realize when ornamentally perched on an embroidered drawing room settee.

Chapter 7

Although she couldn't afford international vacations enjoyed by the likes of Roddy Beck, Helene did take her children away for a week during the summer, usually to another town on Vancouver Island like Parksville. What she saved on airfare she spent on renting a condo so that everyone had their own room. She would never subject her children to the vacations of the 1970s, where a family of five stayed in one hotel room for two weeks and mistook the constant bickering as a form of summer fun. Having a fully equipped kitchen to cook her children's allergy-safe foods was also critical, as every trip to a restaurant put them at risk of a reaction.

But what beckoned her back to Parksville each July was Rathtrevor Beach, a horseshoe-shaped inlet with a shallow swath of ocean only two feet deep at high tide. The azure waters were as clear as a polished gemstone and warm as a bath run by a mother for their child. Miniature crabs darted between periwinkle and scallop shells much to the delight of both the young and old. Discovering bleached sand dollars was the beach equivalent of panning for gold, the hollow circular creatures seeming to contain some kind of satisfyingly unknowable magic. Helene and her children may not have been able to travel to Italy for vacations, but Rathtrevor Beach was an inverted Sistine Chapel ceiling of sand and shells.

However, even if Helene did have the freedom and finances to visit Europe, witnessing the works of Michelangelo would not be the priority. She would much rather head to the coasts of Portugal or Greece, perhaps to hone her skills as a connoisseur of beaches. That's why she had been slightly surprised when her two friends had announced Berlin, a landlocked city despite a surfeit of

53

lakes, as their honeymoon destination. And on that Tuesday morning, when she reached out to Detective Kalinowski at their hotel room in the German capital, the newly married police officer didn't sound entirely enthusiastic about the travel choice either.

"Did you know this is ground zero for Nazi history?" Kalinowski asked.

"Well, yes. But I took a course examining the lead-up to the Second World War at university. And I've watched a lot of movies set during that time. Hitler's connection to Berlin was hard to miss." Not wanting to sound too condescending, Helene added. "But there are other things to explore in the city, I imagine."

"What, like the headquarters of the Stasi during the Communist control of East Germany? A legacy of neighbours reporting on neighbours to get a slightly larger shitty apartment?"

"As a police officer, aren't the misdeeds of the secret police at least a little bit fascinating?"

"I'm on my honeymoon, not a refresher course on State-supported torture."

Helene was sorry that the mood of her friends' trip didn't sound overly romantic, but it made her feel less guilty about making the intruding phone call. She had worked closely with Detective Kalinowski to catch a killer that spring and she knew the officer was still grateful for her help. Helene was in need of information and the Victoria Police hadn't revealed any details of Roddy Beck's demise.

"I'm sure you must have heard about the death of Roddy Beck last weekend." Helene had worried the change in subject from Nazis in Berlin would be too abrupt, but the level of enthusiasm with which Kalinowski responded put her mind at ease.

"Yes, and they've put that bloody Detective Bloom in charge. He's more interested in catching Chinook salmon than criminals. Would have been my case if I'd been home."

54

The level of regret in Kalinowski's voice was more than a little worrying considering she was supposed to be enjoying three weeks with her new bride.

"Well, this Detective Bloom hasn't even sent out a press release and he won't take my calls," explained Helene. "And I'm covering both the death and the story connected to the manuscript Roddy Beck discovered. But before I dig any deeper, I need to know if the case is being considered a murder or at least suspicious."

"Does Alex know you're asking me to look into a case while we're on our honeymoon?"

"Not exactly."

"Let's keep it that way, as she promised to stay off social media as long as I didn't check work emails." Knowing how much her friend Alex loved to post photos of everything from her cappuccino to her cat, Helene recognized that the compromises necessary for a happy marriage had already begun.

Explaining that Alex would return shortly from picking up tickets to a tour of the German Spy Museum, Kalinowski promised to garner any information she could about Saturday's fatality at the castle. She did, of course, warn Helene that she would reveal nothing that would compromise the investigation, but only confirm or deny any suspicions of foul play.

"Make sure you visit Checkpoint Charlie," suggested Helene before saying goodbye. "Such an important symbol of oppression and division."

"Not you too," sighed Kalinowski. "My mother was right; I should have married that pretty dentist from Ladysmith. She was a little too excited about Sunday brunch and Broadway musicals, but at least the only Nazis were in the Sound of Music."

Once she ended the call, Helene realized she hadn't told Kalinowski about the note Zofia had discovered, the one indicating Beck might have arranged to meet someone on the castle's top landing shortly before his death. She appeased her conscience with the thought that the detective would understand the omission, after all, police and journalists, even when not working for a corrupt Communist regime, all had their secrets.

Helene then turned her focus to a list lying on her newsroom desk. She planned to spend the rest of the day trying to get some background on all the players connected to the stories. The first person she needed to learn more about was Mrs. Fernandez, the woman who had caused a stir at the press conference, whose name Roddy's former assistant, Ameer, had unwittingly supplied during their conversation.

Thankfully Fernandez was not a particularly common surname in Victoria, a city where many people's ancestors hailed from places like Sheffield or Dublin. At one point, Greater Victoria boasted two mayors called Murphy, elected in neighbouring municipalities. To their credit, they played up the coincidence for cheeky community fundraisers.

The first local internet hit for a Fernandez was a chef at a tapas restaurant that had a mouthwatering menu; envisioning a plate of papas bravas drenched in a garlic aioli, Helene sadly recalled that she had packed a plain chicken breast and canned corn for lunch. The second link for a Fernandez led to a site for a real estate agent flashing an unnaturally perfect smile. If the numbers were correct, however, the agent did have a very good sales record even in tough economic times.

Helene believed she had finally found the right Fernandez when she clicked on an obituary for a James Bay resident who had died earlier that year. Further searching brought up a photo of the dead man and his wife taken at an event organized by a local senior citizens' centre. The woman smiling behind a table of crochet crafts was the same as the one from the press conference, but in much happier times. It seemed that Maria Fernandez had not only seen her former home destroyed but she had also lost her husband.

Helene was just about to try the old directory number for a Fernandez in James Bay when her producer peered over her office partition.

"What have you got so far?" asked Riya before taking a bite of a donut covered in pink sprinkles.

Helene had been given a lot of leeway to pursue the two stories connected to Roddy Beck and that meant there was one less reporter to cover the daily grind. So she wasn't surprised that Riya wanted to check her progress.

Putting down her phone, she explained, "I have a death that may or may not be a murder. A city councillor who could be on the take. Two widows, one who loved her husband, the other, his fortune. Meanwhile, all anyone wants to talk about is the current housing crisis and a book about a 100-year-old shipwreck." Pausing to catch her breath, Helene realized she wasn't exactly giving herself a glowing progress report.

Riya, however, did not appear concerned about Helene's frustrated investigation. "This should help," she said while passing the journalist a folded paper.

Quickly scanning the single sheet, Helene was delighted to discover it was an invitation to the launch of the newly discovered book by A.J. Beck, to be held at a popular local bookstore two weeks from Friday. Although she was eager to learn more about the novel, *A Grave Journey*, she was a bit surprised the event was going ahead in spite of Beck's death. Perhaps someone was hoping to capitalize on the tragedy, seeking to boost book sales while public interest was strong.

"Are you still taking tomorrow off?" Riya asked casually, as though she didn't view vacations as a lack of commitment to the job.

"Take the day off? Why would I do that?" Helene couldn't remember a reason for booking leave, especially in the midst of covering such important stories. She checked her phone diary for a doctor's appointment, as they were sometimes made months in advance.

Her boss shrugged unhelpfully. "I'm not sure what it was. I think you said something about your sister's birthday. I didn't even know you had a sister. Very close, are you?"

Helene didn't bother replying to her boss's last question as she was too busy being annoyed with herself. How could she have forgotten Lela's birthday? Or have failed to pick up a present? Now she would have to stop at an overpriced downtown boutique on her way home. Perhaps a very expensive scarf made from recycled pop cans would please her sister. Something in the salmon colour she currently favoured for everything from throw pillows to dinner plates.

Although Lela had claimed she would be happy with any gift, Helene knew better than to take her seriously. She could recall Lela on her 8th birthday, standing in the driveway with crossed arms, refusing to ride a grey bicycle because it wasn't pink.

"Yes, I still need the day off," Helene informed her producer. "We're going to the Moss Bay Resort. My sister loves their pools and spa."

Turning back toward the kitchen, perhaps to grab another stale donut from a pack brought in by a colleague, Riya commented, "I'm surprised you can afford that place, considering what I pay you."

What Helene wouldn't admit to her boss, because it would please Riya far too much, is that she would prefer to come to work. Catching a possible murderer held more appeal than getting a massage that came with a criminal price tag.

Chapter 8

Being a seasoned member of the media, Helene considered herself to be undaunted by hostile police officers, aggressive activists and even powerful, overbearing politicians. She was not afraid to ask difficult questions and to repeat them when people were evasive. However, she seemed to lose all her bravado when sitting in a chair at a hair salon or lying naked on a massage table as she was on that Wednesday morning in October. Perhaps the lack of clothing made her understandably less forthright, but she suspected it had more to do with women being raised to not ask directly for what they want.

"I have a lot of neck pain on the right side. You know, from using a mouse all day at work. Would you mind going a bit deeper there?"

The massage therapist grunted in response, indicating she had heard Helene's request, but did not change the position or pressure of her hands.

Faced with such amiable disregard for her wishes, Helene felt oddly powerless and resigned herself to a very costly and ineffectual massage. Her body growing more tense as the minutes passed, she tried to imagine herself somewhere more relaxing, like the newsroom on election night.

At least she had gotten her sister's present right. Lela's eyes had lit up when she pulled a fuzzy coral-coloured cardigan from a plain kraft paper bag. Relieved that the day had started well, Helene had spent an hour in an outdoor hot tub amongst her sister's friends before heading out for her disappointing massage.

Even though her sister had moved back to Victoria less than a year ago, six good friends had shown up for her party. Unlike Helene, she kept in touch with university classmates and former colleagues, cultivating and nurturing relationships like a dedicated gardener. Helene didn't have the time or, frankly, the inclination to sustain so many connections. Her friendship with Alex met her minimal needs for socialization—going out for drinks or taking a walk on the breakwater together once a month. She only needed one dynamic and brilliant blossom for a friend, not a whole bouquet. Admittedly, she was concerned whether the recent nuptials would change this dynamic; it was naive to imagine it wouldn't. Helene didn't make new friends easily, bored by the kinds of conversations that many women seemed to enjoy about sex, hair products and vacation rentals.

But Helene was quite fond of her sister's friends. She had known some of them since her 20s, seeing them at Christmas parties or the occasional backyard barbecue, an introvert enjoying the bounty of her sibling's garden of friends without the responsibility of performing the yard work of relationships. And although they adored Lela, the group always made Helene feel welcome, asking interesting questions about her work as a journalist.

Once she had finished her dissatisfactory massage, Helene rejoined the animated group in the outdoor hot tub. Waiting until her sister was focused on refilling a champagne glass, she snuck a furtive look at her phone: Lela's need to be the centre of everyone's attention at a party hadn't changed over the years any more than her love of pink.

Glancing at the screen, Helene's pulse quickened when she saw there was a missed call and it was from someone named Fernandez. Her plush white robe in hand, Helene told the group she needed to use the bathroom and headed indoors. Lela was merrily describing her latest worst-date-ever and took no notice as Helene left the group.

A waft of cedar and sage greeted Helene when she pulled open the change room door, as even the spa air was curated for the pleasure of wealthy patrons. Along with a row of polished sinks and stacks of fresh towels, the space held lockers for the clients to leave their designer clothing while indulging in hot tubs and spa services. Helene did not have much interest in pedicures or facials; they seemed like an unnecessary extravagance. However, since becoming a teenager, Cleo had taken to painting her nails and her daughter now had rows of bottles lined up on her dresser where stuffies used to live. Helene thought perhaps Cleo had inherited a taste for pampering from her aunt, if those kinds of traits could be genetic. Either way, Helene had resolved to bring Cleo to the spa for a manicure to celebrate her next birthday—what some considered a modern right of passage to womanhood.

Helene was relieved to find that she was alone in the well-appointed bathroom, even the showers silenced of running water. Wanting to ensure she wasn't discovered while on a call for work, she slipped into a sauna that hadn't been turned on. Pulling the door shut, Helene took in the distinct fragrance of the wooden walls and platforms that had been repeatedly baked over time. For a moment she was recalled to childhood winter vacations in the Alberta Rockies, in Banff or Jasper National Parks. Always too skinny and cold to enjoy skiing properly, she had looked forward to unthawing in a sauna after a day spent shivering on perilously swaying chairlifts. At least as a parent herself, she only did activities Cleo and Oscar actually liked. In the 1970s, a child's preference simply didn't factor into vacation plans.

Admittedly, it was slightly challenging to feel like a hard-hitting journalist when sporting a terry towel robe and hiding in an empty sauna, but Helene wasn't planning to ask tough questions of the elderly and troubled Mrs. Fernandez; a bit of background on how the property deal had gone wrong was all she needed. Expecting to speak to Mrs. Fernandez directly, it was a surprise when the phone was answered by a voice that sounded middle-aged. While attempting to come up with a concise explanation for the call, Helene adjusted drooping swimsuit straps under her robe.

"I was hoping to speak to a Mrs. Fernandez. I'm a reporter from Vancouver Island Radio. I was at the press conference on the weekend." Helene never tried to hide the fact that she was a journalist when speaking to someone for the first time. Everyone had a right to know that their words might end up in a story. She knew other reporters like Gary Graham were not so upfront, allowing people to share secrets without realizing who they were talking to.

"Oh yes, I'm the one who returned your call. I guess you didn't listen to the message I left," said the woman. "My mother did want to talk to you, she really loves your radio station. Has it on in the house all day."

"Is she around now? As you may know, the special city council meeting for housing is tomorrow, and I wanted more background on what happened to her."

"Oh no, she's in the hospital. I said that in the message. She had a stroke yesterday. It all got to be too much I think—since my father's death—and Saturday was just too much excitement."

Hearing this news, Helene felt her hopes of uncovering why a property sale might be considered unscrupulous plummet faster than the temperature on an Alberta ski hill. But then she received a reprieve when the woman spoke again.

"I'm her daughter Lucia and I know my mother would want me to tell you everything."

"That's fabulous," said Helene. "I mean, that you're able to talk to me, not that your mother is in hospital. I hope she'll be OK."

"I'm not really sure. She's old and she misses my father desperately. They were very much in love, even after 60 years together. And they had a wonderful life. Right up until when Roddy Beck deceived them."

"So, what happened?" asked Helene at the same time as realizing she didn't have a notebook. Slipping one into her robe pocket while leaving the hot tub might have attracted her sister's attention.

"I must start by telling you about their home. Because that's really what this is all about. They moved into it soon after they were married. My father was a few years older than my mother and already had some savings. Of course, this was in the 1960s when you could get a house in Victoria for under $30,000. Imagine that."

Houses in James Bay were now listed for more than a million dollars, so the days of young couples buying their first home a few blocks from the ocean were long gone. A small inheritance had made it possible for Helene to purchase a bungalow in the community in 2010, but that was before the prices had started to shoot up exponentially year-over-year.

"It was a beautiful brick house on Clarence Street," Lucia continued wistfully. "A wooden porch in front and a large bay window upstairs, I used to sit there and read on rainy days. It was more than a hundred years old, built by a prominent local architect in 1915. Apologies, his name slips my mind, I spent the night at the hospital."

Helene refrained from making any reply. She knew it was better to simply let the story spill out.

"You see, my father was an accountant, but his true calling was taking care of the house and trying to return it to its original condition. Searching for antique doorknobs. Ripping up carpets and redoing wooden floors. He would spend the weekend visiting old buildings slated for demolition, scavenging what he could. And I followed in his footsteps by starting my own window framing company for

63

historic homes. Staying true to the designs and materials of the time."

As Lucia Fernandez described her family and occupation with a compelling if heartbreaking passion, Helene registered a metallic clicking emanating from the sauna walls. Momentarily distracted by the noise, she brushed it off as cantankerous plumbing.

"Anyways, a few years ago the house became too much work for my parents. Mowing the lawn. Replacing the old pipes. Things kept on breaking and I was having to help every weekend. I wasn't spending enough time with my kids or husband. In the end, I encouraged them to sell." The passion in Lucia's voice had been replaced by guilt and regret.

Still perched on the sauna bench, Helene was listening intently to the story, trying to memorize the details she couldn't write down. In deep concentration, she didn't immediately notice the sweat starting to trickle down her back. Suddenly realizing she was getting warm, she unknotted the belt and slipped the robe off her shoulders.

"So, they decided to sell the house and move into a retirement home. The kind where you have your own kitchen but there is also a dining room if you don't feel like cooking. But of course, they wanted to make sure the house would be preserved."

"And that's where Roddy Beck comes in?" Helene couldn't help but interject, eager to discover the tech guru's role in the story.

"Yes, they had used his app to list their house for sale, and it didn't take long before they were approached by a developer. They were shown a proposal, a way to keep the house, but also use the space in the large yard to create more homes. And this was important to my parents, they knew many families were struggling to find a place to live."

The sweat on her hands now making it difficult to hold her phone, it dawned on Helene that the noise she had

64

heard earlier was someone turning on the sauna. At the same time as the heat was becoming distinctly uncomfortable, Helene heard her sister's voice from the other side of the wooden door. Sitting in her swimsuit without even a water bottle, she realized she was trapped—unwilling to interrupt Lucia Fernandez's story, but also afraid to leave the sauna.

"And then what happened?" asked Helene with growing urgency.

"Well, that's what I'm not entirely sure of. Promises were made that the house would be protected, but then a month after they moved out, it was gone. The developers found some kind of loophole. A way to clear the lot and put up an entirely new building and make a bunch more money, to be sure. Broke my father's heart. I mean, Roddy Beck as good as killed my father."

As much as Helene desperately wanted to follow up on this provocative statement, the heat in the sauna was becoming unbearable and her head was starting to spin. She could only wish there was an Alberta snowbank outside the door to plunge into.

"Thank you for talking to me. It's been really helpful. I'll give you a call again soon. I want to talk more about what happened to your parents," Helene hoped she didn't sound as rushed as she felt. "I think it's really important to share their story," she added for good measure.

"Yes, that's fine. And I'll try to ask my mother for more details at the hospital today, if she's up for it. She'll be so thrilled to know that Vancouver Island Radio called."

The fact that someone who was gravely ill could be excited about a call from a radio journalist made Helene a little concerned for the sway of the media.

Slipping the phone back into her pocket and pulling the robe over her glowing shoulders, Helene stumbled out of the sauna to find Lela and several friends observing her graceless exit.

65

"What are you doing?" asked Lela with suspicion, as though they were both still children and she had caught Helene sneaking out of her sibling's bedroom.

Helene attempted to smile enthusiastically while fumbling to fill a cup from a pitcher of water and cucumber slices. "Oh nothing, just trying out the sauna. You know I love a good sauna. And it's definitely good. I mean, the hotness is very . . . hot. Top hotness." Knowing she sounded ridiculous, Helene instead focused on gulping down water.

Lela probably wasn't satisfied with her sister's explanation, but she didn't press the point. Instead, there was a dramatic shift in her tone.

"That's great. We were just gonna try it out." Lela started to untie her own robe. "But in case I forget, I wanted to thank you for coming. It means so much that you took the day off. I know how important work is. And you haven't even taken one call. I appreciate you making my birthday a priority."

With guilt coursing through her body like the waves of heat coming off a sauna stove, Helene watched as Lela and her gaggle of friends entered the overheated chamber. She had a strong suspicion that her sister knew exactly what she had been up to, and that being able to lay a guilt trip on her older sibling was perhaps the best birthday present Lela could have received.

Chapter 9

After arriving home from the spa later that day, Helene was relieved to discover there were enough leftovers for her kids' dinner. It seemed a waste of soaking in a hot tub for hours to immediately dive into domestic duties. Making do with cheese and crackers for herself, Helene purposely put off loading the dishwasher until the morning; rinsing off plates and bowls would pollute the purity of her slothful day.

Before retreating to her bedroom downstairs to indulge in the latest episodes of her favourite British spy series, Helene sat down next to her teenage daughter on the living room couch. Knowing that peppering Cleo with questions about her school day, like an overly eager journalist, would only result in monosyllabic responses and eye rolls, Helene adopted the strategy of a wildlife photographer trying to get close to their subject—stay still and wait to be approached.

Only a few minutes passed before Cleo spoke.

"We had the most annoying substitute teacher today."

Helene simply nodded, conscious that responding too early and with too much curiosity might cause the teenager to retreat to their emotional cave.

"She was taking attendance and had almost made it to the end . . ." continued Cleo.

Unfortunately, Helene could guess what was coming next.

"But of course, she had to stop at my name. 'Unger, Unger? What nationality is that? Ukrainian?'" Cleo imitated the abrupt, authoritative tone of the substitute.

Having experienced the mockery of schoolteachers drawing attention to her unusual last name in the 1980s,

Helene was disappointed but not surprised that nothing had changed.

"And rather than get into the whole, it's Mennonite, which isn't a nationality, it's a religion, because people moved around a lot back then, so it's like being Jewish but we eat paska not challah . . . well instead of getting into all of that, I just said it was Greek."

Taking another bite of a cracker and brie, Helene weighed up her possible responses. If she criticized her daughter for lying to the teacher, it could shut down communication for days. Furthermore, she was impressed by Cleo's knowledge of breads and their corresponding religions and wanted to make her feel good about that. In the end, she decided to make the relationship with her daughter the priority.

"That's hilarious sweetheart. I've always wanted to be Greek. I think they have much better parties than Mennonites."

Cleo's earnest features were fleetingly altered by a grin, all the confirmation Helene needed that she had made the right choice when interacting with the local teenage wildlife.

Heaving herself off the couch, a day spent in steaming water taking its toll, Helene stopped to kiss her son on his blond head. Oscar had already described the day's events in great detail, chattering happily in the car on the drive home from school. A spelling quiz had gone badly, a lunchtime game had been fun, but Adam had tried to take his favourite game trading card. Now laying on his stomach on the daybed, her son was engrossed in a violent video game that would have appalled her pacifist Mennonite grandparents.

"I saw that boy at school today," muttered Oscar while keeping his eyes affixed to the screen.

"What boy?" Helene asked distractedly, thinking only about her soft bed.

"The one from the castle."

"The castle? There was a boy at the castle?" asked Helene, trying to shake the hot tub haze from her head.

There was a massive explosion on Oscar's video screen, which put a smile on his face. "Yeah. He wanted to play catch but we had to go listen to your work thing where that lady started yelling."

Helene could only assume the heat from the sauna session had cooked her remaining middle-aged brain cells. She couldn't recall seeing other children at Saturday's press conference. Nor did she know of any reporters whose kids attended the same school. Too tired to probe any further, she simply replied, "That's nice," and made her way downstairs to her beckoning bedroom.

"We need to be out the door in ten minutes!" After a rare restful night's sleep, Helene once more found herself in the throes of the daily battle to leave the house on time. Her shouting was mostly for the benefit of Cleo, who was in the bathroom, applying make-up with the precision of Cleopatra. For his part, Oscar sat by the front door in his coat, eager to see his friends on the playground that morning.

"Do you have your clarinet?"

"Yes."

"Your binder?"

"Yup."

"Your runners for gym?"

"I'll grab them."

Before leaving the house each day, Helene went through all the items Oscar needed for school. On too many occasions she had received an urgent call halfway through the morning from annoyed teachers, asking how he was supposed to participate in music class without his instrument. At 11, her son could describe the precise phases of a black hole collapsing, but he had no aptitude for remembering where he had left his pencil case. Sympathetic to his absent-minded nature, Helene knew the best way to manage the situation was daily routines, not parental reprimands.

Once Cleo emerged from the bathroom and lunchboxes were shoved into backpacks, the family of three hurried from the house to the car. Thankfully it had been warm overnight, so Helene didn't have to use an old scraper leftover from her years in Edmonton to get frost off the windows.

After dropping her kids off at school, Helene headed in the direction of Victoria City Hall. The special council meeting on housing started at 10:00 and she wanted to get a good seat in what was sure to be a crowded room. However, she did make a slight detour to pass by Craigdarroch Castle, as she hadn't been near it since Roddy Beck's death on Saturday.

When she arrived at the mansion, Helene drove slowly through the circular parking lot. A group of tourists were clustered near the main entrance, waiting for the museum to open, an indication that the recent ghoulish events had probably increased attendance rather than reduced it—hardly a winning recommendation for the human race. Helene had to look away when she realized the group was standing on almost the exact spot where Roddy Beck's body had landed.

A few minutes later, when she was stopped at a traffic light on Yates Street on her way to City Hall, Helene rolled down the car windows in the hopes a strong breeze would clear her mind. The tech guru's screams as he fell to his death were on replay, and it wasn't until she was seated in one of the rows reserved for the media in the City Council Chambers that she managed to push away the unwanted memories.

Like the building's exterior, the Chambers' decor appeared largely unchanged since the 1970s. Plush carpeting and wood paneling gave off the impression of dated luxury, like the office of a Russian oligarch. The council members sat at a horseshoe-shaped table: the mayor seated at the top of the arch—the pinnacle of municipal power.

Helene was glad she had arrived early as the room was filling up with members of the media and community. When it came to issues like bike lanes, dog parks and building height restrictions, Victoria had many politically engaged residents, making it sometimes difficult for council to ever accomplish anything. And the growing population on the South Island created a need, not just for more housing, but also for updated and expanded infrastructure. However, many people who had bought homes 50 years ago didn't want anything to change, preferring that the community, like the City Hall decor, remained unaltered.

Just past the hour, the mayor called the meeting to order, and quickly dealt with the preliminary business of council. Although now seated, the municipal leader Irma Strauss was extremely tall and never slouched to hide her height like women of a certain generation were taught to do. She was surprisingly blunt for a politician and sometimes grew impatient in the wake of the endless protests against progress. Helene normally didn't have much appreciation for politicians, finding them either too earnest or too phony. But she respected the mayor and her attempts to manage a beautiful city through growing pains; as the parent of a moody and attractive teenager, Helene could somehow relate.

The discussion on housing was led off by the politician for whom Helene had less regard. Wearing a tweed jacket with actual leather patches, Rupert Davies could only have looked more like a minor member of the British aristocracy if he was cuddling a corgi.

"We are here today to discuss the development proposed for the 100-block of Menzies Street in James Bay. The plans put forward have received approval from council, however a last-minute petition has been started in opposition to the project."

The James Bay housing scheme was listed as the main item on the council meeting agenda, but Helene assumed the allegations of council corruption made by Mrs. Fernandez would also come up. After all, her complaints were connected to housing in the island community.

After Councillor Davies had made his opening remarks, the floor was opened to members of the public.

Several residents took turns at the microphone to share their concerns that the picturesque neighbourhood was being overwhelmed by a rapidly growing population. The area had narrow streets, a congested grocery store parking lot and, at the height of summer, it was invaded by cruise ship passengers, horse drawn carriages and pedicabs. The need to protect historic homes was also raised: the fact that they were often only one or two bedrooms made them vulnerable to the promoters of densification.

These arguments against development were already familiar to Helene, and she was starting to despair of learning anything new at the council meeting. But just when she was considering slipping her notepad into her backpack, a man in grey slacks and a worn fisherman's sweater stepped up to speak.

"My name is Thor Jacobsen, I am a retired government analyst, but please don't hold that against me." The man with a weathered yet dignified face flashed the council a disarming smile and then continued speaking with a slight accent. "I have been paying great attention to the changes going on in our city, and although we are undeniably in the midst of a housing crisis, we must never drop our guard against corruption. I am not in agreement with Machiavelli, that the end justifies the means."

Every journalist in the room was now staring at the man in anticipation of his revealing something worth reporting.

"I have not only talked with Mrs. Fernandez about the manner in which her home was inappropriately approved for demolition, but I have also been given leaked private documents showing that Roddy Beck, may God rest his soul, planned to allow the home of his great-grandmother, A.J. Beck, to be destroyed."

In response to this statement, a ripple of gasps crossed the room. Even the normally unflustered mayor removed her glasses, used her shirt cuff to clean the lenses and put them back on.

"Not satisfied to make money from his unethical apps, he was going to destroy his family's own historic home and create an 'immersive book experience' for tourists . . . whatever dystopian hell that is."

Shouting immediately broke out in the room, residents declaring the imminent ruination of James Bay. The media added to the chaos by pelting questions at members of council, not giving them a chance to respond before asking another. Order was only restored by Mayor Strauss banging her gavel on the table and threatening to adjourn the meeting. She thanked Thor Jacobsen for his information and then asked the next speaker to come forward.

For another two hours, residents took turns at the microphone, either to call for an end to all development or to push for apartments to be built on every remaining empty piece of land. However, nothing was shared that rivalled Thor Jacobsen's alarming revelations. And once the meeting was brought to a close, a scrum of journalists formed around the man responsible for creating a brief ruckus in the room.

73

Emerging from the building 15 minutes later, Helene was in such a rush, she almost tripped over a pair of long legs belonging to an emaciated woman sitting on the ground near the City Hall entrance. Perhaps in her late 20s, her brown hair was pulled back into a disheveled ponytail and she was wearing a stained green coat. A large backpack and several overflowing reusable shopping bags perched against the brick facade all but confirmed she was living on the streets.

Although Helene wanted to put together her radio story before her media competitors, she did stop long enough to hastily retrieve a $20 bill from her purse and hand it to the girl whose face lit up with both surprise and gratitude. The journalist made it a habit to give even just a few dollars whenever she encountered someone living rough. She only hoped that her spare change might bring momentary relief from hunger or memories of childhood trauma.

Caring for the less fortunate was one maxim from her Mennonite upbringing that she still followed, even if she didn't attend church or eat paska bread at Easter. She recognized that it was in some ways down to the lottery of life that it wasn't a younger version of herself—or God forbid an older incarnation of her daughter—who needed to survive off the generosity of strangers while enduring their judgment.

She also knew that the lack of housing only added to the misery faced by people living below the poverty line, and the idea that Roddy Beck might have been taking advantage of the crisis to pay for the upkeep of an oceanfront home fuelled her desire to uncover the rot which was starting to smell like a beach at low tide.

74

Chapter 10

Upon her return to the office, Helene's coworkers were less interested in her news from City Hall than she had expected. To be fair, they were busy working on their own stories including the release of a high-profile sex offender into the community and a cyclist ending up in hospital after being struck by a drunk driver. In fact, the early afternoon newscast included one tragic story after another and if Helene hadn't worked in radio, she would have been tempted to turn it off.

Thankfully, her producer could tell she needed someone to bounce ideas off of and beckoned her into the glass-fronted office.

"How's the ankle?" Helene asked, spying that the cumbersome brace on Riya's injured limb had been replaced by a beige wrap.

"It only hurts when I laugh," Riya replied. "And walk, but worse than that, somehow Vancouver found out about my accident and they want me to do a first-person article about failing at pickleball."

Helene was surprised by this request since her producer rarely wrote stories anymore, having become firmly established in her role of guiding the news agenda, not so much contributing to it. However, pickleball was unquestionably an endless source of controversy and, therefore, media interest. That summer, the District of Saanich had tried to convert a section of an off-leash dog park into pickleball courts, as players were having to wait hours to use the existing facilities. Needless to say, the dog-owning community managed to get thousands of names on a petition to stop the proposal, ultimately triumphing over the less-organized pickleball players. She suspected another showdown was imminent between the predominantly senior sports enthusiasts and the pet owners, as green space on the South Island was under increasing pressure.

"I don't quite get the push to share my misadventures. It's not like I'm the lovechild of Roddy Beck and a former Olympic figure skater. I guess whatever gets clicks. Granted, it's been a while, but I'm sure I can pump out a few hundred words of self-indulgent drivel," said Riya. "But let's get to the real news. What's the latest from city council and the people you've spoken to?"

Plopping herself down in an uncomfortable chair probably chosen to discourage lengthy office visits, Helene did her best to explain the numerous threads to the story she had uncovered so far: Mrs. Fernandez's house being destroyed by a developer; Roddy Beck's alleged plan to replace his great-grandmother's home with a tourist attraction; his ex-wife's claim to RoddTek Inc.

"What are the police saying?"

"Right, the police. Just need to follow up with my source." Helene hadn't heard back from Detective Kalinowski in Berlin, but it was noon in Victoria, and the honeymooners were nine hours ahead, so it was still early enough to call. And who knows, she might even be doing her friend a favour by rescuing her from a musical featuring singing Stasi. Discussing the details of a possible murder would be a relief in comparison.

"I also need to check in with the daughter of Mrs. Fernandez, she told me her mom ended up in hospital a few days ago. I think partly due to stress. I want to see if she learned any more details or perhaps Mrs. Fernandez is well enough to talk."

"Sounds like you have enough to stay busy. Don't let me keep you."

After making the abrupt dismissal, Riya added, "Now I just have to come up with a headline for my own story. I am thinking of running with: 'The Punishing Perils of

Pickleball' or 'Pickleball: Fun Fitness or Courtside Calamity?'"

As Helene left the office and returned to her desk, she allowed a passing thought of sympathy for the editor assigned to work with her producer, hoping they had been well-trained in constructive feedback.

While logging back onto her desk computer, Helene felt the cell phone in her pocket buzzing. Glancing at the screen, she had to chuckle; Detective Kalinowski's ears must have been burning in distant Berlin, as the message was from her.

> Not clear if Roddy B was murdered
> Interviewing family and employees
> Let you know if hear more

It seemed that the police weren't getting any further than she was in discovering what had led up to Roddy Beck's fatal fall at Craigdarroch Castle that Saturday. Helene did have to wonder whether, under the pressure of a police interview, Professor Bosko would share the note she had discovered. Surely, she had to realize the Victoria Police Department, although by no means perfect, did not function like secret police during the height of the Cold War.

Helene was texting back a thank you along with well-wishes for the rest of the honeymoon in Germany, but another message from Kalinowski buzzed her phone before she could hit send.

> Alex says hi
> And can you visit Daisy?
> Separation anxiety

Last spring, during Helene's investigation into an art curator's death, Alex had announced she was adopting a cat. The writer had decided it was time to create change in her life, making journalism less of a priority or at least not the only one. And letting a pet into her home turned out to be a sort of trial run for allowing Detective Kalinowski into her heart.

Ahead of her honeymoon in October, Alex had researched accommodation options for Daisy for while she was away. In the end, the place she had chosen seemed to be more of a high-end hotel than any kind of kennel Helene was familiar with. The brochure on Alex's coffee table had boasted abundant indoor cat perches, an enclosed outdoor nature park and meals of fresh fish.

After texting a promise to visit Daisy, Helene spent the next several hours putting together radio and web stories on the tumultuous city council meeting on housing. Once she had picked out the best quotes from Thor Jacobsen, she emailed Mayor Strauss for a response, but received a very bland statement about the challenge of providing new housing quickly while ensuring community buy-in. In her writing, Helene was careful to describe Roddy Beck's purported plans to tear down a historic home to make room for a tourist attraction as allegations. The tech guru was dead so he technically couldn't sue for libel, but there could be other financial players involved who could claim damages.

Her stories filed and vetted, Helene walked past her producer's office on the way to the water cooler. Riya was leaning forward and typing furiously, perhaps experiencing a rush of inspiration for her pickleball story. After refilling her bottle, Helene observed that her colleagues all seemed to be similarly occupied, so she assumed no one would notice if she slipped out of the office an hour early. Not wanting to attract attention by saying goodbye, Helene simply packed up her backpack and turned off her computer before exiting the building.

It was a short drive across the Bay Bridge to the cat resort, as Helene referred to the boarding facility in her own mind. She was relieved to find street parking outside the business located on the ground floor of a trendy condo development style known as "mixed-use" because it was both residential and commercial. When she walked up to the entrance, the glass front doors swept open automatically, reminding Helene of the spa where Lela had her birthday party earlier that week. The air was also scented, this time with a combination of catnip, potting soil and old couch. There was an undertone of urine as well, which she did her best to ignore.

After being shown to the room where Daisy was lounging in a patch of sunshine streaming through a windowpane, she received a curt glance from the feline who then turned on her back to allow for tummy rubs. While obligingly stroking the warm belly of the pampered beast, Helene couldn't help but smile at the thought of her friend's anxiety. The situation reminded her of Cleo's first week at daycare—Helene had impatiently watched the seconds tick away on the office clock, worried about whether her daughter had choked on the grapes she shouldn't have provided for lunch or gotten soaked in the rain that hadn't been in the forecast. But when it came time for pick-up, Cleo didn't want to come home, happily trying to force her way down the slide in rubbery rain pants her mom had remembered to pack after all.

Before leaving the upscale feline facility, Helene took a few photos of the recumbent cat which would hopefully put her friend's mind to rest and allow her to focus on having as much fun as was possible while taking in Berlin's problematic early 20th century. The plush furnishings and instrumental guitar music made her think that if Alex had really wanted to relax on her honeymoon, she should have booked in at the cat resort. Leather collars aside, there were certainly fewer mementos of fascism.

There was still a half hour before the sun set over the breakwater, and Helene was considering stopping by

79

the promenade to take a few shots. The ribbons of clouds across the sky would likely reflect the fading sunbeams, creating a rose and lilac layered cake overhead. But as she made her way across the blue bridge and through downtown Victoria, she decided to drive down Clarence Street in James Bay first. Lucia Fernandez had said that this had been the location of her family home before it had been demolished and Helene wanted to see what kind of construction had been completed so far.

Turning right off busy Niagara Street, Helene recalled interviewing a couple who lived in a garden suite in one of the older wooden houses on Clarence. They had created an art piece by hanging old teacups and teapots in a tree, broken china blowing in the wind, golden rims glinting in the sun. The quirky composition that could have come from the pages of *Alice in Wonderland* attracted both tourists and locals alike who snapped surreal photos of the branches heavy with chipped-crockery fruit. The spot was especially popular in spring when the cherry blossoms burst from slumber, nestling the delicate china in clouds of pink.

The project was dedicated to the man's late grandmother, a celebrated educator and intrepid solo female traveller in the 1930s. Eleanor Palmer was a teacher at Central Middle School on Fort Street in Victoria, and she was remembered for her patience with struggling students and her marvelous stories of travelling up the Yangtze River. Needing a photo for her online article, Helene spent hours trying to capture the perfect shot, one that reflected both the legacy of unconventionality and affection.

Since it was now October, the teacup tree, as it was referred to by locals, was mostly bare of leaves and blossoms, so the cups and saucers hung a bit dejectedly from the denuded branches—reinforcing the notion that Victoria lost much of its luster in the fall and winter.

Rolling down the window, Helene examined the construction site on the other side of the road. It appeared that three single family lots had been cleared for the project, and she had no way of knowing which area had belonged to the Fernandez family. But the fact that their lot was now included in a larger project made Helene suspect that the destruction of the house had always been in the planning. This meant that any promises made to preserve the historic structure were intended to be broken.

A wooden placard describing the project was fixed to a wire fence encircling the site and thankfully Helene was parked close enough to read the details. A dozen three-bedroom townhouses were being constructed, with a completion date just six months away. A bike room and an electric vehicle charging station were listed among the building amenities.

For all Helene's commitment to follow up on any possible unscrupulous treatment of Mrs. Fernandez and her husband, she recognized the incredible demand for this kind of housing. For many years developers had built only one- and two-bedroom suites in Victoria as this maximized the price per square footage. But city council had made it clear they now wanted homes for families, so parents and their children could walk to the grocery store, library or the James Bay farmers market on Saturdays in the summer.

Surveying the construction site before driving back to the home she was privileged to own, Helene could not ignore a growing sense of ambivalence toward the housing issue. On the one hand, she agreed with Thor Jacobsen, that the end didn't justify the means—tricking the Fernandez family into allowing their cherished house to be destroyed could never be considered ethical. But she also thought that the spirit of Eleanor Palmer would delight in the happy chatter of children tumbling from the front doors of these new homes. This begged the larger question, did young laughter justify greedy lies?

January 8, 1904
Early Afternoon

I believe it was much to my credit, considering my inauspicious surroundings, that I managed to fall into a short, deep slumber on a feed sack after we departed from Port Townsend. Perhaps it was merely the overwhelming relief of having left the last American port of call, and knowing Canadian shores lay ahead. Or more likely, it was the utter exhaustion of being in a constant state of alarm since fleeing the home I shared with my husband. The rolling of the ship may have also played its part in encouraging somnolence, akin to the tender rocking of a mother. Ironically, it was a sudden, sharp tossing of the vessel, which caused the cargo to slide from one side of the boat to the other, that brought me back to a state of wakefulness, as though a baby had been rudely ejected from its cradle.

Once I had readjusted my cap, which had become displaced while I dozed, allowing strands of long hair to escape, my focus was drawn to a striped rubber ball bouncing down the corridor between the wooden crates. The patter of light footsteps followed the sphere until I found myself under the curious gaze of a ruddy-faced boy. He stared at me without apology, his mouth hanging open in surprise. He then leaned in a little more closely, as if scrutinizing whether I was friend or foe.

"I believe your ball travelled down that passage." I pointed my finger toward the bow of the ship, which continued to reel side to side energetically. "But take care of the wooden boxes."

The boy, who appeared to be about eight years in age, had obviously taken the spirit of the mariner to heart as he gave me a brisk salute before decamping in pursuit of his wayward toy.

Once the child had moved along, I exhaled in relief, still believing it wise to avoid becoming the object of any person's attention, no matter how junior in age. But my respite was short-lived as the step of sharp heels rapidly approached. I pulled back into the shadows, hoping my drab garb would blend into the ship's hold.

"William, come back here this instant!" As the woman spoke, the vessel heaved violently to the right, and I could not resist an instinctive attempt to break her fall by reaching forward. In the process, my cap was once again dislodged, this time releasing the full cascade of my hair. The woman grasped at the edge of a crate to pull herself into an erect position, briskly straightening out her tousled skirts. I took this opportunity to once more shove my locks under my woolen head gear. I was unsure whether the woman had noticed my brief but undeniably feminine appearance. Under my breath, I cursed my own vanity for deciding against shearing my mane like a sheep at the commencement of my journey.

"I do beg your pardon," the woman stammered, seemingly more concerned with her own deportment than any confusion around my sex. Dressed in a sturdy, deep blue skirt and jacket, and appearing to be in her early 20s, the woman was what would be considered undesirably thin by my husband's set. But I saw a flicker of intelligence in her eyes which made me believe she might be a sympathetic soul, even if my cause were to be exposed.

"I wish I could blame the rollicking of this ship on the captain's lack of sobriety, but I think he is doing his best in trying circumstances. The waves appear to be tremendously fierce," said the woman.

"Waves?" I asked, not wanting to speak long enough to reveal my upper-class cadence. Despite having played

small roles in Christmas pantos, I thought mimicry of the diction of a deckhand was a bit beyond my acting skills.

"Have you not been up top in the last hour? It's all quite frightful, water washing over the deck, the crew running hither and thither. The evening meal has even been cancelled as the tables will not stay fixed to the floor. Seems a storm has come up swiftly and caught everyone unawares."

The young woman paused her speech to examine me with a more careful eye, I shifted uncomfortably while enduring the visual inspection. She must have established that I posed no threat as she then carried on, "Just give me a minute to locate my charge and then you can come up top with us. Heaven knows I am not going to get paid if I lose him on the journey. I'm Miss Beck by the way, Clara Beck." The woman extended a hand, which I did not dare grasp for fear of revealing my well-kept hands.

"Bert," is all I muttered, as politely as a one-word answer would allow. I had assumed Miss Beck was the mother of the boy, but as she hitched up her skirt to set chase, she did exude the energy of a woman whose life had not yet been fully etched in stone by marriage and motherhood.

I surmised Miss Beck was a governess, and a capable one at that, as she soon returned with the tousled boy clutching his ball.

"Join us in the social hall," she said, and then, as if sensing my desire to remain unseen, she added, "Most folks have retreated to their cabins." Miss Beck then turned and playfully dragged the boy up the stairs, not waiting for my response.

I knew I should stay hidden in my current location, but quite frankly, I had been living in isolation for such a great length of time, physically as well as emotionally, so an offer of company was very hard to resist. Even before I had embarked on my daring escape, I had play-acted my life, *going through the motions of a contented wife while sharing my plans with no one. Miss Beck also seemed like a well-timed portent of a successful and happy new beginning. And after all, we had left the last American port, so I believed it most unlikely that my journey could now meet with disaster.*

Chapter 11

The following morning Helene woke to the sound of rain cascading over the sides of the blocked eavestroughs outside her bedroom window. In an attempt to mute the drumming, she placed a pillow over her head—for as much as she was grateful to own a house, the upkeep and yard work was often too much for the single mother to manage.

After reluctantly departing from bed, Helene was preparing breakfast in the kitchen when the radio news announced that a major island road was as obstructed as her home's eavestroughs. Twisting and narrow, Highway 4 was the main access to the communities of Tofino and Port Alberni and it had once again been hit by a rockslide. Since it was the route taken by locals, tourists and truckers to the west coast of the Island, Helene knew that the radio station would be doing special coverage of the closure. Therefore, when she arrived in the newsroom a few hours later, she was not surprised to be asked to help out. And in some way, she was grateful—after spending a week trying to establish whether a death was a murder and a property deal was unethical, it was a relief to deal with immediately tangible problems, like food and gas supplies running low.

It took several hours and dozens of phone calls, but the journalist was quite pleased when she managed to track down a trucker who was stuck waiting to get through on the highway. The exhausted driver did an interview on the afternoon radio program, sounding frustrated and raw. Helene considered this to be live radio at its best: ordinary people trying to manage in extraordinary circumstances, a refreshing break from the curated vacuous statements regurgitated by politicians.

While covering ongoing emergencies, the day tended to pass quickly in the newsroom, and this time was no exception. Riya had ordered lunch for the team and most reporters managed to take a break long enough to scarf down a slice of pizza. Helene ended up working an hour late, which she didn't mind even though it was a Friday. It made up for leaving early the day before, and she preferred an office where a boss wasn't watching the clock, trusting employees would get their work done.

By the next morning, the rain had stopped and the sky was completely clear, as though the clouds themselves had decided not to get out of bed after the previous day's heavy work. Since it was October, Helene wanted to take advantage of the good weather so she badgered her two children into taking a bike ride. She was determined to make them put down their electronic devices and explore the outdoors, even if they loathed every moment of it.

It took an hour of wrestling with bike pumps and panniers before the family was ready to hit the road. Not that they would ever admit it, but Helene suspected her children were begrudgingly excited about the adventure as Cleo was wearing a new lip gloss and Oscar had a pair of birthday binoculars dangling from his neck.

Thankfully they only had a short journey along calm streets before they could ride on the wide separated bike lanes on Dallas Road. The path for cyclists and pedestrians had been built during the height of the COVID pandemic, allowing people to escape from their homes but still feel safe near strangers. A virus that stole the breath of millions could not compete with the purifying breeze rolling off the coastal beach. Helene loved the elevated trail because it was completely set apart from car traffic, as she never felt comfortable taking Oscar and Cleo on busy roads. Reading newscasts that included the deaths of young children from traffic collisions made her overly cautious when it came to urban cycling.

The wind was at their backs as they peddled eastwards toward Clover Point, passing by a lengthy green space on their right which was an off-leash dog park with a spectacular ocean view. On the other side of the road, Beacon Hill rose above the surrounding land, making it a popular sledding spot when snow made a rare appearance in Victoria. Next to the gentle hill, a totem pole by Kwakwaka'wakw carvers stood proudly almost 70 years after it was erected; an eagle was perched on top, perhaps surveying its hunting ground.

The only frustration Helene had with the protected and picturesque bike path was that it ran out after three kilometers. Once it reached Clover Point, cyclists were forced back onto the roadway, albeit a quieter section of the oceanside route. However, Helene preferred to leave Dallas Road and lead her children through the sleepy residential streets of Fairfield.

Travelling along neighbourhood roads allowed Helene to gaze at the charming wooden houses, which were often grander in style than those populating James Bay—the wealthy residents of Victoria building to the east. And perhaps it was her training as a journalist, but as she viewed each veranda or arched trellis, she imagined the lives of the homeowners, not unlike how a child creates adventures for their dolls. But quite different to the stories in her daily newscast, these tales always had happy endings. It was a way of balancing the scales of joy and misery in her mind.

Having glided along the cozy streets of Fairfield, the next section of their bike ride took them through markedly different scenery—the meandering rows of graves in the historic Ross Bay Cemetery. Occupying almost 30 acres of beachfront land, the graveyard was more than a century old and many early prominent citizens of Victoria were buried there, including several premiers and the painter Emily Carr. The expansive burial ground was a popular spot for both walkers and cyclists, and those who appreciated its slightly melancholy elegance.

A shout from behind let Helene know that her children wanted to make a stop, so she pulled over and dismounted.

Taking a drink from her water bottle, she observed her daughter laying down her own bicycle next to the path and taking out her cell phone. At first, she assumed Cleo wanted to check for text messages from friends; after all, she had been off the device for 20 minutes, but Helene was delightfully surprised when the teenager instead started snapping photos.

"Cool," was the sole comment made by the 14-year-old as she knelt down to take a close up shot of a barely legible inscription on one of the nearby graves.

Helene hadn't considered that the cemetery's Victorian Gothic overtones would naturally garner interest from her daughter.

"It belonged to a woman," Helene said as offhandedly as she could manage, not wanting to scare off her daughter with facts.

"The grave?" asked Cleo.

"No, the land where the cemetery was built," Helene continued, "Isabella Ross. The first female landowner in the province. Officially that is."

"That is so awesome. Why does no one ever talk about things like that? The stuff that women did."

Helene was aware that any response she made now would come off as too political—a lecture on the erasure of women from history books, their achievements always overshadowed by the actions of men. She chose to remain silent instead, content in the knowledge that her daughter was awake in the world.

"Look at that one." This time it was her son who had spoken. "It says they were only seven years old." Oscar was crouching in front of a derelict gravestone, tracing the moss-covered letters as though they were written in braille.

"I didn't know they put children in places like this," he said. "It seems awfully lonely."

"Yes it does. But perhaps they are happy to have a visitor today," replied Helene.

Straightening up, Oscar looked at his mom and said, "Maybe the children just wanted to be near their mother. I know I would want to be close to you."

Helene had to turn away to hide her tears. She was grateful to have such a compassionate and affectionate son, but she worried about how he would cope in a world where these characteristics could be viewed as weaknesses.

And then the conversation about children and parents and death brought to mind the articles she had recently read on the sinking of the S.S. Clallam—the doomed voyage that A.J. Beck had apparently survived and written about in her newly discovered novel. Contemplating the surrounding sea of gravestones, Helene recalled the fact that some of the victims of the maritime disaster were buried in Ross Bay Cemetery.

Quickly searching on her phone for the list of those who perished on January 8,1904, it didn't take Helene long to find the two names she was searching for. What was not quite so simple was trying to understand the graveyard's grid system, laid out in a badly drawn PDF she kept having to zoom into, trying to identify the letters and numbers of rows.

Deciding to make a game of it with her son, a morbid treasure hunt on a sunny Saturday afternoon, she showed him the names on the list and the general area in which they were supposed to be buried. Due to either his young eyes or his spiritual sensitivities, Oscar was quickly able to track down the grave in question.

IN SACRED AND
LOVING MEMORY OF
JEANNIE GERALDINE
AND JESSIE MACDUFF
BELOVED WIFE AND ONLY DAUGHTER OF
A J.C. GALLETLY
WHO LOST THEIR LIVES BY THE
FOUNDERING OF THE SS CLALLAM OFF
TRIAL ISLAND JANUARY 8th 1904

Helene and her son Oscar silently stood in front of the concrete cross, erected by a father and husband who had experienced a loss deeper than any ocean, an icy grief that would have made drawing breath a labour.

For some reason, this disaster more than a century ago seemed profoundly tragic and pointless to Helene, more so than the death she had witnessed at the Craigdarroch Castle a week past. Perhaps it was the idea of these two women dying together, each using their fading strength to give comfort to the other, thoughts of their own demise secondary to the possible survival of their loved one. Selfless in the face of extinction.

A passing cloud cast a shadow over Helene and Oscar and she pulled him tightly to her. He made no protest, merely wrapping his arms around her waist, an action of compassion and gratitude beyond his years. For a moment they were each other's lifeboats in a world that was cruel without apology or explanation.

Chapter 12

On rare occasions, Monday didn't feel like a Monday at all. At the start of the workweek, Helene had woken up refreshed, for once not even resentful for having to get out of bed. She packed the school lunches efficiently and even had time to wash her hair. More shockingly, her children got themselves ready with a minimum of urging, and they were dressed and waiting by the door for their mother by 7:45 with binders and instruments secured in their backpacks.

Helene suspected the Saturday bike ride had done them all good, the ocean air and view providing a sort of spring cleaning for the mind in late October. Cleo had come home with dozens of stark yet beautiful photos of the cemetery, while Oscar was less restless than usual—a result of the mother and son spending quality time together.

For her part, Helene's interest in the book A.J. Beck had written about the *S.S. Clallam* disaster was heightened, visiting the graves of two victims somehow transforming the story from black and white to vivid colour. Although it was 12 days away, Helene was keenly anticipating the book launch, imagining that she would spend the future weekend devouring the novel between loads of laundry.

In the meantime, Helene knew she was overdue to uncover something concrete on how the Fernandez property deal had gone wrong. With that goal in mind, after dropping off her still suspiciously docile children at school, she headed to City Hall once more. Making her way along the narrow roads of the capital city, Helene reminded herself to get reimbursed for all her parking payments from the last week, as leaving her car on the downtown streets seemed to be a growing habit.

The promising start to the week continued as Helene managed to maneuver her car into a spot directly in front of City Hall and then, once she had entered the building, a man held the elevator door open for her.

"Beautiful weekend," said Helene in place of a thank you.

"Yes, if you are into endless hours of sunshine. I mean, it's not for everyone. Think of the bats."

Helene turned to look at the man who had made such a cheeky response to a stranger first thing on a Monday morning. Appearing to be about ten years her junior, he was wearing dark jeans with the cuffs rolled up and a well-pressed white shirt under a blazer. With glasses perched on a prominent nose and slightly thinning hair, he was handsome in an intellectual way, like someone who refused to apologize for spending too much time in libraries.

"Yes, but how do we even know when the bats are happy. Do they have little bat smiles?" Helene replied, wanting to show the man that he wasn't the only one who could be sassy first thing in the morning.

A moment later the elevator doors slid open, and the man moved forward to exit, but first he turned and looked directly at Helene. "Fools are those that believe smiles are a sign of happiness."

Taking in the poetic insult, Helene was disappointed to discover that Monday was behaving like a Monday after all. As she tried to shake off the odd encounter, Helene stepped out of the elevator and examined the signs on the wall for directions to the right office.

At the end of the hall, an orange door with a square glass window led into a large room divided by a long counter for serving members of the public. There were no staff in sight which wasn't entirely unexpected since it was first thing in the morning. Helene waited patiently for several minutes for someone to appear, but then resorted to repeatedly tapping an ancient looking desk bell. The old-fashioned clang of the silver mechanical device made her feel like a 1950s housewife trying to return a fur stole. And her unease only increased when the handsome man from the elevator finally walked out from between rows of filing cabinets, holding up a half-eaten bagel.

"Sorry to keep you waiting," he said in a way that made Helene feel like she was in the wrong.

Considering making a quip about bats not having breakfast at dawn, Helene instead resolved the best way to overcome the tension in the room was to get down to business.

"I'd like to see the property records from 143 Clarence Street, please." Helene had asked Lucia Fernandez for the exact address of her parent's home the night before.

"Have you filled out the forms?" the man asked laconically, as though he already knew the answer.

"What forms?" Helene did not like the direction this conversation was going.

"The ones we email you, when you request to see property records."

"No. I didn't know I had to email first."

"You thought you could just walk in here and see the records?"

Helene glanced around the expansive office that only held the two of them. "Well, if you aren't too busy. And once you've finished your breakfast, of course." Helene wasn't sure why she added the last comment, but it was the right decision. The man's face broke into a playful smile.

Placing his bagel on the counter and scattering sesame seeds everywhere, the clerk then reached into a cubby, pulled out several forms and pushed them in Helene's direction.

"You can fill them out at that table in the corner. There are pens in the cup," he said. "I should be done my breakfast by then."

Helene had to resist gawping as the man turned on his heel and disappeared behind the rows of cabinets. But then she realized, despite his apparent rudeness, he did seem willing to help her.

Once Helene settled herself in the corner desk, placing her backpack on the linoleum floor, an awareness dawned that a peculiar clerk wasn't the only challenge she would encounter that morning: instructions at the top of the form stated that the legal owners of the property were the only ones authorized to request records.

However, since she had succeeded so far, despite failing to follow protocols, Helene decided to keep going in that direction.

On the line where it asked for the first and last name, Helene wrote, Maria Fernandez. Shrugging off any protests from her conscience, Helene absolved the misrepresentation by reminding herself that sometimes in journalism lies were necessary to uncover the truth. And once the initial untruth was committed to paper, Helene quickly filled out the rest of the form.

A loud rumble from Helene's stomach was a reminder that she had skipped breakfast, so she surreptitiously ate the remains of a granola bar retrieved from her jacket pocket before making her way up to the counter. She half-hoped and half-feared she would end up being served by the same clerk again. This time she did not have to resort to ringing the bell to get help as the man was quick to appear.

"So, Mrs. Fernandez," the clerk said the name with exaggerated emphasis, as though he knew what Helene was up to. "You seem to have filled out everything correctly." His tone implied "correctly" did not mean the same thing as "honestly."

The man then picked up the papers and shuffled them into a neat pile. "It should take about one week to process the application, and then you can come back to review the property records."

"One week!" Helene protested, evidently City Hall worked on slower timelines than newsrooms. "But what takes so long? Don't you have to just go back there and pull the file?" Helene immediately realized that her condescending description of the clerk's job would probably not entice him to rush her request.

"It's a little more complicated than that," the clerk replied defensively. "And we have other applications to process."

Helene took a moment to look over her shoulder to double check that there was no one else lined up for service. And although the empty room bolstered her cause, she decided to switch strategies, hoping honey worked better than a hammer.

"I would be incredibly grateful if there is any way you could possibly expedite this request," she said while smiling sweetly, "I need my niece to help me go over them. And she is leaving for university on Friday. Studying architecture."

"University? That starts in October?" the clerk asked without attempting to hide his incredulity. Helene was almost offended by his doubt.

"It's a school in Zurich. Very exclusive. Their term starts late." Wondering how far she would have to stretch her tale, Helene was relieved when the clerk begrudgingly acquiesced. She didn't think for a moment that he was convinced by her lies, but perhaps he just appreciated the break from the monotony of his job.

"Give me a couple of hours. Come back around 11:00. But don't tell anyone I did this for you," warned the clerk.

"Oh, I wouldn't dream of it," responded Helene, hoping that no one ever found out about her tactics either, managing to violate multiple journalism guidelines before a second cup of coffee.

Deciding it wasn't worth driving back to the newsroom for such a short amount of time, Helene topped up her parking meter and made her way to one of her favourite local cafes. She arrived during a mid-morning lull so there were lots of empty tables in the back room.

After logging on to her laptop, Helene checked for emails, but didn't see any messages that couldn't be ignored a little longer. She was half-way through rereading one of her online stories from the previous week when her cell phone rang.

"How did it go at City Hall this morning? Did you get what you needed? Is there any proof Roddy Beck was up to no good?" Riya's numerous questions indicated that she had probably already consumed several doses of caffeine that morning.

"I'm just waiting around for a clerk to come up with the papers I need. It was supposed to take a week, but I talked him into speeding up the process."

"Good to hear you haven't lost your ability to manipulate people."

Not entirely sure her boss's comment was a compliment, Helene asked brusquely, "Was there something you needed?"

"Right. Yes. I called to let you know the police sent out a statement minutes ago. It says they are continuing to investigate the death of Roddy Beck and have not yet determined if it was a homicide. They are appealing for more witnesses to come forward. They basically said nothing," scoffed Riya.

Helene wondered what kind of witnesses the police were hoping for, as it would have been difficult for anyone below the landing to see how events had unfolded even if they had thought to look up. Helene recalled that the view from the ballroom was blocked by the walls of a short stairway. Perhaps the investigators should instead hire a medium to communicate with the spirits roaming the halls of

98

Craigdarroch Castle. They might have witnessed the untimely death of Roddy Beck between games of billiards.

"But I also learned through the grapevine that they released the body. The funeral is on Wednesday. I assume you'll be going."

Helene felt a rush of excitement at this news, a gathering of the tech guru's friends and family would be a great opportunity to survey all the suspects in one place. The people who loved him would be sure to show up, and the ones who hated him, even more so. The challenge would be determining whose grief was as authentic as the newly discovered manuscript.

Assuring her boss she would attend the funeral, Helene ended the call, and ordered a mocha from the cafe barista. During her university days, she had worked in a funky coffee shop in Vancouver to help pay tuition and rent. She recalled that there was something uniquely satisfying about creating artisanal drinks topped with foamed milk or whipped cream, each specially prepared coffee was a work of art in its own way. The techniques for making a cafe latte or cappuccino had specific steps including running hot water through espresso and steaming a tin cup of milk. This unvarying routine was so unlike her current confusing investigation into the death of Roddy Beck, which was more like trying to put a coffee bean back together once it had been through the grinder.

Before returning to her seat, warm coffee mug in hand, Helene made sure to tip the barista generously; her current job may be more frustrating, but it was also better paid.

Between sips of rich mocha, Helene checked her text messages. She saw that there was one from Detective Kalinowski in Berlin, letting her know about the police press release that her producer had already mentioned. She sent a quick reply thanking her friend and wishing them another great week in Germany. She suggested they take a train ride, perhaps to visit a medieval castle nestled in the Black Forest. The trip might kindle some of the fairytale romance that had been missing from the honeymoon so far.

Although the clerk had told her to come back in a few hours, once she had finished her drink and responded to a few more emails, Helene decided to return to City Hall. Patience was not considered a virtue in her profession, and she thought her presence might incentivize the man to locate the file a little more quickly.

Walking into the property records office for the second time that morning, she was pleased to find that there was still no one else waiting to be served, however, Helene did have to resort to clanging the desk bell to summon the clerk again.

Fears that her early arrival might be a source of further irritation turned out to be unwarranted, as when the man came into sight, he looked harried in an entirely different way. Blazer discarded, his well-pressed shirt now rumpled, he anxiously pushed his wire-rimmed glasses against the bridge of his nose.

"I think I may have to call the police!" he stammered.

"The police?"

"Yes, the file is missing!"

"Which file?" she asked with trepidation.

"The one you asked for!"

"Well, as much as I think the file is important, I am not sure the police are going to share your concern." The last thing Helene needed was to be questioned as to why she wanted the property records of Maria Fernandez when she wasn't Maria Fernandez.

The man gestured toward the banks of files behind him. "But nothing like this has ever happened before. It's a disaster!"

If this clerk thought a missing file was an emergency, then Helene believed it was a good thing he hadn't become

100

a journalist. Who knows how he would have handled an earthquake or planes flying into buildings.

"Listen. Why don't you go back and check again. Make sure it's gone."

"Are you saying I don't know when a file is missing?" The clerk spoke with indignation while taking the opportunity to restore some of his dignity by straightening his shirt collar.

"Not at all. You just seem like someone who likes to be thorough." Helene knew a compliment was the best way to defuse the situation. "And there must be some kind of log of who accessed the files, or a record of applicants. You can go through those as well."

Looking slightly mollified, the clerk replied, "Yes, that's true. There are a few places I can check."

"Great, why don't you do that, and then let me know what you find," Helene suggested nonchalantly.

Helene's comment managed to diminish the clerk's distress at least temporarily. In response, he grinned, stating, "I can do that. But first you are going to have to tell me who you really are."

Chapter 13

Helene had skipped the last funeral she had been invited to and, years later, she still wrestled with the decision to stay away. It was six months into the COVID pandemic when her mother was diagnosed with rapidly progressing dementia. Less than three weeks passed between her being admitted to hospital and Lela's call to say she was gone. Their mother had died at 80, which seemed young for someone so stubborn. Helene had always thought of her like a monarch who would vociferously resist giving up their throne. But in some ways Helene was grateful that death had come quickly; her mother had been terrified of waking up in a hospital, the staff and the surroundings so jarring after living in the same bungalow in a verdant academic Edmonton neighbourhood for half a century.

In death, as in life, Helene's mother made everything as difficult as possible. She died at the point in the pandemic when people were only meeting outside; offices, restaurants and airplanes were places the virus lurked. So, Helene had to weigh paying her last respects to her late mother against her own health and that of her children, and the living ultimately took priority. It was, in fact, because she was a mother that she did not attend the funeral of her parent.

Perhaps she would have made a different decision if her relationship with her mother hadn't been dysfunctional for decades, if not always. To describe her mother as the woman who raised her was a stretch. That's because her mother's mental illness was like having a third greedy and volatile sibling in the house.

To friends and neighbours, her mother appeared simply eccentric. A gifted musician who would insist on hosting a spontaneous picnic in the park while friends attentively listened to her playing a concerto on an alto recorder. She was also very fond of painting, and her pastel watercolours hung on every wall in the house, mostly of the same lilac tree in the front yard during different seasons. At the university, her mother was a popular lecturer in medieval music, and she often stayed later after class to chat to her adoring students. Perhaps this is what made Helene most resentful toward her mother and the community: that no one recognized how her frequently unconventional behaviour could turn toxically bizarre.

As children, Lela and Helene would sometimes wake to find sheet music spread across the kitchen table, her mother examining each arpeggio and coda for an encrypted warning about the mafia. The fact that they lived in a city in northern Alberta, and not New York, did nothing to diminish her mother's obsession with the criminal underworld. These incidents happened on what Helene classified as good days, when she and her sister cooked their own meals from scraps in the fridge and took money from their mother's purse to buy the things they needed, like a first bra. On the worst days, their mother was transformed into a swaying banshee—her angular form backlit by the large living room window. She would grasp and shatter whatever was within reach, including any sense of stability for her two daughters. Accusations were hurled at Helene and Lela about how they had once again betrayed their own mother. The specifics of their treachery were never clearly laid out, but that hardly mattered to the terrified children, and later, mortified teenagers. As an adult, Helene did not recall these episodes in their entirety but as fractured moments. As if her brain could only manage a single note of discordant memory at a time, not the whole song.

Their father was long gone by this point, having never returned from a sabbatical he had taken at a university in Italy when Helene was 12 and Lela nine. He had apparently moved in with a pastry chef and never looked back. Helene could hardly blame him, if she could have divorced her mother she would have, but children didn't have that luxury. As an adult, she knew she should feel more resentment toward him for abandoning his young daughters. However, after being married to her mother for 15 years, Helene believed he deserved a bit of happiness. Or maybe her heart just couldn't handle hating both her parents.

The funeral for her mother had ended up being very small, and the few friends in attendance believed that COVID had kept Helene away. But three years later, as she entered the church where the service for Roddy Beck was being held, Helene experienced a familiar rush of regret. Pandemic concerns aside, her mother's funeral would have been a last chance to not only say a final goodbye to her intellectual, artistic and neglectful mother, but also to mourn her own corrupted childhood. And yet, looking around at the cast of characters filling the pews for Roddy Beck, some of whom were now familiar, Helene understood grieving was always complicated.

"I see you made it."

Immediately recognizing the voice, Helene looked askance as the disreputable reporter Gary Graham slipped into the pew next to her. He was eagerly eyeing the crowd, as though waiting for the mourners to start brawling. She was only grateful he had left his trademark Blue Jays hat at home.

"Personally, I wouldn't have missed this for the world," Gary continued, "Although I expected something a little more glamorous for a guy who was rolling in it. They didn't even hire a choir. I just love those gospel numbers."

Helene had hoped that by not replying to Gary's remarks he might shut up, but then she remembered he was a radio host, and monologue was his preferred style of conversation. So she came to the same conclusion as

105

Churchill in the Second World War: appeasement was the wrong approach.

"You know, funerals are such tragic affairs," said Helene. "The loss of a loved one. A life taken before their time. There is only one thing that could make it worse."

"What's that?" asked Gary, making no attempt to hide his salacious anticipation.

"Having to listen to you talk through the whole thing."

Helene received an offended smirk in response, but gratefully, no more commentary was forthcoming.

"Friends and family, we are gathered here today to remember the life of Roddy Beck," the minister began speaking as if he too had been waiting for Gary to be quiet. "Roddy was one of those rare individuals who had a bright mind for business and technology, but also for creating community. He was the very best of men and his memory will be cherished in the hearts of those who loved him." An indignant snort could be heard echoing down the church nave, possible pushback against the sanitizing of Roddy Beck's character.

Helene was all too familiar with the tendency to absolve the dead of their sins. Politicians were remembered for the economic programs they spearheaded rather than the profits they skimmed through shady side deals, musicians were celebrated for the songs they had written for a lost generation while giving their own children money in the place of love. And maybe that is what truly kept her away from her mother's funeral, she could not endure the mourners heralding her parent's idiosyncratic personality as though it was a qualification for sainthood.

The priest spoke for a few minutes more and then, after a brief shuffle, he was replaced at the pulpit by a man in a well-cut suit in charcoal grey rather than traditional black.

"I've been a friend of Roddy's since high school and I am honoured to share a few words about him today. And yet, I still can't believe that someone so extraordinary has been taken from us." Handsome and exuding wealth, this man was the kind of individual who was so steeped in privilege that he was probably dumbfounded as to why everyone else did not share his smooth path to success.

"Roddy always stood out, even when he played football back at Vic High. You could tell he was meant for bigger things in life. Raised by his grandmother, he didn't let losing both parents so early in life hold him back. In fact, I think enduring hardship taught him how important it was to be strong and to not let anything or anyone stop you." As the man offered up vapid observations of his friend's life in the manner of a motivational speaker, Helene couldn't help but tune him out. She instead took the opportunity to examine the crowd.

At the front of the church, Roddy's ex-wife and Zofia Bosko were sitting in the pew closest to the pulpit. Adrianna Beck was stunning in a black wool blazer and skirt, a string of oversized pearls accessorizing her outfit like a chain of moons against a midnight sky. Zofia, who lacked such talent for materialism and vanity, wore a grey turtleneck that appeared worn out even from a few rows away. Helene wondered if the two women from very different worlds were acquaintances or even friends, or if they had just ended up sitting next to each other due to a mutual sense of self-importance.

In the row behind the two women, Mayor Strauss and Councillor Davies sat in the middle of the pew. It was interesting to see them together as Strauss was usually more left-leaning in her support for bike lanes and green roofs, while Davies often spoke up for those who wanted to maintain the status quo. Perhaps it was just a matter of politicians sticking together at a public event, but Helene struggled to believe they might have carpooled to the funeral. It was hard to imagine Rupert Davies would deign to ride in Irma Strauss's electric Mini.

As Helene was attempting to recall the name of a familiar looking figure occupying the same row as the mayor and councillor, her attention was abruptly brought back to the speaker.

"Some people might have questioned the tactics Roddy used to get ahead, but I believe this was the secret to his success: do what is necessary and don't ever apologize."

Helene was intrigued by this remark. It sounded like praise but could be perceived as a criticism of Beck's ruthless business tactics. Apparently, this childhood friend had decided against presenting an unflawed version of the dead. Perhaps he was settling an old score when Roddy Beck was in no position to protest. Examining the faces of the other mourners, Helene wondered how many of them had really liked Beck. Perhaps he was someone who was easier to love when he was dead. He wouldn't be the first.

Taking in the bounty of memorial flowers and the luxurious casket occupying the centre aisle, Helene knew that it was possible to possess opposing emotions about someone. Despite the neglect and narcissism, her mother had supported Helene's decision to become a journalist. She had helped her daughter financially to go back to university and bragged to friends when Helene had landed her first media job. This might have been because her mother had a great appreciation for poetry and novels, and seeing Helene's stories in print was like having an Anaïs Nin in the family.

Not wanting to reawaken the ambivalence she felt toward her dead mother, Helene let herself become distracted by the footsteps of a late arrival. She turned in her seat to spy a woman standing at the foot of the aisle, almost like a bride waiting for the music to commence. But the woman who appeared to be relishing the disturbance she

108

had caused was not suitably attired for either nuptials or a funeral, as she wore a bright red dress and a matching hat perched at a jaunty angle. And if her outfit left any doubt about her disrespect for the proceedings, her look of disgust made it clear that if Roddy Beck had any second thoughts about being dead, she was there to make sure they came to nothing.

Chapter 14

The reception for Roddy Beck's funeral was held at the palatial home of his almost-ex-wife in Moss Bay. Perhaps Adrianna wanted to play host in order to solidify her claim to the tech guru's fortune or to simply assert final control over her dead spouse's legacy despite their imminent divorce. Either way, it was clear she could afford to feed the dozens of mourners who had passed through the elegant foyer and were now mingling on the marble floor of the sunken living room. A 12-foot glass table running along one wall held generous fruit platters, charcuterie boards and hefty tubes of uncut salami. There was no knife on the table so Helene wasn't sure if the cured meat was for display or if guests were meant to tear off chunks with their teeth. The buffet also boasted miniature desserts ranging from mille-feuille to cream custards. Having eaten a substantial breakfast before driving to the funeral that morning, Helene still found herself wondering how long she would have to wait before filling up one of the gold-rimmed plates with food.

As people continued to arrive and the initial awkwardness of a party for the dead had yet to pass, Helene took a moment to survey the paintings gracing the tall beige walls in the foyer. She would have expected such an ostentatious home, with its spiral staircase off the main entrance and wide ocean-facing windows, to have a collection of abstract art. Possessing a worth that came mostly from competing auction bids as opposed to any identifiable artistic talent, canvases covered in random red streaks or geometric shapes were usually the preference of the rich. The often-incomprehensible art was a status symbol, proving they could afford to spend millions of dollars on something that lacked inherent value or beauty.

However, Helene had to begrudgingly admit that Adrianna Beck had a sophisticated and specific taste in art, owning a collection reflecting a personal fondness rather than the offerings from a Sotheby's catalogue. The wealthy homeowner had acquired landscape paintings of Vancouver Island scenes, the artists interpreting familiar sites with dynamic colours and unsettling angles. In the main hallway there was a work depicting an expansive view of Ross Bay Cemetery at dawn, the ocean blues bisected by a shimmering path of tangerine sun. Helene knew the vantage well, having taken photos of the same vista from Clover Point on early weekend mornings. The artist had managed to capture not only the scape but also the feeling of inhabiting the promontory, as though the salty wind that swept across the grassy peninsula was emanating from the artwork.

"That was one of Roddy's favourite paintings." Zofia Bosko had joined Helene in the main entrance. "It was the work he bought after selling his first website. And even after he separated from Adrianna and moved out, he always meant to come back and get it."

Helene did not know why she was so disappointed that it was in fact Roddy Beck who had possessed a discerning eye for art, not Adrianna. The man had so many talents, she would have preferred him to be unremarkable at one thing at least.

"Then Adrianna asked for it as part of the divorce agreement. To be cruel," mused Zofia. "You don't know how to really hurt someone until you have loved them." This comment made Helene curious as to why this academic knew the details of Roddy's proposed divorce. Their relationship must have gone beyond working on A.J. Beck's newly discovered book together. She wondered if they had been lovers despite a 20-year age difference.

"What a fantastic home! Totally fantastic!" An older woman wearing faded jeans and a leopard print blouse joined Zofia, her hair appearing to have been bleached into near non-existence. "This place is the dream we all want. A dream the Communists tried to take from us."

"Mother, no politics. We're at a funeral."

"The funeral is over. This is the party!" The woman spoke in a loud voice with a slight accent. A few people turned to stare in her direction.

Helene was about to introduce herself to Zofia's parent, but the woman had other plans. Walking up to the abundant display of food, she picked up one of the tubes of salami. She then reached into her suede purse, pulled out a Swiss Army knife and cut off a chunk of meat.

"Pretty good," she reflected. "Not Polish, but still pretty good."

"Oh god, I knew I shouldn't have brought her. But she was so desperate to see the inside of the house." Zofia was obviously mortified by her mother's behaviour, which made Helene like her a little more. Being embarrassed by a parent had occupied much of her childhood.

"It's OK," Helene offered, "Everyone needs a little light relief at a funeral. And I think your mother may have broken the ice. Or cut the salami, as the case may be."

Zofia smiled in response to her kindness.

"It's funny," Zofia said, "I could never really tell if my mother, Ludmilla, liked Roddy or not. The few times they met, she never spoke much. But afterwards, she always went on about his success. And his wealth."

Helene imagined that if Zofia's mother had come to Canada as an impoverished immigrant, then Roddy Beck's achievements would have represented the fruition of the ultimate capitalist dream. Although belonging to the family of a very famous writer, he had quite a few advantages and he wasn't exactly self-made.

"We never had much money when I was growing up. My mother worked double shifts as a cleaner to pay for everything. The ultimate single mother," further explained

113

Zofia. "And that's why working on this book project with Roddy meant so much. I was finally able to support her. Pay her back for everything she had done." Then she abruptly asked, "Are you any closer to figuring out who killed him?"

Caught off guard, Helene knew her reply sounded defensive, "The police haven't even decided if it was murder or not."

"Yes, but the note I gave you? Someone was threatening him!"

"Well, I have come across a few people he seems to have upset."

Zofia looked confused, "Everyone loved Roddy! Except whoever killed him, obviously." Not waiting for an answer, Zofia added. "After my interview, the police asked for permission to search my home. They went through my basement and took away some oil cans."

"Oil cans?"

"Yes, the kind you use for greasing a bicycle chain."

Zofia's attention was suddenly drawn back to her parent who was making a beeline for a pristine white couch with a plate piled high with food. The academic immediately headed off in her direction, perhaps in hopes of making an interception.

Helene was reflecting on the possible ways bicycle chain oil might have been used in a murder when she felt the cell phone in her pocket buzzing. Moving to a quiet spot behind the imposing staircase to check her messages, Helene expected it to be her boss wanting an update from the morning. However, she was pleased to find it was actually a text from the city clerk looking into the missing property records. A little too pleased, if she was honest.

No luck tracking down records
Must be a forged name on file release
Sincerely, Tristan

Helene wasn't sure which amused her more. The fact that the clerk was behaving like a newly deputized sheriff or that he put his name at the end of his texts like a 19th century correspondence.

At funeral reception
But eager to hear more

After sending the reply, Helene did wonder why she was sharing details of her morning with the clerk but put it down to reciprocal enthusiasm.

To avoid any unnecessary concern, she added some context.

Funeral is for work
Not anyone I was close to

Except, literally, when he died, Helene thought, recalling Roddy Beck's body lifelessly sprawled on the pavement.

Knowing she had to get back to mingling at the reception and eavesdropping on the guests for possible motives for murder, Helene gave herself a few moments to wait for a reply from the clerk. She was not disappointed.

Way to make my job seem boring

Grinning as she put away her phone, Helene admitted to herself that she had been a bit lonely since Alex had gotten engaged to Kalinowski. Recently her friend had been less available for the little snarky exchanges that made life more tolerable.

There were now enough people helping themselves to the buffet that Helene didn't feel self-conscious grabbing a snack. Picking up a plate, she took a large chunk of Camembert and a handful of crackers containing cranberries and nuts. She would need to wash her face and hands after she finished eating to remove all allergens as this food was high-risk to her children, but for the moment she would enjoy indulging in the rare treats. In the newsroom, the only free food on offer was either pizza or donuts, or the occasional indigestible culinary creation of a local restaurateur being interviewed on the radio, usually combining chocolate and jalapeño peppers.

Plate in hand, Helene found a place to hover near the living room windows which offered a panoramic ocean view, as though one of the room's landscape paintings had come to life. While studying the other guests, she attempted to divide the Camembert into bite-sized pieces with a cracker.

Mayor Strauss and Councillor Davies had gone their separate ways, each now holding court to a small group. Admittedly, Davies, in his dark suit and polished shoes, appeared more comfortable in the extravagant surroundings. His audience was listening attentively, sharing subdued smiles at what Helene assumed were the councillor's riveting anecdotes. The mayor and her entourage seemed slightly unsettled in comparison. When there was a pause in conversation, Strauss would glance nervously around the room, as if expecting a journalist to take a photo of her cavorting with the wealthy.

Playing the part of the hostess, Adrianna Beck was too busy overseeing the numerous staff to mix with the guests. Directing the waiters to refill half-empty glasses or to remove a disarranged fruit tray from the buffet, she reminded Helene of a captain of a ship directing a crew in battle. She could understand how even a manipulative businessman like Roddy Beck had lost his favourite painting to his commanding almost-ex-wife.

Then, like a shot over the bow, the woman who had shown up at the funeral in the flashy red dress entered the opulent house and stood at the edge of the foyer, which

116

overlooked the sunken living room. Boldly meeting the gaze of those who were staring at her, she gracefully made her way down the three steps in lethal looking stiletto heels. Helene, like any seasoned journalist, headed in the direction of the well-dressed danger rather than away from it.

"Helene Unger, Vancouver Island Radio," the journalist introduced herself to the intriguing interloper.

"I know, we spoke on the phone the other day. And I've seen your byline photo." The woman extended her hand in greeting. "Lucia. Lucia Fernandez."

Connecting the voice from the sauna phone call to this guest made sense since the woman's dress and hat were the colour of flames. The daughter of Mrs. Fernandez appeared to be in her late 40s, beautiful in a severe sort of way, her sharp features framed by jet black hair hanging in a bob like a helmet.

"What a bunch of hypocrites," Lucia said while motioning to the other guests in the room, "Acting as if they care about anything besides money. But that's what Roddy Beck deserves, since that was the only thing of importance to him."

"How's your mother doing? Is she out of hospital?" Helene asked, hoping to draw the intense woman into a less dramatic but more informative conversation.

"Better. I think they will release her soon. But her heart. It'll never be the same."

"I thought you said it was a stroke. She has heart issues too?"

"Yes, when my father died, it lost any reason to keep beating. That's why I came here today. To make sure the man who destroyed my parents' lives is really and truly gone."

If Roddy Beck had been murdered, Helene felt like she was speaking to someone who might have volunteered for the job. The elder Mrs. Fernandez was probably too feeble to push the tech guru from the top landing at

Craigdarroch, but her daughter seemed extremely able-bodied and willing. In addition, her bitter words were similar to the threatening tone of the note Zofia Bosko had discovered clutched in Roddy Beck's hand. The only problem was that Helene didn't recall seeing Lucia at the castle press conference, and the bitter woman hardly seemed capable of making a quiet entrance. Helene did wonder whether the police had spoken to the daughter of Mrs. Fernandez. Not for the first time, she wished Detective Kalinowski was working the case, not strolling along streets of cobblestones.

Possibly seeking a fresh audience to shock, Lucia moved on from Helene, heading in Mayor Strauss's direction. The journalist couldn't help but feel sympathy for the municipal leader, hoping she had taken some fortification from the buffet table before the imminent attack. At the castle press conference, Mrs. Fernandez had levelled questions about the complicity of city officials in Roddy Beck's unethical property deals and, at the funeral reception, her daughter appeared determined to get answers.

"I hate it when she gets like this. But her mother going into hospital has only made things worse." The words were spoken by a kind-looking man who now stood next to Helene. "I'm Charles. Lucia's husband. And minder, apparently. I need to get her out of here before she causes a scene."

Introducing herself to the man, Helene restrained from adding that she thought the opportunity to avoid drama had already passed.

"She loves her parents just a little too much. Some people do. Even her dad, with his passing, he's become a sort of martyr." The husband offered a rueful smirk. "Sorry, I'm a psychologist. Not supposed to analyze your own family. But it's hard to resist, considering the circumstances."

118

"I'm not sure I loved my mother at all," Helene blurted out, and then was immediately taken aback by her own disclosure.

"It's OK," the man said, as if sensing her embarrassment. "People say things around me. It's always been that way. Partly why I went into this profession. And you should know that not feeling a deep connection with your parents can make someone incredibly strong out of necessity. Honestly, I wish my wife could be a little less attached."

Helene and the man watched as Lucia grabbed a glass of wine from a passing waiter, downed the contents in one go, and then continued to grill a very uncomfortable looking mayor.

"If you're a psychologist, can't you help her become … less attached?"

"It doesn't work that way. I can understand what's wrong, but somehow my powers to heal seem to end at my own doorstep. Frustrating is too small a word."

"What can be done?" Helene asked, surprised to find herself in the midst of an intense conversation with a virtual stranger at a funeral reception.

"Love them, as best you can. And if you can't do that, then you should probably leave."

Helene wasn't sure if the psychologist was talking about his own marriage or her damaged childhood, but apparently the old adage was true: you could love them or leave them.

However, staring down at the swirling pool of funereal guests, Helene wondered if someone had chosen a third option when it came to dealing with Roddy Beck: not to love or to leave, but to kill him.

Chapter 15

Although she had consumed a small brick of cheese at the funeral reception, and could hardly imagine being hungry ever again, Helene decided to take Oscar and Cleo out for dinner at their favourite restaurant. It was partly because she hadn't had time to go grocery shopping, but she also wanted to have some fun with her kids. After leaving the funeral reception she couldn't shake the shadow of her mother's death and her own mortality. Spending the rest of the day in a newsroom broadcasting grim headlines had failed to brighten her mood.

Helene viewed her children as a failsafe cure to overthinking life and death: Oscar offered reports of his badly behaving classmates, while Cleo gave updates on her strategic maneuvers between high school cliques. How could anxiety about the pointlessness of human existence compete with the descriptions of Noah grinding crackers into the petri dishes being used by Alicia for her science fair project?

Due to their severe allergies, there were only a couple restaurants in Victoria to which Helene felt comfortable taking her children. That evening the vote was for a sushi spot close to home where Oscar and Cleo enjoyed vegetables wrapped in rice. Because of their food restrictions, the staff knew the family well, and arranged their sushi in entertaining ways. So if her children's classroom anecdotes hadn't been enough to push aside melancholy musings, then a tempura carrot volcano certainly was.

By the next morning, Helene had managed to shake off the despondent emotional hangover from the funeral and was left with a keen sense of wanting to make every day count. The journalist felt a renewed determination to uncover the truth behind both Roddy Beck's business dealings and his untimely death.

Helene decided that returning to the RoddTek head office was as good a start as any to resume her search for answers. The previous day, she had spotted Beck's former assistant, Ameer, lurking at the fringes of the funeral crowd, appearing more like an observer than a mourner himself. Tracking down his personal email from the company website, she was pleased to receive a prompt and obliging reply to her request to talk further. Perhaps the assistant wanted to set the record straight after Adrianna Beck had crashed their last conversation.

Ushered into Roddy Beck's upscale former office once more, Helene resisted the siren call of the deep leather couch and instead perched on the seat of a taller and firmer chair. Ameer made himself comfortable behind the substantial desk, as though his appointment as CEO would be imminently confirmed. He even went so far as to possessively arrange a few of the silver-framed black and white photos on the desk before their conversation really got going, as if they held pictures of his own family, not Beck's.

"What can I help you with today?" Ameer asked directly. "I'm hoping now that the funeral is behind us, you want to discuss the bright future of RoddTek, not dwell on the past."

"Well, until the mystery of Roddy's death is solved, that may be a bit difficult."

"Mystery? It was an unfortunate accident. Roddy was simply not risk averse. Not in business. And, apparently, not when it came to heights."

"And yet the police are still investigating," Helene insisted but then changed tack. "However, I didn't come here to talk about that. I was really hoping to find out more about one of his business projects. At a recent city council meeting someone claimed that he wanted to tear down A.J. Beck's former residence and turn it into a tourist attraction."

Appearing to take a moment to consider how much to disclose, Ameer eventually replied, "Yes, that was one of Roddy's pet projects, and he was trying to keep it under wraps, as he knew there would be community pushback. But now that he's gone, and it'll never come to fruition, I'm sure there is no harm in discussing it."

"It's just such a strange thing to do. To destroy the home of his great-grandmother. A woman who is Victoria's most famous writer. Especially if he wanted to uphold her legacy."

Ameer grinned as he offered an explanation. "But that's what most people don't realize. Roddy didn't venerate his great-grandmother like everyone thought. In fact, he told me once that she had ruined his life."

"Didn't she die long before he was born?"

"Yes, but his family idolized her and anything associated with her was treated like a holy relic. His grandmother, A.J. Beck's daughter, she inherited the home and it was packed with books and memorabilia. And that's where Roddy lived after his parents died, so his childhood was spent in a sort of museum to the writer. My sense was he never got much attention—he couldn't compete with his great-grandmother even though she was dead. Probably what drove him so hard in business."

"Remind me what happened to the parents," she prompted.

"They were killed in a car accident on their way to a big party at Government House to honour A.J. Beck. So, he thought she was responsible for their deaths."

"Only in the most convoluted way," protested Helene.

"Yes, but Roddy was very young when it happened. I think five years old. He needed someone to blame."

"What about his uncle? I heard him mentioned at the press conference. Why didn't he take in Roddy instead of his grandmother?" Helene inquired.

"I'm not really sure, except that he was a single man. I think in the '70s they thought a child needed a female caregiver, even if it was an indifferent grandmother. Not that it sounds as though the uncle would have been any different. He's been the caretaker for A.J. Beck's house for the past 20 years and he only contacted Roddy when he wanted money for its upkeep."

"But at the press conference Roddy made it sound like his uncle was a father figure. 'Taught him how to be a man.'"

"Yes, Roddy was always good at telling a story people wanted to hear. Maybe he got that talent from his great-grandmother."

As if revelling in his newfound freedom to talk about his boss candidly, Ameer leaned forward and pressed a button on the office phone.

"Sheila, can you bring us two coffees? And maybe a few cookies if there are any left over in the kitchen?"

After releasing the button, the assistant leaned back in the chair and surveyed the room with greedy eyes. Helene wondered how long he had been yearning to lord around the place like he was in charge. Depending on how much abuse he had received as an assistant, she couldn't blame him.

"Of course, the immediate future of the company is going to be revealed on Friday." Ameer said, tantalizing the journalist.

"Why on Friday?" asked Helene, willing to play along.

"Because that's the reading of the will." Ameer replied smugly, clearly believing his position leading the company was secure despite Adrianna Beck's previous claim that her almost-ex-husband had left everything to her.

"And where's that happening?" inquired Helene, trying to keep the eagerness from her voice.

"In Vancouver," said Ameer. "I suppose I'll have to take a helicopter over." His days of waiting with the common folk in lengthy ferry lineups to get off the island were in the past and Ameer was beaming like a schoolchild who had taken first prize.

For her part, Helene was less concerned with transportation, and more with how she was going to finagle an invite to the will reading.

To keep the topic going, she asked, "Why is it being held in Vancouver? Wouldn't most of the beneficiaries be from Victoria?"

Before Ameer had a chance to reply, a woman entered the room carrying a tray of coffee mugs and containers of sugar and milk. When she laid down her burden, Helene spied four chocolate chip cookies on a side plate. It seemed snacks lasted longer at the tech office than her newsroom.

Once the woman had departed, and Ameer added milk and sugar to his coffee, his explanation continued. "The executor lives there. Harold Webb. Perhaps you remember him from the funeral? He delivered the eulogy."

It was not difficult for Helene to recall the man who had spoken at the front of the church, a rugged and attractive face delivering a slightly problematic review of his friend's life.

"I didn't even think readings of the will were still a thing," said Helene.

"They are when millions of dollars are at stake."

"Well, I look forward to hearing the details."

"I'm sure there won't be any big surprises," replied Ameer confidently.

Helene didn't bother contradicting the man, despite her strong notion that the one thing the will would contain was surprises for someone. And definitely not happy ones.

Indulging in a sip of the fragrant coffee, Helene started to pack up her notebook and recorder. At the same time as she was preparing to leave, one of the photos on the desk caught her attention. It was a black and white scene featuring a much younger looking Beck lounging on a pub bench surrounded by friends.

"That's the Barge and Whistle, isn't it?" guessed Helene, thinking she recognized the old English decor.

"That's right," Ameer confirmed. "That was Roddy's favourite hangout during his university days. Claimed he got the inspiration for his first website while having a pint there. You can see Harold in the photo too."

Lifting up the picture to examine the details, Helene did spot a younger version of the man who had spoken at the funeral. More hair, less weight, the same conquering smile.

As she placed the photo back on the polished desk, she accidentally bumped another silver frame. It was holding a recent photo taken in front of the Empress Hotel in Victoria's Inner Harbour, a snap showing Roddy Beck standing next to Zofia Bosko, his arm wrapped around her shoulder. It was difficult to determine if the gesture was intimate or simply friendly, but once again Helene wondered about the exact nature of the relationship between the tech guru and the academic.

While waiting for the hallway elevator, Helene tried to devise a plan to get an invitation to the will reading in Vancouver. She was convinced that many of the questions plaguing her investigation would be answered by the contents of the will. Her thoughts were interrupted first by the bing of the elevator arriving and then by the alert of a text message.

Watch out for blooms!

Stepping into the elevator, Helene reread the text. Why was Detective Kalinowski concerned about her pollen allergies, especially in mid-October? Helene texted back a puzzled looking emoji.

A few minutes later, when her car's Bluetooth device alerted her to a phone call from the Victoria Police Department, understanding dawned, albeit too late: autocorrect had turned the name 'Bloom' into 'blooms'. Not for the first time, she cursed a technology that made corrections like a schoolteacher who knew everything about words and nothing about how people used them.

"I understand that you witnessed the death of Roddy Beck." Detective Bloom's gruff voice boomed out of Helene's car speakers, prompting her to turn the volume down.

"Yes, and I gave a statement to an officer who was on the scene." Helene was grateful there wasn't too much traffic on the highway while she navigated the conversation with the police detective.

"But you didn't think to come in for an interview? Even though you were the first to see the body after the fall?"

Bloom's pointed question once more conjured up images of Beck's bent limbs. She did her best to ignore them and focus on passing a minivan.

"I wasn't aware that I was supposed to volunteer for a police interview." Helene knew her reply was probably brasher than was advisable, but the detective had the bedside manner of a dentist who didn't believe in anesthesia. "I assumed you would have called if you wanted to speak to me again. And I did send several emails asking for an update on the investigation."

Ignoring her response, Detective Bloom continued, "I just happened to hear you on the radio yesterday afternoon, your story about Beck's funeral. Funny that you didn't mention you personally witnessed his death."

127

Feeling more exasperated than intimidated by the police officer, Helene brusquely asked, "Is there something I can help you with?"

"Yes, you can come in first thing tomorrow for a formal interview, as part of our murder investigation."

"Did you say murder?" Helene didn't even attempt to hide the excitement in her voice.

"Yes, we've just sent out the press release," confirmed Bloom. "The death of Roddy Beck is now being considered a homicide."

After agreeing to arrive at the police station no later than 9 a.m., Helene spent the rest of the drive home going over her interviews from the last week with people who had known Roddy Beck. As each person's face came to mind, she couldn't help but wonder if it was the mask of a murderer.

January 8, 1904
Afternoon

In a matter of hours, the seething of the ocean was so wildly violent that it had become necessary for passengers to cling to some fixed object to remain upright. I had indeed joined Miss Beck in the social hall and we did our best to remain seated on a sofa bolted to the floor. My stomach did lurch unhappily as the vessel tossed from side to side and I was grateful I had eaten a mere thin crust of bread for breakfast.

My earlier concerns about the other passengers paying too close attention to my person had been all but discarded. Whether they were a coal merchant or a stoker, all occupants of the vessel now had one thought in mind: their own survival.

In the same way, my hesitation in trusting Miss Beck had dissolved soon after I arrived topside before the storm had fully erupted. Our conversation had quickly evolved from tentative and formal to warm and sympathetic. There was no doubt in my mind she had detected my class and sex, but I also surmised that she was a kindred spirit. She had explained how she had come into her occupation. Her charge and his mother had lived in Seattle whilst their father conducted business in the lucrative coal trade on Vancouver Island. However, a few months earlier, the mother had died of a summer flu, and Miss Beck had been hired as a governess. On that day, she was escorting the boy to take up residence with his father in Victoria and would stay on to instruct him in his studies. I was most impressed by her level of education which included a fluency in French and an understanding of algebra. But at that moment she was taking on the role of mother, not teacher, to the boy whose excitement over the tossing of the boat had evolved into a frightful panic.

"Your father has promised an invitation to the Craigdarroch Castle. Have your ever set your eyes upon a real castle before? Maybe this one will even have a dragon!"

The boy's face was briefly illuminated at the thought of encountering a magical beast. But almost immediately the gale force winds were once again the only monsters on his mind.

While attempting to keep my own hope afloat in the terrifying storm, I moved briefly to the door and overheard a man in a fine suit yelling to a slightly less well-dressed one that the boat was now taking on water. The social barriers which would have previously kept these two passengers from having an exchange had been swept away by the storm. Preferring to know the truth, no matter how terrifying, rather than relying upon the possibly unfounded speculation of strangers, I managed to waylay a crew member who was running across the slick tiles of the social hall as quickly as possible without losing his footing.

"My dear fellow, how grave is the situation?"

Despite the tempest pitching the vessel, the sailor still had his wits about him enough to look confused as to why the speech of an upper-class gentleman was being delivered by someone who appeared to be a deckhand. I had taken on my husband's most imperious tone, one that I knew anyone of the lower classes would instinctively defer to, no matter my dress.

"It's the deadlight, sir, it's come away. And the engine room is filling with water, right enough."

My knowledge of boats did not extend to a "deadlight" but I knew with certainty that water in the engine room posed the gravest of dangers.

"The stewards are sure to be passing out the lifebelts at present. You best be securing one for yourself." The *young man spoke in a lilting Irish accent before doffing his cap and then moving on to more urgent matters.*

"What did he say?" Miss Beck asked in a whisper, so that her charge would not overhear. I must have taken on my role as a man in earnest as my first instinct was to lie to my companion, to protect her feelings from the dreadful truth. But then I realized this was exactly the sort of infantilizing treatment of women by men that I so abhorred.

"I think the danger could hardly be greater." I spoke directly into her ear in a way that was far too intimate for our short acquaintance but seemed appropriate given the gravity of the situation. After explaining we needed to acquire the lifebelts, I reached for her hand and held it tight as we moved out onto the deck.

The sight which greeted us on the promenade could hardly have been more terrifying. Thundering waves crashed over the boat, tossing the vessel about like a rag in the washtub of an angry maid. I sensed a lack of forward motion and was in the midst of morbidly speculating whether the engine had ceased to function due to the ingress of water, when the captain appeared on deck.

A man of average height and sturdy frame, the grey pallor of the boat's master did nothing to inspire confidence in his authority. I was at too far a distance to comprehend the orders he shouted, but as the crew immediately began to uncover the lifeboats, I understood the worst was truly coming to pass: the ship was in a state to be abandoned. In the chaos of the unfolding disaster, I could almost wonder if my husband was in league with the winds, in trying to thwart my escape.

The word was soon passed along that it would only be women and children allowed into the lifeboats, and Miss Beck and her charge were urged forward.

In the crush she reached back for me and yelled, "Show them who you are! You must reveal your true self!"

I gave her hand one last squeeze before she was dragged away by the crowd. There was no logical explanation for why, in that moment, I did not remove my cap and expose myself to be a woman. But I had somehow married myself to the fate of a man, whether that would be to enjoy my freedom unhindered or to die bravely as the occasion demanded.

Chapter 16

"And what made you decide to remove your children from the press conference?"

"There was a bit more yelling than I was comfortable with."

"Not because you thought there was going to be a murder?"

"How would I know there was going to be a murder?"

"But you ended up with a dead body at your feet."

"I can't quite see how that's my fault."

Using the pause in the conversation to scratch the substantial stubble on his hefty chin, Detective Bloom seemed genuinely frustrated that Helene had not yet confessed to being a conspirator in the murder of Roddy Beck. The police officer was well over six feet tall and his bulk overflowed from either side of a straining plastic office chair. Built like a lumberjack but wearing a creased suit, his sheer size was probably an asset when it came to intimidating a suspect.

This wasn't Helene's first visit to the police station. Last spring when she was covering the death of the museum curator, Detective Kalinowski had requested her presence for several interviews. At the time, she had found their exchange to be a contest of who could cause the other to reveal key details of their own investigation. Her experience with Detective Bloom was more like facing a firing squad of accusations, perhaps meant to exhaust her into an accidental admission of guilt. At that moment, she could only wish her friend a speedy return from Berlin in the hopes she might take over the investigation into Beck's murder. However, removing Bloom from the case would probably prove more difficult than extricating him from the contorted chair in which he was currently embedded.

"And why did you bring your children along anyway? Do they normally join you at press conferences?" asked Bloom, his voice rich with incredulity.

Drawing the line at having her parenting choices challenged, Helene decided it was time to push back.

"I came here to discuss the investigation into the death of Roddy Beck. You have no evidence linking me to the crime, so I am free to leave at any time. Either start asking relevant and respectful questions or I am going back to work. I too, have a job to do." Helene credited this speech not so much to her journalistic understanding of the legal system, but to watching too many crime shows. And the desired effect was forthcoming: the bully backed down when faced with a bully—or at least someone standing up for themselves.

In a tone that was now bordering on collegiate, Detective Bloom said, "Well then, help me out. You were there. You saw him die. Help me bring his murderer to justice. I know you don't like giving up until the guilty are caught—almost as satisfying as reeling in a feisty sturgeon at sunset."

Helene assumed Bloom was referencing the part she played in the investigation of the curator's death. She had to wonder how Detective Kalinowski had described her role to the other officers and was unsettled at the thought of the police discussing her actions over an apple fritter. She decided to give Bloom something else to chew on.

"You must have figured out that the control of a multi-million-dollar company is up for grabs—always a good motive for murder. And so far, several people seem to think they're entitled to it."

"There's the ex-wife," conceded Bloom.

"Almost-ex-wife," corrected Helene.

"There aren't any children to fight over it." Bloom added without acknowledging his mistake.

"But the assistant seems to think of himself as a sort of progeny."

"No one leaves a company to their assistant."

"Well, don't tell him that."

Bloom took a moment to consider before speaking again. "I suppose it doesn't matter what Beck intended to do. It's what the assistant *believed* he was going to do. And if the upstart thought he would end up with a fortune, that's motive for murder. And we'll know soon enough anyway."

"Know what?" Helene couldn't help asking, accepting she was being baited.

"The details of the will. Having a copy sent over as we speak."

Helene experienced a rush of frustration. It wasn't fair that the police had access to more information than she did. How was she going to arrange an invite to the reading of the will? And what about seeing witness statements and autopsy reports? What kinds of secrets did they contain? It was like she was forced to take a photo with a 50 mm lens while police had access to a telephoto.

For a fleeting moment, while sitting on the wrong side of the interview table, Helene contemplated whether a career in law enforcement might have been a better choice than journalism. Imagine being able to compel people to submit to interviews? There could even be a special penalty for politicians who answered a question with a question. But despite the tantalizing thought of holding several slippery provincial ministers to account with more than a microphone, she had no desire to spend her days writing up criminal charges rather than radio stories. And sometimes people were more willing to share information with reporters. Recalling the note Zofia had shown her, the one Roddy Beck had clasped in his dead hands, Helene felt a renewed sense of confidence in her own investigation, even though

135

she was currently occupying a room frequented by criminals.

"What about the can of oil?" Helene had decided it was time to turn the tables on the detective, show him that she had her own sources of information.

"How do you know about that?"

"People talk to me. You know, without me hauling them into a police station first thing in the morning."

"You need to keep that piece of information to yourself. That can not go on the radio."

"Fine," agreed Helene, "but I don't want to be treated like a suspect anymore. I wasn't in the castle when the murder happened. And I would hardly have brought my children along if I knew it was going to be the scene of a crime."

As Bloom didn't look fully convinced, Helene added, "You know that I know Detective Kalinowski. We worked together, sort of. And now I think it's fair to say she thinks of me as a friend. I'm sure you consider her a good judge of character."

Put in the position of having to either doubt a fellow police officer or trust a journalist, Bloom seemed reconciled to a truce.

"The door hinges were oiled. To the balcony on the landing. I've been told that technically it's called a Juliet balcony, from Shakespeare or something. Just a small one off the windows, not really meant for standing on. And the lock had been messed with. You can see scratches on the plates from being picked. It wasn't supposed to be open, according to the staff. Creates a hazard for tourists."

Thinking that this could simply be evidence of a castle enthusiast trying to get an exterior view, Helene had to remind herself that she was a journalist, not a detective. Maybe they could see a crime where she could not. But Bloom registered her doubtful look.

"And there were minute traces of oil on Roddy Beck's back. Exactly where someone would have placed their hands if they'd pushed him over the edge. The same oil that was on the door hinges." Bloom then shrugged his massive shoulders and said, "I'll admit, it's all circumstantial. But it's enough to elevate the case to homicide."

At that moment Helene knew she had a decision to make. Reciprocate the exchange of information or keep working in isolation. Not wanting to give herself time to overthink her choice, she blurted out, "I found a note on the body. Right after he fell."

Since the police were officially investigating a murder, Helene had resolved it was important for them to know about the note. But she wasn't going to get Zofia Bosko into trouble by disclosing that it was actually the academic who had discovered the threatening writing and withheld it. Helene couldn't see what difference that detail would make. Also, she needed to maintain a good relationship with Zofia.

A red flush reached Bloom's neck, but he managed to keep full-blown anger at bay as he asked tersely, "A note?"

"Yes, and I brought it along." With that remark, Helene pulled the plastic bag which contained the crumpled and blood-stained paper from her pocket. In an attempt to redeem herself, she said, "I put it in a baggie, just in case you needed to check for fingerprints."

Too annoyed to offer praise for her methods of preserving evidence, Bloom picked up the plastic bag, and, without taking the paper out, read the message aloud.

Meet me on the fourth floor landing
after the press conference
or I will tell her everything.

Putting the bag down on the table in a controlled manner, Bloom said, "You know I could detain you for interfering with an investigation. For concealing evidence."

Helene didn't think it would be helpful to defend her actions by pointing out that this was her first formal police interview.

"However, I'm willing to overlook this overdue disclosure because of your 'friendship' with Kalinowski." Taking a deep breath, as if swallowing his exasperation, he then asked, "Do you have any idea what the note means or who wrote it?"

Seeing this question as a chance to make her way into Bloom's good books, Helene wanted to offer the detective something.

"Could it be connected to his imminent divorce? A secret that would give the other party more ammunition?"

"What kind of secret?"

"Hidden assets? An affair? It's usually money or sex."

Showing more interest in the latter possibility, Bloom probed further, "An affair? With who?"

Helene didn't have a ready candidate to put forward as Beck's lover. Despite harbouring concerns about how close Zofia was to the tech guru, she hadn't lied about being the one to find the note to then offer the academic up to Bloom. She decided to buy some time. "I'm not sure. But he was handsome and rich, so he couldn't have been short of willing women. Or men for that matter."

"That's true," Bloom agreed, not seeming to mind that handsome and rich were not two adjectives that would be included in his online dating profile if he had such a thing.

As the conversation seemed to be stalling, Helene decided to pick at another thread. "If it's not money or sex, what about revenge? He seems to have made some shady property deals through his HomeHitch app. Have you found anything there?"

"We are pursuing that line of investigation. However, the woman who apparently caused a ruckus at the press

138

conference, Mrs. Fernandez, she's still in hospital. Doesn't look good if police start harassing people while they are hooked up to a heart monitor. Her daughter was pretty freewheeling with the accusations, but we need to speak to Mrs. Fernandez herself."

Helene was going to ask the detective if he had looked into any community backlash to the plan to demolish the home of A.J. Beck, but her phone chose that moment to start buzzing. Glancing down at the screen, she saw that the caller ID simply stated "Victoria." Concerned that it could be a teacher calling from school about her children having an allergic reaction, she asked, "Do you mind if I take this?"

"No, I think we're done for now. I'll wait outside until you're ready," said Bloom before collecting his papers and hefting himself out of the office chair, which groaned in relief.

"Hello?" answered Helene once the detective had left the room. "Helene speaking."

"Good morning, it's Tristan. From the property office."

Helene's mind made the quick shift from preparing to deliver emergency instructions to a panicking teacher to having a chat with an oddly attractive if idiosyncratic city clerk.

"Oh right, how's it going?" asked Helene, feeling the adrenaline ease off.

"I'm well. Where are you?"

The clerk's question was a bit abrupt, and Helene was not entirely certain she wanted to disclose that her morning had been spent in a police interview room, so she decided to give a vague answer. "On my way to work. Got a late start today."

Making no attempt to hide his disappointment, Tristan said, "Too bad, that probably means you don't have time for a coffee."

Now finding the clerk's directness flattering, Helene also thought she needed a chance to decompress before heading from the police station to the newsroom.

"You know what, that sounds great. Where do you want to meet?"

"Why not Cafe Monico?"

"The place on Yates Street? But I've heard their coffee isn't any good."

"Exactly," replied Tristan. "No one goes there. We'll have the place to ourselves. I don't want anyone to overhear what I have to tell you."

After ending the call, Helene told herself that the not unpleasant thrill she was currently experiencing was due to her curiosity about the forthcoming information the clerk was going to share. She tried to suppress any suspicion that she was in fact looking forward to hanging out in an unpopular coffee shop with the peculiar property records clerk. A few minutes later when she was saying goodbye to Detective Bloom at the police station doors, she felt only the slightest twinge of guilt when he asked to be kept up to date on any important information she came across. Despite her initial misgivings about the officer, he was starting to grow on her. And she wouldn't want to get on the wrong side of a man who looked like he could wrestle a grizzly into submission.

Chapter 17

Helene believed the Yates Street cafe's lack of success might have less to do with the quality of the coffee and more to do with the poor design of the seating—the steel chairs with straight backs reminding her of schoolroom furniture designed to punish students. In addition, the sloping floor of the coffee shop caused the chairs to shift suddenly from one leg to another like an occasional earthquake. The whole point of a cafe was to sip a warm drink while enjoying distracting conversations or contemplations, which was next to impossible to do while sitting on a contraption that was as cozy as a post-modern art installation. If Helene ever decided to open her own coffee shop, the seating would be entirely chaise lounges and worn couches rescued from alleys. An infinity of throw pillows would ensure the comfort of all customers.

However, when Tristan walked through the front door, Helene was struck by the thought that he was also an oddly designed chair. Possessing a face that was striking rather than attractive, and a demeanour best described as eccentric, he retained an undeniable charisma, like a favourite but threadbare settee. Maybe it was simply that he seemed to embrace his own singularity, and confidence was the most irresistible quality.

Realizing she had been staring at the city clerk a few seconds too long, Helene flashed a welcoming smile and then returned her attention to the tolerable coffee she had ordered.

"I've been trying to decipher the signature of whoever approved the release of the missing property records for Mrs. Fernandez's home. As far as I can tell, the name doesn't belong to anyone who works in property records. I checked twice."

Tristan had acquired his own steamed beverage before sitting down across from Helene at a square table that was affixed to the floor. He hadn't yet taken a drink, immediately jumping into an update of his progress.

Picking up the photocopy which Tristan had brought along, Helene examined the signature.

"G. Lindbergh? G. Longfellow? Can you make it out?" asked Helene.

"I thought maybe Livingston, but it's really hard to tell," said Tristan. "Most likely it's fake. No one with a name like that has worked at City Hall or is on council."

Impressed by the thoroughness of the clerk's research, Helene hypothesized, "So, someone stole the property records and signed a false name."

"And only City Hall staff would have been able to access these files," added Tristan.

"But why?" Helene deliberated out loud, while readjusting herself on the metal chair that had rocked to the right. "Why would someone want to steal a property record?"

"Well, obviously to cover up a crime," said Tristan point-blank.

"Doesn't that seem like an awful lot of drama for the property records office?"

The clerk looked mildly insulted by her comment. "It isn't all sorting through filing cabinets and putting the correct stamps on forms, you know."

"Of course," Helene quickly replied by way of an apology, but she had put Tristan on the defensive.

"Think about it. I'm responsible for the records of the biggest asset most people will ever possess—their home. And owning property is becoming the great divide between the haves and have-nots. And it's not just Victoria, it's happening around the world," lectured the clerk.

"You sound like you're organizing a revolt," joked Helene, in an attempt to make Tristan relax, but the clerk continued in the same vein.

"I'm sure you know how it works. If a family has property, they can pass it on to their kids. But trying to break into the housing market without help is practically impossible these days."

In reaction to this intense social commentary, Helene suddenly burst into laughter. The startled look on Tristan's face prompted her to explain, "It's not you. It's this morning. I spent the first half in a police station being questioned about a murder. And now I'm sitting in a coffee shop listening to your treatise on the new class system." Looking up at the cafe's wall menu, she said, "I wonder if they serve anything stronger than caffeine here."

Tristan was finally distracted from his hobbyhorse. "A murder? Police station? And you accuse me of high drama!"

Realizing she had revealed more than she had intended, Helene tried to offer a satisfactory explanation that didn't invite more questions.

"It's to do with the death of Roddy Beck. I was there. When it happened. That's why the police wanted to speak to me. To know if I saw anything."

"You saw him die? That's awful!" declared Tristan. "Have you talked to anyone about it?"

"What do you mean? Like a therapist?" asked Helene, genuinely flummoxed. "Honestly, it never occurred to me. I've been too busy trying to figure out if it was murder, and if so, who might have done it."

As Helene picked up her cup to take another drink, Tristan mulled over what he had just heard.

"Wait, did you say Roddy Beck was murdered? Isn't that the tech guru who set up the deals between homeowners and developers? With his app HomeHitch."

"That's right," Helene cautiously agreed.

143

"And don't tell me. He was involved in the sale of Mrs. Fernandez's home?"

"That's what I understand."

"You're saying, these missing property records might actually be connected to a murder?" Tristan's voice was growing in volume with each statement.

"Quite possibly," replied Helene as nonchalantly as possible.

"Well, don't you think that if you are going to involve me in a murder investigation, you might give me a heads up?" demanded Tristan.

Putting down her coffee cup, Helene replied, "I don't actually remember inviting you to get involved. You sort of invited yourself. And to be fair, I wasn't sure it was a murder until this morning." With more gusto than she really possessed, she added, "Feel free to walk away, now that you do know."

Tristan took a moment to consider his options before replying. "And go back to retrieving records for people lucky enough to buy homes before 2001, but think the younger generation eat too many avocados and that's why they don't own property? Not on your life." He then looked at her eagerly, "What's next?"

"But what if you lose your job?"

It was Tristan's turn to smile. "It's worth the risk. And who knows, maybe I could figure out what I might want to do with the rest of my life. Start a housing co-op. Or build a bat sanctuary."

This was the second time the clerk had mentioned the flying nocturnal creatures since they had met and Helene was tempted to ask about this apparent preoccupation, but she didn't want to derail the conversation. Instead, she said, "We need to find out who took out those property records. And I think you're right, our strongest lead is the signature. I know it's fake, but perhaps you could compare it to other samples from staff members."

144

Tristan's eyes brightened. "You mean, conduct my own forensic handwriting investigation?"

"Sure," agreed Helene, thinking she was not the only one who had watched too many police procedural TV shows. "But don't confront anyone about it. Come to me first. Remember, this could be connected to a murder."

Shrugging off her warning, Tristan asked, "What are you going to do?"

Quickly replaying that morning's conversation with Detective Bloom in her head, and the one she had had the day before with the assistant Ameer, Helene came back to the same inevitable conclusion. "I need to get myself invited to a reading of the will."

"Roddy Beck's?"

"Yes, it's happening in Vancouver on Friday. I want to find out who benefits from his death."

Without missing a beat, Tristan asked, "Do you ever do normal things, like visit art galleries or go out for dinner?"

Helene wasn't sure how to interpret this question, which almost sounded like an invitation. She nervously blurted, "I'm a single mother. I don't really do things in the evening unless it's for work. Too busy unpacking school lunches."

Registering the look of disappointment on Tristan's face, Helene experienced immediate regret. She knew the words "single mother" were like bear spray to most men. And then she had to stop herself and ask why she cared whether Tristan wanted to go out for dinner or not. He was probably ten years her junior. Besides, she had given up on dating years before COVID made hiding at home socially acceptable.

Flustered, she pulled on her coat and picked up her bag. "I'll let you know. How it goes. In Vancouver. If I do go."

Before Tristan could offer up any further response or even a farewell, Helene was out the door and standing on the sidewalk under a grey sky. A chill breeze was a panacea to her warm cheeks.

While driving back to the newsroom, Helene mulled over the new clues—Detective Bloom describing the oil on the door hinges and the victim's back, Tristan trying to decipher the name on the property records release form. She didn't know if the two inquiries were linked but it was impossible to ignore the shared connection to Roddy Beck.

Shortly after arriving in the newsroom, Helene was flagged down by Riya who asked if she had time to do a quick write-up for the web on a rare turtle discovered on a Vancouver Island beach. Aquarium staff were rehabilitating the reptile and had sent some photos. Helene didn't mind obliging her boss's request.

More than a dozen years ago, when Helene started out as a journalist, she had dismissed articles featuring the rescue or heroics of adorable animals as intellectual fluff. She thought the media should focus on important stories, like systemic discrimination in healthcare. However, after writing endless stories about human wickedness, she now viewed the occasional entertaining tale of animal antics as a respite from the bleakness. And the fact that these stories received thousands of clicks on their website meant other people were desperate for a distraction as well.

Once she had filed her turtle story for both radio and web, the puzzle that had been tugging at the back of her brain since her meeting with Ameer was brought to the fore: how to get an invitation to the reading of the will in Vancouver.

At first Helene debated asking Zofia to bring her along, assuming the academic was invited herself. But, after further consideration, she realized it was probably up to the executor to decide who was allowed into the room. This meant she would have to make her request to Harold Webb himself, a man she knew little about beyond his friendship with Roddy Beck. But recalling the expensive cut of the suit he had worn to the funeral and his elegantly coiffed hair, Helene knew exactly the direction her appeal should take.

"I am writing a feature article about Roddy Beck's life and legacy and, I know, as someone he respected and even looked up to, it's important to include you in the piece." Having made it past the phone receptionist to be directly connected to Webb, Helene was doing her best to stoke the man's sense of self-importance. After all, some people still considered journalists as brokers of fame and Helene was happy to use this fallacy to her advantage.

"You've known Roddy since high school, so you'll be able to provide unique insight into his life and character. What made him tick. What drove him to work so hard. Really, I don't think anyone else can offer this perspective." Helene hoped she wasn't laying it on too thick, but she knew that people with an oversized ego couldn't resist being described as exceptional. "If you have any photos of the two of you together over the years, I would love to share those. People want to get to know the 'real' Roddy."

"I can definitely do that," Harold replied, letting Helene know her sales pitch had hit home. "I probably knew Roddy better than anyone. And we had so many shared passions, like sailing and golfing. Nothing made him happier than a day spent out on the green."

Bristling at anyone using the words "passion" and "golf" in the same sentence, Helene then proposed, "I can come over on Friday. To Vancouver. I feel it makes for a better interview to meet in person."

"Let me check my schedule," Harold replied. "I think I have squash in the morning and then I have the will reading in the afternoon. Friday's a bit busy it seems."

"The reading of Roddy's will? That's perfect!" Helene enthused as though she had received an invitation. "That will add such a great angle to the piece. Are you the executor? I mean, that just shows how much Roddy trusted you."

"I'm not actually sure that's the done thing. To invite journalists to a will reading," Harold said with some alarm.

"But you're the one in charge! Surely it's up to you, who can and can't be there?"

"I suppose that's true," Harold cautiously agreed.

"Then it's all set. I'll arrive in the late morning."

After arranging a specific time and place to meet on Friday, Helene hung up and took a deep breath. If she ever lost her job in journalism, perhaps she should consider pursuing a PhD in psychology—specifically manipulation through flattery. Helene would have been ashamed if she wasn't so pleased with her success in securing an invitation to the reading of Roddy Beck's will.

Chapter 18

The sweeping view from the deck of the *Coastal Celebration* ferry was as impenetrable to ugliness as the ship's steel hull was to water. Leaning against the cool railing, Helene watched as waves lapped against Gulf Island beaches while sailboats elegantly slipped through the surrounding cerulean waters. In the distance, the delineation between the shifting sky and restless ocean was difficult to detect, as though air and water had finally managed a union after an infinity of separation. And as the mutable marine landscape passed by, Helene scanned the waters for a flash of fin because for ferry passengers, the phrase "winning the lottery" had nothing to do with money and instead it meant spotting a pod of orcas up close. And Helene knew how thrilled her son would be if she came home with a photo of a surfacing creature.

As the ferry entered the ocean canyon that was Active Pass, opposing shores of two islands seemingly just out of reach, Helene once again contemplated what it would be like to live on a smaller island. Considering she was an introvert and found the company of most people exhausting or boring, an isolated place like Gabriola or even Mayne Island should have been appealing. But Helene was the kind of solitary soul who still wanted the option to be around others, if not necessarily speak to them, which was why Victoria's James Bay neighbourhood was a good fit. Besides the company of her children, she could indulge in the introspection she craved without ever drowning in loneliness. She wanted a friendly exchange on a breakwater trek to remain a possibility despite preferring to take her walks alone.

Although the Gulf Islands possessed too much wilderness and not enough coffee shops, Helene also knew that she would never again make her home in Vancouver. She had lived in British Columbia's biggest metropolis in the 1990s, when she had ingested Canadian history lectures at Simon Fraser University by day and downed cheap highballs at the alternative Luv-A-Fair dance club by dark. And after the DJ had played the night's final anti-establishment song by Rage Against the Machine, there was nothing she loved more than cycling home at 2 a.m., quite drunk, pushing the pedals of her dilapidated bicycle through the cool air, the city transformed under moonlight into a hushed but more intense habitat.

However, the anonymous urban chaos which proved a worthy distraction from the pressure to choose a career when she was younger, was totally unappealing to her as an older adult. Between caring for two children and working full time, her days already had too much noise, and on the weekends she needed to decompress by kayaking or taking a walk on the windswept breakwater.

The rising costs of the ferries and hotels also discouraged her from taking her kids to Vancouver even for a short getaway. In addition, her Victoria-raised children seemed quite overwhelmed when confronted with the bigger city's traffic and human congestion, sticking close to her side as though they were half their age.

However, on that morning at the end of October, Helene was excited to be making the journey. She hadn't been anywhere since the height of COVID, and the return to the stomping grounds of her youth seemed like a manageable place to start. Thankfully, travelling on a large ferry evoked none of her lingering fears connected to smaller watercrafts.

After manipulating Harold Webb into inviting her to the will reading, and then convincing her boss that the venture would add enticing details to her coverage, Helene was really only able to go to Vancouver for the day because Lela agreed to pick up Oscar and Cleo after school and to give them dinner. Helene was a little surprised that her sister was free on a Friday evening since this would normally be a prime date night. But lately Lela had brought up the subject of men a little less frequently, which could mean one of two things: she was getting over a very bad man or she had met an extremely good one and was afraid to jinx it. Helene was ashamed to admit that the second scenario scared her more, as it put her sister's heart at greater risk. She also knew it was dangerous to come to depend on her sister to help with the kids as she was liable to move to a new city with only slightly less forethought than she moved on to a new man.

But while standing on the broad port deck of the *Coastal Celebration* ferry that bright morning, Helene let her worries about work and parenting slip away like the vessel's watery wake subsiding into the ocean currents. For the 90 minutes it took to travel from Swartz Bay Terminal on Vancouver Island to Tsawwassen on the mainland, she wanted to recall what it was like to be 25 years old and to be a little bit lost and a little more free: to be a boat without an anchor, but to know she could sail to any port.

However, any romantic notions about what it was like to be young and poor in Vancouver were vanquished when she boarded a crowded city bus from Tsawwassen Terminal to the closest Skytrain station. In Victoria, Helene drove to work on weekdays, but the rest of the time she walked or cycled around James Bay and downtown. Decades had passed since she had taken public transportation and things hadn't improved over time. The proximity and even the smell of strangers was especially jarring after revelling in the cleansing ocean breeze. Helene wished she had been successful in convincing Riya to pay for her to bring a car on the ferry. But the extra $190 round trip was not going to get a pass from a producer who asked

151

people to pitch in for station coffee. Helene knew the only reason she was being allowed to go at all was because her recent story about Roddy Beck's funeral received more web hits than the latest orca video.

The day was turning out to be prone to extremes when a few hours later she found herself sitting across from Harold Webb in a restaurant where the price of a steak was only slightly less than the money she saved by not bringing a car on the ferry. In a classic navy boat-neck sweater and faded jeans, she had felt like an incognito movie star when lounging on the ferry deck. However, in the high-end establishment with cedar tables and puce hanging lamps, she couldn't help but wish she had worn something more professional.

"Thanks for coming to Vancouver for the day," said Harold while picking at a plate of breaded squid and jalapeño peppers. Helene thought it was a good sign that he thought she was doing him a favour by attending the reading of the will.

"Did you come over by helicopter?" Obviously, Harold was wealthy enough to patronize the pricey service.

"No," replied Helene with feigned regret, "they were all booked up."

"Oh well, the seaplanes aren't so bad either." Harold picked up two large pieces of squid that were stuck together and pulled them apart before popping one after the other into his mouth. "I get so hungry after squash. Would you like something?" he offered, motioning to the menu. "We still have time before meeting the others."

Rather than trying to explain that journalism ethics prevented her from accepting gifts and meals, Helene simply responded, "I'm fine. I had a big breakfast." Immediately after speaking, a loud growl emanated from her stomach, putting paid to her lie, but Harold was enjoying his seafood appetizer too much to take notice. She resolved to slip into the bathroom to inhale a granola bar at the first opportunity.

After finishing his food and paying the bill, Harold drove them back to his office, explaining that they were going to use one of the corporate boardrooms for the will reading. He dropped Helene off at the room first, saying he had to collect the documents. Making herself comfortable in a chair that bounced enthusiastically every time she shifted her weight, Helene could not quell her own sense of buoyancy. She remained confident the details of the will would reveal a possible million-dollar motive for wanting Beck dead.

"What the hell are you doing here?" The bark of the voice from behind caused Helene to lurch forward against the polished table.

Spinning around a little too quickly in the chair, Helene was confronted with a vision of the tastefully attired Adrianna Beck standing in the doorway. "Harold invited me to attend the reading. To shed more light on your late-husband's legacy."

"Harold?" Adrianna raised one well-curated eyebrow while speaking. "Someone's getting cozy with the press."

Helene decided to ignore the remark and spun her chair back to facing the table, albeit more cautiously. However, it wasn't long before her presence was once more the source of attention.

"Helene! I didn't know you were coming." This time it was Zofia Bosko who had made the remark after entering the room, but her tone was markedly warmer than Adrianna's had been.

"I'm sorry I didn't have time to warn you. Actually, I wasn't sure you would be here either," explained Helene.

"I know," said Zofia. "Isn't it strange? But maybe he set aside funds for a university endowment. That's my hope anyways."

Guffawing from the other end of the boardroom table, Adrianna made it clear that her aspirations were not so selfless.

The last individual to enter the room before Harold's return was Roddy Beck's former assistant Ameer. He made no remark about Helene's attendance at the will reading, but simply took a seat across the table from Adrianna. To Helene, it appeared like a subtle declaration of war.

Thankfully, Harold didn't make them wait much longer and he was soon situated at the head of the table.

"I want to thank everyone for coming today. I know you had to make the trip to Vancouver, but this is where Roddy wanted the will read. On neutral territory, as it were." Harold took the time to make eye contact with each person in the room, probably a technique picked up at a leadership course.

"I have made a copy of the entire will for each of you to take home and I'm not going to go through all of it right now. But I think it's important to lay out the financials, so the future of the company he worked so hard to create is not in limbo. Before I begin, however, Roddy wanted me to start by apologizing to you, Adrianna. He wanted to let you know he is sorry for everything."

"What the hell does that mean?" exclaimed Adrianna.

Facing her from the other side of the table, Ameer smirked in reaction to her alarm, assuming any loss for her meant a victory for him.

Not offering further insight, Harold then picked up the papers in front of him and started reading.

"I, Roddy Beck, of sound mind and judgment do, in front of several witnesses, declare that the entirety of my fortune, excluding the family home, does go to Zofia Bosko."

A shocked silence hung in the air for several beats before Adrianna Beck jumped out of her chair. "What the hell? That can't be true! He left everything to her?" The furious woman pointed at Zofia as though expecting the others to join in her outrage. "She's not even family! This can't be legal!"

For her part, Zofia looked equal measures astonished and mortified. "I didn't ask for this," was all the response she could manage.

Ameer was watching the scene unfold with an amused smile, right up until Harold Webb started reading the next section of the will.

"In addition, I leave my controlling share of the company to Zofia Bosko, who will have final decision on the new CEO of RoddTek."

Although he remained seated, it was now Ameer's turn to be devastated. "But he said, if anything happened to him, he would make sure my role was secure in the company. I always thought he meant … I mean, who's going to appoint the boss's old assistant?"

"Actually, he did specify in the will that you were to stay on as the advisor to the new CEO, Ameer. He even included a small pay raise."

"Never mind your job," broke in Adrianna. "He's given all my money to her!" Helene didn't think it was a good sign that the woman was referring to Zofia as if she wasn't in the room. "And I helped him build the company at the start. I invested my savings!"

"He did leave you the house, Adrianna. He knew how much you loved it," Harold said in an attempt to placate the angry woman.

"And what was the point in sleeping with you, Harold, if this was all I was going to end up with?"

"But you only asked me to make sure Roddy didn't cheat you in the divorce," Harold replied.

"Well, there wasn't much point in that if he was just going to cheat me in death, was there?" Glancing around the room with indignation, Adrianna suddenly seemed to remember there was a journalist present. The beautiful woman then took a moment to collect herself, tugging down the hem of her tailored suit jacket and flipping her unruffled hair over her shoulders. "I guess it's time to talk to my own lawyer because this doesn't end here. You can count on that." Following this declaration, and while still managing to appear elegant, Adrianna marched around the table and exited the room.

Zofia was the first one to speak again, and she made her appeal directly to Harold. "Why did he do this? I don't understand. We were good friends. But nothing more. I didn't ask for the company or the money."

"Roddy didn't explain his decision to me," replied Harold quite calmly considering the fight with his lover. "And I admit, it does seem a little unusual. But this is what he wanted. He told me himself. Although, of course, he didn't expect to die so soon."

Ameer abruptly stood up and addressed the room. "Well, there is a first time for everything, and for once I agree with Adrianna. This is not OK! In the past, I protected Roddy's secrets because he promised to take care of me. But now? Now, I won't stay silent any longer." With that pronouncement Ameer dramatically pushed his way through both sides of the boardroom double doors. As the heavy doors closed with an anticlimactic hush, Helene could only wonder if Ameer's secret was the same as the one referred to in the threatening note Roddy had been clasping in death.

Still sitting at the head of the table, Harold shared an apologetic smile with the two remaining women. Despite the brave face he was putting on, Helene suspected he regretted inviting a journalist along that day.

Although not quite certain about the fallout from the extraordinary provisions of the will, the 25-year-old Vancouver version of Helene, who used to fiercely dance to grunge music calling for the downfall of the rich, couldn't help but revel in the afternoon's eruption of frustrated greed and resentment.

Chapter 19

After attending the will reading in Vancouver on Friday, Helene was grateful to have a weekend to mull over the astonishing and confusing revelations. Ahead of the event, she had assumed that whoever benefitted from Roddy Beck's demise would be the prime suspect for the murder. But since Zofia Bosko stood to inherit most of the fortune, Helene's theories were upended. The academic had always insisted a homicide had taken place, even giving the journalist the threatening note Beck had been clutching in death—hardly the actions of someone trying to get away with a crime. Zofia also appeared genuinely shocked to be named as the main beneficiary of the tech guru's fortune, but perhaps this was a double bluff to throw Helene and police off the scent.

When it came to the other people in the room, Helene was utterly disgusted by Adrianna Beck's outrageous display of entitlement. The fact that the woman was sleeping with her husband's lawyer only further confirmed her lack of integrity. And at the same time, since she was surprised by the contents of the will, this meant she could have still been expecting to benefit from her husband's death. This was also true for Ameer, who had counted on being promoted in the wake of his boss's demise.

As the competing theories tugged her brain in different directions, Helene decided to go kayaking as a form of distraction. But while she was packing her gear, Cleo asked if she could come along, having shown an interest in going out on the water during their recent bike ride to Ross Bay. Helene was delighted to spend time with her daughter, and as far as her son was concerned, he didn't mind staying home alone as he was busy building a Lego replica of a creature from his video game.

Since Helene owned only one kayak, she called up a shop along the Gorge waterway in Victoria and made arrangements for a two-hour rental. The tidal inlet and its calm currents were the perfect spot to try out the water sport for the first time, the paddle to Craigflower Bridge and the return trip made for an easy venture. She also rented a second wetsuit for Cleo, hoping that the tight orange neoprene outfit didn't put her daughter off kayaking before she even got onto the water.

"Must I?" Cleo asked while holding the wetsuit away from her body like it was a rotting fish, even wrinkling her nose as though it smelled, which it did a little.

"Absolutely," said Helene, "you'll need it if you fall into the water."

"I know how to swim!"

"The biggest danger is not drowning, it's the cold," said Helene while packing their lunch into a waterproof bag. "It would only be a matter of minutes before you would slip into hypothermia."

"But the shore is so close!" her daughter argued.

Putting down the things she was arranging, Helene looked at Cleo directly. "This is non-negotiable. Wear the suit or we don't go."

"All right," capitulated the teen, "but don't you dare take a photo. I will die if my friends see me looking like a pumpkin sausage with a zipper. And I'll never speak to you again."

Despite Cleo's frustrated grunts as she pulled the clinging material over her swimsuit, once she was nestled in her kayak and gliding through the water, the teen's mood improved. The girl had always been a good swimmer due to her powerful shoulders, so she took to the paddle sport naturally and Helene soon found herself having to make an effort to keep up. She knew the day was rapidly approaching when Cleo and Oscar would be better at sports than she was and this fact inspired both delight and sadness—she would miss her reign as the supremely capable parent.

It didn't take long before the pair fell into a steady rhythm, paddling for several minutes and then taking short breaks to enjoy the view of the verdant banks on either side of the watery pathway. To the left, substantial homes with private docks offered a glimpse at the lives and the lawns of the wealthy, and, in the other direction, a long narrow park ran along the Gorge, a green space for everyone regardless of income. Ignoring a twinge of guilt, Helene snuck a picture of her daughter cutting a ribbon through the water with her kayak, not for social media but for her own private collection of parenting triumphs.

"Do you want to pull into the beach and have a snack?" asked Helene about an hour later. They had almost reached Craigflower Bridge in the community of Saanich and the waterway was busy with kayaks, canoes and paddleboards.

"Sure," agreed Cleo. "I kind of have to pee anyway."

Pointing the tip of her kayak at the beach near the bridge, Helene had only taken a couple more strokes when Cleo let out a scream.

"MOM! There's water in the boat!" she exclaimed. "There's not supposed to be water in the boat, right?"

Adrenaline flooding her bloodstream, Helene experienced a flush of complete terror as her lifelong fear of boats reared up like a tidal wave. However, her instincts as a mother took over, and she quickly managed to achieve the dead calm required for handling emergencies. Her children's anaphylaxis had trained her for just such moments.

"We're almost to the beach. Just keep paddling as fast as you can. Pull hard with every stroke," Helene instructed in rapid-fire. "The water isn't very deep and we will soon be able to stand. But paddle, baby, paddle."

161

Drawing up next to her daughter, the pair pulled their rapid strokes in unison, however Cleo's vessel soon started to drag from taking on water.

"OK sweetheart, the water is shallow now. I want you to tug the skirt up and free yourself from the kayak." Cleo's boat had sunk below the midline and Helene didn't want it dragging her daughter under. "Just one strong pull, Cleo. Do it now!"

Following her mother's instructions, Cleo separated herself from the kayak and splashed into the water. Once she managed to stand up, the waterline was just above her waist, and the teen trudged up the beach. Helene caught the line at the bow of her daughter's kayak and she slowly towed it to land.

"What the hell, Mom?" The mother and daughter lay on a patch of grass above the beach, trying to catch their breath. The two kayaks were resting just out of the water in front of them.

"I'm so sorry, Cleo. Nothing like this has ever happened to me before."

"I know you like to spend memorable time together, but I didn't think we'd be reenacting *Titanic*," said Cleo with exasperation. For her part, Helene was relieved that her daughter could already make a joke about their near disaster.

"Next time, I'll just take you to the mall to buy that lip gloss you've been asking for," Helene offered apologetically.

"Thanks mom, but I'd rather go with a friend. You can just give me the money," Cleo replied.

Knowing that her daughter might be taking advantage of the situation, Helene still said, "That's fine sweetheart. Whatever you want."

After she had rested a little longer and used the park bathroom, Helene went down to examine the boats. She had decided to let Cleo paddle her own kayak that morning, not knowing how well the rental vessel would handle. Going over the interior, she couldn't spot any obvious holes in the hull. Next, she turned the boat over, and checked the bottom for cracks, but what she found was much more distressing: there was a stab line running along the bottom of the kayak, damage that wouldn't have been caused by a hard beach landing. Even more concerning, there was a flap of long tape half covering the slit. Her brain was slow to put together what had probably occurred, as it resisted the thought that someone had wished her harm. However, in the end she accepted a long cut had been made in the kayak, and then it was taped up so water wouldn't start to fill the boat until she had been paddling for a while and would probably be in deep ocean water.

"What happened, Mom?" Cleo had come up to stand next to her mother.

Not wanting to scare the teen by letting her know she had possibly saved Helene's life because she had prevented her from going out on the open ocean that morning, Helene simply said, "I may owe you two lip glosses."

After a quick call to the rental shop, the owner helpfully offered to come pick them up in a vehicle that could carry both kayaks on the roof. Helene heard the relief in his voice when she explained that it was her boat that had almost sunk, not one from his collection. When he arrived and looked at the malicious damage to her kayak, he looked like he wanted to pepper Helene with questions. She just shook her head and motioned to Cleo, making it clear she didn't want to talk about what had happened in front of her daughter. So, they loaded up the boats and made the short drive back to the shop, the owner offering Cleo half of a chocolate bar on the way, which she happily accepted after checking the ingredients for nuts.

"I guess that's it for you and kayaking," commented Helene after they had transferred the damaged vessel to their own car outside the shop.

"It was actually kind of fun. Right up to the bit where I almost drowned," Cleo said in a surprisingly chipper voice. "Too bad you didn't record it for YouTube. Would have gotten so many hits."

Helene had to laugh out loud at the fact that her daughter was more concerned about boosting her social media presence than going down in a kayak.

"I did take one photo of you. Before everything went sideways," Helene disclosed. "I can send it to you. You looked great."

Her daughter took a moment to consider, not wanting to appear too eager. "I suppose," Cleo said. "As long as you can't see the orange spandex travesty."

On their way home, they picked up an order of cheeseburgers and french fries from Big Wheel Burger in Cook Street Village. It was her daughter's favourite meal and Helene was eager to spoil her.

As they were pulling into the driveway, Cleo offered to help her mother unload the kayak from the car roof but Helene demurred. Her daughter had not yet spotted the slit in the boat's bottom and she wanted to keep it that way. She waited until her daughter had gone inside the house before maneuvering the vessel off the roof and dragging it to the backyard, making sure the strip of tape was still attached at one end.

Helene took a shower to wash off the salt water before making Oscar a hot dog and steamed carrots. She then retreated downstairs to her bedroom, making sure the door was firmly closed behind her. Arranging the pillows before settling onto the bed, Helene texted Alex in Berlin, to see if she was available for a chat.

She had to wait a few minutes for a response and was wondering if the couple might be at a show, but soon enough Alex texted her back, telling her to call on the hotel phone.

"It's a good thing I'm not the jealous type," jested Alex right off the top.

"And why's that?" Helene played along, despite the serious reason for calling her friend mid-honeymoon.

"I understand you've been sending my wife secret text messages."

"They weren't exactly secret. I just didn't want to bother you," said Helene. "And you're going with 'wife'? Seems a bit domesticated."

"I know, but I'm not a giant fan of 'partner' either. Sounds like we work at a law firm."

"Well then, how are you and the wife enjoying Berlin?" asked Helene.

"I'm loving it. Like walking through the pages of history books. We went to the Reichstag yesterday and did one of those audio tours. But I'm not sure Karolina is having as much fun. I think she would have preferred some place like Bali. More infinity pools, fewer mementos of a police state."

Although they may not have picked the best honeymoon destination, Helene thought it boded well for the marriage that Alex was at least cognizant of her new spouse's discontent. For Helene's part, it was going to take a while to get used to Alex referring to Detective Kalinowski by her first name, Karolina.

"But I don't think you called to get an update on the trip," surmised Alex. "What's up?"

Pulling a giant duvet over her legs against the lingering chill from the morning paddle, Helene said, "I think someone may have tried to get at me." She still wasn't exactly sure how to phrase what had happened. "Attempted murder" seemed hyperbolic.

"I went kayaking with Cleo, and my boat, the boat she was in, started to sink. Don't worry, we made it to shore.

165

And she's OK. But when I examined the hull, it had a cut in the bottom."

"Are you saying that Cleo almost drowned in a kayak because someone sabotaged your boat?" exclaimed Alex.

"I guess that's one way of putting it," replied Helene, whose anxiety was spiking once more. And then, with a stab of guilt, she remembered Alex's life had been put in danger last spring when Helene was investigating the death of the museum curator. She hoped she wasn't retraumatizing her friend.

"I'm sorry. Maybe I shouldn't have talked to you about what happened. Is Detective Kalinowski, I mean, Karolina around?"

Alex's outraged reply was a balm to Helene's uneasy and exhausted heart: "Excuse me! I was your friend first. You come to me with your troubles. Especially if they affect Cleo and Oscar. I may not be able to do much or personally lock anyone up, but friends tell friends their problems, and my marriage, or your latest investigation, will never change that."

"OK," replied Helene, happily contrite.

"That being said, I'm going to pass you to Karolina. She's been listening this whole time and looks like she is going to arrest me if I don't let her talk to you," Alex joked, but then in a much more sober voice added, "I love you and your amazing children. Don't ever forget that."

"I love you too." Helene wasn't sure if she had ever said these words to Alex before, if not, they were definitely overdue.

"Someone caused malicious damage to your kayak?" Kalinowski stated bluntly once she was in possession of the phone.

Helene recounted the story once more, adding the detail of the tape which she presumed was meant to come free once she was in deeper water. When she finished the story, there was a long pause on the other end of the line.

"As much as I hate to involve Detective Bloom, I think you should let him know what happened. Someone made a serious attempt to cause you harm." Kalinowski then asked, "How did the interview go, by the way, with Bloom?"

"It was a bit rough at the start, but once he figured out I probably wasn't a murderer, things improved. He confirmed they are treating Roddy Beck's death as a homicide," said Helene. "We even bandied about some theories, and I would say things were almost cordial by the time I left."

"Cordial? Detective Bloom? I thought he only had two speeds. Gruff and gruffer." Kalinowski chuckled at her own joke and then continued, "It's Saturday, so I'd send him a text before calling, in case he's reeling in a big fish." At first Helene thought Kalinowski was metaphorically referring to a criminal being caught, but then remembered Bloom's outdoor pursuit.

"Sounds good and thanks for your advice," said Helene. "What day do you guys come back?"

"We still have another entire week. I don't know what we were thinking, booking such a long honeymoon in Berlin. I might ask if we can spend a few days in Paris."

"That's a great idea. Give Alex a chance to practise her French."

"Alex speaks French? Wow. I think I like that."

With that final exchange, Helene said goodbye and let the honeymooners get back to getting to know each other. Although she was a bit jealous of their romance, Alex's reassurance about the importance of their friendship was consolation enough.

Not wanting to let her nerves build up further before contacting Bloom, she immediately retrieved his card from her backpack and sent him a text.

When you have time, please call
Concerns about safety

Helene knew the message was a bit vague, but she also thought that sending a text about a leaky kayak was not going to make much sense either. However, she didn't have to worry about not sounding urgent enough, as a reply was quick to arrive.

Do NOT leave house
Be in touch ASAP
Another body at that damn castle

Another death? At Craigdarroch Castle? Who could it be? Helene's first thought was that someone had murdered Zofia because she stood to inherit Beck's fortune. And then she had to wonder if in fact the murderer had struck again, after failing to drown her in a kayak.

Checking that the crowbar she kept under her bed was still in place, Helene wasn't sure which scared her more: the fact that the killer might have struck again, or that the grumpy detective was so worried about her wellbeing he willingly disclosed that there had been another death before the investigation was official.

January 8, 1904
Late Afternoon

The cruelest rub of death can sometimes be the proximity of hope. And this was certainly the case when attempts were made to remove the women and their young from the beleaguered steamboat. Through the sleet and the rain, the rocky beach of a small Canadian island appeared to be perhaps just two miles away, not an impossible distance to cross in a lifeboat. The grey shoreline in the distance offered a tantalizing refuge from the savage storm. However the efforts to send the vulnerable to safety, which started as a sort of ordered chaos, quickly devolved into a horrifying maritime massacre.

The women and children were ushered from the middle deck, which had offered some protection from the lashing wind, up the stairs to the exposed top of the vessel where the lifeboats were located. I followed a short distance behind the throng, resolute in my decision to maintain my identity as a man, and not to take a seat in the boats that could otherwise allow a mother and infant to be saved. It is impossible to describe why I felt so keenly that my own destiny was coupled with the fate of the battered vessel, but as a young girl I had always resisted changing a plan once it was set in motion. Perhaps that is why I stayed in my suffocating marriage for so long. And as the vessel lurched from side to side, I knew my stubbornness might perhaps be the deciding factor in my survival or demise.

As the first group clambered into a lifeboat many shed tears while others tried to keep a brave face so as not to terrify the younger occupants even further. My attention was drawn to a tall young woman in a grey silk walking suit adorned with a pearl necklace who was providing *assistance to the mothers, passing over their infants once they were seated in the vessel. Couples clasped hands as long as they possibly could before the wives were thrust forward and the men were pulled back into the crowd; a romantic oceanic expedition tragically transformed into a hasty final parting of lovers. I gave up a small token of thanks when I saw that Miss Beck and her charge were not numbered in the initial lifeboat party. Like the storm that raged all around us, I had concerns I could not quell, about the safety of this plan to abandon the vessel.*

The lowering of the lifeboat went as smoothly as could be expected in such a powerful and twisting wind. After much perilous rocking and near misses of the side of the boat, the small vessel finally landed in the waves. However, just as I exhaled in relief, a man half-crazed from fear shouted, "By God, this boat don't go without me!" Then, to the collective horror of all who watched, the man jumped from the deck of the S.S. Clallam, attempting to join the women and children below. The force of the man's landing did overturn the steel lifeboat, dumping all the occupants into the frothing and frigid waves. I watched with utter dismay as desperate grasping hands flailed and then disappeared beneath the water's surface.

As my heart and head reeled in sickened shock, I had to wonder if what I had witnessed was anything less than murder. Was there no limit to the selfishness of men? Was there never any escape from the evil perpetrated by the male of the species against the female? It seemed that not even in the nucleus of a storm could a man's ego be suppressed. The fact that the individual who was responsible for the numerous deaths of women and children had also drowned in the incident was of no consolation. I only hoped he was taken directly from his watery grave to a fiery hell.

Rousing myself from a dizzying stupor, I watched in dumbfounded dread as the crew prepared to launch a second lifeboat, despite the deadly outcome of the first venture. Understandably the women in the crowd resisted being ushered into the boat, one well-dressed older lady even wrenched her arm free from the grasp of a crew member.

I had already witnessed too many previously inconceivable events that day to start doubting the veracity of my vision, but the scene which next unfolded was so appalling, that it could have come straight out of a child's penny dreadful.

As the women continued to put up resistance to being forced into the lifeboat, several of the crew members brought out firearms as a form of brutal encouragement. I could only fathom the logic behind this action: were they planning to shoot the passengers they were attempting to save? The spectacle was increasingly not unlike watching a band of pirates compelling their victims to walk the plank. In the end, the women gave up their fight, and some were even dropped into the vessel. I realized at that moment that the crew had allowed the bellwether sheep to decide its own fate to stay on land at the start of the voyage, but now, the women were not granted the same privilege of self-determination.

I dared not take a breath while the second boat was being lowered, my body paralyzed by desperate wishes that this lot would have a chance at survival. It was an interminable few minutes of watching the vessel being battered by the powerful winds, like a cat's toy on a string, before it finished its descent with a massive splash. The lifeboat had a rough landing with some immediately lost to the sea as others managed to cling on. It did not take long before the sleet and rain swallowed even the outline of the vessel.

The partial success of the previous launch meant the remaining women were slightly less resistant to getting into the third lifeboat. I experienced both relief and dread as I watched Miss Beck and her charge step over the vessel's low gunwale. She gave me a small brave wave and I returned her gesture all while fear did grip my heart. Knowing this was the final lifeboat to be launched, I did consider for a short moment tearing off my cap and throwing in my lot with the women and children. And yet, some unseen hand held me back.

This time disaster struck quickly, even before the vessel had reached the water. The craft was making its journey down the side of the steamship, when an intense gust thrust the lifeboat against a lower guardrail. The collision of wood and metal flipped the craft upside down, and the screams of the terrified passengers as they fell into the raging ocean shall forever haunt me. I forced myself to scan the surface for Miss Beck, but she had been immediately swallowed by the merciless waves. It did not take long before all calls for help faded.

Collapsing backwards, I inhaled sharply, and used my choking breath to curse a God I had long mistrusted: an apparently all-powerful male deity who abandoned women and children to monstrous deaths with as much care as a vigorous breeze heedlessly whips autumnal leaves from gnarled branches. It was almost unfathomable that amid an ocean squall the prejudice against my sex was still inescapable. It was as though the hate was imbued into the very essence of the rain which cut bitterly against my tear-stained cheek.

Chapter 20

It was early Sunday morning when Helene received a call from Detective Bloom who sounded like he hadn't slept much the previous night; he paused frequently, as if to collect his tired thoughts.

The police officer asked Helene to explain in detail how the ill-fated kayak trip had unfolded, and when she described the slash in the hull, half-covered by tape, he agreed she had reason to be concerned. However, he said his team was too busy collecting evidence at the castle to examine the kayak immediately. He instructed her to keep the vessel under a tarp and make sure the tape stayed in place. Helene suspected that after being submerged in the Gorge, there probably weren't any fingerprints or forensic clues to find. However, she did appreciate how seriously Detective Bloom was taking her concerns.

"Are you going to tell me who died?" Helene couldn't end the phone call without at least trying to learn more about what had occurred at Craigdarroch Castle.

"Off the record?" asked Bloom.

"Absolutely. I won't publish a name until you give me the go-ahead."

As she waited for the detective to come to a decision, the faces of all the possible victims swirled in her mind like a child's kaleidoscope. Zofia Bosko for inheriting the fortune. Adrianna Beck for threatening legal action. Mrs. Fernandez or her daughter because they had made allegations of deceit.

"It was Anderson," Bloom reluctantly imparted.

"Anderson?" Helene was confused. She hadn't come across an Anderson so far in her coverage of Roddy

Beck's murder. There was no way another death at the castle could be totally unrelated, could it?

"Ameer Anderson," the detective clarified.

"You mean the assistant?" Helene felt a shock wave pass through her body. She had been in the same room as him just two days previous, when he was very much alive and very angry. And now his body was a lifeless shell.

"Which brings me to something I wanted to ask you about. I've got a copy of Roddy Beck's will, and it seems a bit odd to me. A guy like that leaving his fortune to some professor he hired a year ago to work on an old book by a dead writer."

Helene decided this wasn't the time to explain the possible ramifications to the canon of Canadian literature in the discovery of an unpublished novel by A.J. Beck, so she let the detective continue talking.

"And I understand you managed to get yourself invited to the will reading on Friday. I won't ask how, I know journalists have their ways, but can you tell me the reaction to the news that the professor was getting the lot?"

Not seeing any reason to hold back on the events she had witnessed, Helene said, "Well, it's fair to say you aren't the only one who was surprised by the provisions laid out in the will. I mean, both Ameer and Adrianna were really angry. But I guess since Ameer is the latest victim, he could hardly be the murderer."

"I don't remember saying he was murdered," interjected Bloom brusquely.

Helene was taken aback. "Sorry, I just assumed. Since he was found at the castle where Beck was killed. How exactly did he die?"

"That's the kind of information I'm gonna keep to myself," Bloom replied. "Wouldn't want to jeopardize the investigation."

Although Helene was annoyed by the lack of further details, she was grateful the detective was still talking to her.

"Oh, I remember one more thing from the will reading and it was to do with something Ameer said."

"Well, make it quick. I've got to meet with the team in five minutes to go over everything we've got so far."

Helene tried to transport herself back to the boardroom in Vancouver. Remembering exactly what had been said after Harold had explained Zofia was the main beneficiary of the will. "Ameer was really angry, obviously."

"You said that already," commented Bloom impatiently.

"And he made a sort of threat."

"A threat?" The detective was now very interested. "A threat against who?"

"It wasn't like that. He said he had been keeping a secret for Roddy. But that he had expected some kind of reward for his silence. So after the will reading he announced he wasn't going to keep the secret any longer."

"And did he give any clue as to the nature of the secret?"

"No," replied Helene, "he just stormed out of the room."

Helene thought she could hear Detective Bloom scratching his bristled chin over the phone as he took a moment to consider what she had told him.

The police officer then asked, "Did anyone else in the room react like they knew what he was talking about? Look worried or upset?"

"Not really. Adrianna had already made a dramatic departure after revealing Harold Webb was her lover. Zofia still seemed stunned from the news about the will. And Harold Webb, he didn't show much reaction to any of it."

"Roddy Beck's lawyer was his wife's lover? That's complicated," considered Bloom. "And Beck had his own secret that Ameer knew about, perhaps the reason either or both of them were murdered."

Helene did not think it was wise to draw attention to the fact that the police officer had just confirmed he was investigating another homicide.

"But what do you think I should do? About the kayak incident."

"Is there any point in me advising you to take a break from doing stories about Roddy Beck? At least until things calm down a little."

Helene replied, "I can hold off for a day or two, but as far as I know, the book launch is still this Friday. And I must cover that. I *want* to cover that."

"Book launch? What book launch?" Bloom sounded more than a little irritated, like he wasn't used to his investigations involving castles and kayaks and literature. He was probably longing for a good old-fashioned pot-shop robbery.

"It's for the book they discovered. It's being shared for the first time at a store downtown on Friday. Everyone will be there."

"Not sure I've ever heard of anyone being killed over a book before. Control of a lucrative company, sure, but not some story."

Although Helene was certain that the novel was connected to the killing of Roddy Beck, she did not yet have any evidence to convince the detective otherwise.

"I'm OK with you hanging out at a bookstore, but can you at least avoid going out on the water anytime soon?"

"I'm not sure how I would even do that, considering my kayak is damaged." As she spoke, Helene couldn't help but wonder what it would be like to attempt to paddle again. After watching her daughter sink lower and lower into the Gorge, would her old fears of watery depths return with the strength of a king tide? While she tried to shake off a fresh bout of anxiety, she said, "I will do my best to avoid unnecessary attention, but I'm on the radio most days. People know where to find me."

Although Helene wasn't going to give up her job as a reporter to stay safe, after ending the call with the detective she did spend the rest of her Sunday at home with her kids. She was slightly reassured by the fact that if someone wanted to make a second attempt to harm her, they would at least have to ring the doorbell. She instructed her children not to answer the door themselves, which was no burden to them since it meant they didn't have to interrupt their reading or video games.

When she returned to the newsroom the following morning, her colleagues' noisy chatter drowned out her fears for at least a few hours. She put off questions from her producer about what happened at the will reading by saying there were a few facts she needed to double check. Helene wasn't worried about another reporter scooping the story as she was the only one who had gone to Vancouver. To buy herself a few days to figure out how the latest killing might be connected to the inheritance, she proposed putting together a story on Beck's estate for Thursday, ahead of the book launch on Friday which seemed to satisfy Riya.

Since she didn't have a deadline for the day, Riya asked if Helene would mind doing a story for the afternoon news run about the latest petition to stop a housing proposal for Moss Bay. In recent years, Helene had covered this kind of opposition many times so it would be an easy assignment, which meant her brain could continue mulling over the killing of Ameer Anderson while she pasted together predictable quotes from outraged residents.

In many ways Moss Bay was like a shrine to the heyday of the single-family home. Generous yards were divided by wooden fences often painted in the same colour as picturesque porches no one ever seemed to use. The tallest building in the leafy residential community was only ten stories and the structure was resented by neighbours for blocking ocean views. There was even a quaint village square which boasted an organic grocery store and a bakery selling overpriced muffins. However, the area lacked some basic but unsightly amenities like a gas station, which could be found in the adjoining more prosaic District of Saanich.

The tree-lined streets and abundance of bookstores might give the impression of a restful and contented community. And yet, if a proposal was put forward to alter the housing stock to include more rentals for low-income families, a shocking militancy immediately awoke among the residents. Petitions boasting slogans such as "Preserve our Homes" were soon blooming with signatures like a cherry tree erupting in spring. Passionate speeches were delivered at packed city council meetings detailing the woeful ramifications of a 20-unit apartment building. And so, it had been apparent for many years that under the veneer of this idyllic community was an intolerance of an existence that wasn't at least solidly middle class—a defence of beauty that was, at its core, quite ugly.

The latest proposed development was planned for one of the few busy roads in Moss Bay. Helene assumed the location would make the project more palatable to the community since it wasn't destined to defile an overly serene streetscape. But when she parked her car half a block from the ongoing protest, Helene could see a throng of people waving placards and chanting slogans. As she approached the crowd on foot, she spotted a table holding a tea urn and scones, supplies to keep up the strength of the crowd in the style to which they were accustomed.

Helene needed to get a couple of clips for her radio piece, so she tried to identify the organizer. Scanning the mostly middle-aged faces, she was shocked to discover the daughter of Mrs. Fernandez in the group.

"What are you doing here?" asked Helene after approaching the woman who had traded in her stiletto heels for silver running shoes.

"And you call yourself a journalist?" Lucia Fernandez had stopped shouting at passing vehicles long enough to answer Helene. "I think it's pretty obvious what I'm doing."

"But is this what your father would have wanted? Even he knew people needed homes. That's what you told me."

"Well, they need to find someone else to build them. These are the same bastards who destroyed my parent's house."

"But aren't you just punishing the people trying to find a place to live?"

Lucia Fernandez rested the end of the sign she was holding on the ground and turned to address Helene. "It sounds like you're taking sides in this fight. I thought journalists were supposed to be unbiased—just holding up a mirror to the world."

"Perhaps I'm tired of seeing that mirror reflecting people struggling to find a place to live. Tired of hearing about old people who can't afford jacked up rents now living out of cars. Or others trying to survive on disability having to choose between food or housing." Even as the words poured out, Helene knew she had lost any veneer of professionalism. But the sight of the affluent protesters had caused something to boil over in her heart.

Helene's words hung in the air and she waited for the woman to tell her she wasn't fit to cover this story. However, Lucia's response was instead sympathetic.

"I get what you're saying. I really do. But I just don't want greedy developers to be taking advantage of the situation. Of everyone's desperation. And I'm not sure how to stop that from happening."

"If you figure that one out, let me know. I will write the story. In the meantime, can you point me in the direction of the organizer? I need to get a couple of quotes for my story."

After conducting an interview with a woman in a form-fitting black down jacket and expensive knee-high rubber boots that would never go near a puddle, Helene made her way along the busy road back to her car. Despite the momentary rapport she had shared with the daughter of Maria Fernandez, she couldn't help but wonder if the woman had visited Craigdarroch Castle on the weekend. But asking people for an alibi for the killing of Ameer Anderson was probably the exact opposite of what Detective Bloom imagined as keeping a low profile. And even though Mrs. Fernandez and her daughter had a reason to wish Roddy Beck harm, what could possibly be their motivation for killing Ameer? Believing that Lucia was more interested in attacking developers than murdering assistants, Helene kept her low on the list of suspects.

Chapter 21

Since it was necessary to provide balance to every story, Helene conducted a short phone interview with the Moss Bay mayor about the protests while still sitting in her car. She had hoped he would offer a strong justification for the apartment project like the shortage of affordable rental stock or the lack of new construction. However, the politician instead delivered a lengthy speech about the need to listen to community voices and provide public consultation. In the end, he sounded more supportive of the protesters than the project, which made Helene feel like she was writing lopsided news copy.

Knowing she needed a strong pro-housing voice, Helene decided to take advantage of the slow burning animus between the mayors of Moss Bay and Victoria. About ten years previous, the province had imposed a contract on the two communities to share policing costs. The leaders of Moss Bay resented this arrangement since the offences committed in their tony neighbourhood mostly involved elderly drivers failing to yield to a stop sign. Victoria on the other hand, attracted all the urban chaos from the surrounding suburbs, resulting in higher rates for assaults and vandalism. Since their emergency workers were also on the front lines of the toxic drug crisis that plagued the streets of the core, the capital city politicians expected regionwide support.

Believing that Mayor Strauss would jump at the chance to provide an understated critique of how Moss Bay was resisting building new affordable housing, Helene stopped by City Hall on her way back to the newsroom. She tried not to question why she wasn't also trying to do this interview by phone from her car, all the while ignoring the niggling hope that she might again bump into Tristan in a City Hall elevator.

"Can I help you?" The woman had come up from behind, making Helene jump in her skin. The journalist had knocked twice on the mayor's office door causing it to swing open, now she felt like she had been caught committing a break and enter.

"I was just wondering if Mayor Strauss was around," she explained defensively. "I wanted to do a short interview for a radio story. Do you know where she is?"

The stout woman in her early 60s possessed an air of authority despite her short stature and she all but rolled her eyes in response. "I believe Mayor Strauss is on a tour of a new green roof on a local microbrewery." The woman's scornful reply made evident she had seen a few mayors come and go as well as many trendy initiatives.

"Are any of the other councillors in their office?" Helene asked hopefully, trying to remember who else was strongly pro-housing.

"I believe it was a group tour. Or at least everyone wanted to go along. Might have had something to do with the free lunch in the brewery."

"Right then," Helene said, "I'll have to try again later."

"It is always best to arrange an appointment," said the woman.

"Well, the news doesn't always work that way," replied Helene, which wasn't going to make her any friends.

Before turning to make her way back down the hallway, Helene couldn't resist peeking past the half-open office door. She had never seen the inside of the mayor's domain and she was intrigued to spot several framed vintage posters for folk music concerts. It made sense that Strauss would support local arts initiatives, but Helene struggled to picture the gavel-wielding politician garbed in a tie-dye dress and swaying to the music of Joni Mitchell. She supposed the mayor had to have ways of unwinding after drafting parking bylaw amendments.

Taking the nearest stairs to the floor below, Helene rationalized a visit to the property records office by telling herself Tristan might have an update on his investigation into the mystery signature. She was curious as to whether he had had any luck comparing the penmanship to writing samples of other City Hall workers. However, when she looked through the plate glass door, Helene saw that a young woman in a checkered dress was standing alone behind the counter. Disappointed, she headed to a nearby stairwell and descended to the ground level of the building.

Resigned to the complete failure of her trip to City Hall, Helene was trying to come up with another local politician or advocate who could share their support for the Moss Bay housing project. Deep in thought, she brusquely marched out the City Hall front entrance and, at the last minute, had to dodge left to narrowly miss colliding with a stranger's coffee cup. Checking her clothing to ensure she was stain-free, she was about to offer her apologies when she realized it was Tristan standing in front of her, a good-natured smirk brightening his features.

"I was looking for you!" Helene blurted out before she could think better of it.

"Well, the happy news is, you've found me," replied Tristan, who was enjoying her candid response. "But you also appear to be rushing away."

Adjusting her backpack which was slipping off her shoulder, Helene said, "Yes, I've got to get back to work. I was trying to get a quote from the mayor, but she's off drinking beer somewhere."

"I hope you aren't putting that in your newscast!" laughed Tristan. "Although that might finally capture the attention of the 18-to-35-year-old demographic so highly sought after by politicians."

"Radio stations too. You have no idea how many strategic plans we have to attract younger listeners. But sadly, most fans of the radio are boomers."

The short exchange having ended, Helene and Tristan simply remained facing each other on the sidewalk outside City Hall. Not sure she could take the tension any longer, Helene was forming the words to say goodbye, but Tristan spoke first.

"Should we go for dinner tomorrow?" Tristan asked abruptly, and then endured his own moment of discomfort. "I have some updates for you," he added, as though to justify the invitation.

"Yes," replied Helene, not quite able to fit her enthusiasm into such a small word.

"OK. I'll text you."

"Good," she said, now starting to worry that she had come down with some rare monosyllabic disease.

With the dinner plans solidified, and a need to escape their awkward standoff, the clerk slipped past Helene and into City Hall.

It took Helene ten minutes to drive back to the newsroom but a bit longer than that for her mind to refocus on her housing protest story. She couldn't quite understand how her investigation into the death of Roddy Beck had led to her agreeing to go on a date but she knew that the prospect of conducting a flirtatious conversation over a breaded appetizer scared her only slightly less than the prospect of being hunted by a multiple-murderer.

Under deadline to finish her story, Helene resorted to calling up a strident housing advocate to get a clip for her radio piece. As a journalist she was grateful that passionate activists never failed to pick up the phone or offer an opinion, but from a more human perspective she did worry about whether they ever took a break from their cause.

Once she had packaged her radio piece, Helene wrote up a matching article to go on the web. Thankfully,

184

she had remembered to snap a few photos at the protest in Moss Bay. Although she preferred to take pictures of breakwater sunsets, she didn't mind that photography had now become an important part of her job—it allowed her to exercise a different sort of creativity beyond writing.

As she was about to pack up her bags and pick up her kids from school, Helene's departure was momentarily delayed by a text message from Alex, asking if she could give her a call in five minutes. Helene replied that she was just about to get into her car, so it was the perfect time to chat.

"Paris is absolutely fabulous!" Alex cheerfully proclaimed once the friends had connected.

"Have you been to the Louvre?" asked Helene.

"The Louvre? That place is like a prison for paintings. Those interminably long hallways packed with hordes of tourists looking stunned and lethargic from a diet of tasteless 'jambon et fromage' baguettes. No thanks." Honking cars could be heard in the background as though Alex was standing on a cobbled street corner.

"But you're having fun?"

"Oh yes, we visited the Musée d'Orsay today to see a special exhibit on Art Nouveau furniture. Honestly, sometimes I feel like I was born at the wrong time. The craftsmanship that went into every piece is just incredible. There was a stained-glass lamp I desperately wanted to steal. But since I just married a police officer, that probably wouldn't be a great idea."

Helene recalled that her friend usually had a calendar hanging in her kitchen featuring paintings by Gustav Klimt—classical female figures ensconced in geometric forms, like dark swans in a pond of gilded waterlilies.

"Have you eaten anywhere good?" Helene felt obligated to ask anyone visiting Paris about the food. She only hoped her friend had found something more to indulge in than ham and cheese sandwiches.

"Oh yes, there's this great little place called Le 404," Alex replied enthusiastically, pronouncing the numbers in a perfect French accent. "North African. Amazing décor. The best couscous I've ever had. And it's in the 3rd arrondissement near our hotel." Her friend sighed deeply, as if recalling the flavour of her last meal. "But I didn't call to talk about couscous," she said with some regret, "I wanted to tell you how the assistant was killed."

Helene had to resist stomping on the brakes in reaction to her friend's declaration. Of all the possible reasons for the late-night call from France, details from the latest death had not been what she was expecting.

"Does Karolina know you are calling to tell me this?" Helene inquired with some skepticism. "And how did she end up telling you?" It was true that during their last investigation, Detective Kalinowski and Helene had openly discussed the leads they were each pursuing. But sharing forensic details from an ongoing inquiry with her new bride did seem slightly out of character for the police officer.

"She didn't so much 'tell' me, it was more that she left her phone open to a downloaded report while taking a shower in the hotel room."

As Helene waited in the left lane for a break in traffic to turn down Johnson Street, she had to consider whether obtaining this information from Alex was going to put the recent nuptials in jeopardy. In the end, curiosity won out— not the first time romance had taken a backseat to journalism.

"OK then, how did he die?" Helene assumed Ameer had not also been a victim of a long fall from a window like Roddy Beck, but as far as stabbing or shooting, she hadn't seriously considered the other options. And even if she had, there was no way she could have predicted the answer.

"A cricket bat to the head." Alex shouted down the line as a particularly noisy vehicle rumbled by. "And then he was shoved down a laundry chute."

"A cricket bat? Like the kind you use to play cricket?" Helene was incredulous.

"Yes, they found wood fibres that matched an antique one from the castle. Apparently, it might have been used by Pierre Berton in the 1930s. I guess the murderer wasn't too worried about desecrating Canadian history."

Helene was still trying to process a cricket bat being a murder weapon, but she also needed clarity on the second half of what Alex had told her.

"What did you say about a laundry chute? He was pushed down it?"

"That was probably the killer's intention, to hide the body, but it was very narrow, according to the report. And he got stuck. His legs sticking out the top." Alex managed to say the last bit in a serious tone, but Helene was now imagining a pair of legs extending from a shaft in the wall like an overgrown plant with feet.

"Which part of the castle was it in?" She didn't recall a laundry chute near the family bedrooms or the billiards room—its function much too banal to be in sight of the wealthy residents who simply expected their well-pressed clothes to appear in their closet everyday.

"The servants' quarters. Apparently, you get to them from a separate staircase."

"Yes, I saw the passage leading to the other side of the castle when I was at the press conference," Helene recalled.

"The chute had been nailed shut decades ago but someone must have opened it with a file or hammer."

Helene considered all her friend had revealed before asking, "When do they think Ameer was killed?"

"The pathologist couldn't be totally sure. Since the body had been moved and hung upside down, but the

187

window for the time of death was from late Friday night to early Saturday morning."

Thinking about the tight timing, Helene presumed the killer must have been in contact with Ameer shortly after he returned from the will reading in Vancouver. Did that mean the details of the inheritance led directly to his death or were their plans already in motion? Either way, the murderer had a predilection for making people fall from great heights: Roddy Beck from the elevated castle landing and Ameer Anderson down a laundry chute. Admittedly, the second scheme was frustrated by a too-narrow passage, but the intention was the same—a final journey downward, perhaps to propel the victims to Hell.

Chapter 22

Helene took it as a small mercy that the skies were clear on Wednesday evening. She had decided to take advantage of the absence of rain to enjoy a quick walk along the breakwater after work—a sort of intermission between the newsroom, parenting and the final act of the day, a date with Tristan. A ridge of clouds above the Olympic Mountains was lit up in faint shades of pink and tangerine, but the sunset fell short of spectacular. This was a relief to Helene who didn't need the distraction of photography, as she was busy mulling over candidates for a murderer ahead of her dinner date. Trying to figure out who was responsible for the two deaths was not unlike picking a meal from a menu, but these choices came with different motives rather than sauces. Just like ingredients that make up a recipe, a mixture of greed, lies or longing for vengeance had to simmer into a concoction that drove someone to kill not once, but twice. But for each candidate she considered, it was difficult to come up with one reason for both Roddy and Ameer to die.

Revenge for destroying a home.
Betrayal in marriage.
Greed over an inheritance.
Desperation to hide a secret.

Helene knew the upcoming book launch might also be connected to the crimes, but she just couldn't figure out in what way. The story of the shipwreck had been written more than a hundred years ago; how could it contain information that would be a threat today? Perhaps it would become clear after reading the tale of the maritime disaster.

The one benefit of relentlessly re-examining the events leading up to the murders was that Helene's anxiety over the dinner date had taken a back seat. It wasn't until she was tugging open the front door of the narrow Victorian-era house that had been converted into a restaurant that her apprehension for the evening encounter returned. As was her habit, she had arrived early for the meeting and had assumed the waitress would be showing her to an empty table. However, Tristan also believed in punctuality, and he gave her a broad grin as she wove her way across the wooden floor to join him.

"I love this place," commented Tristan as Helene got settled. She placed her backpack on the neighbouring chair, suddenly wondering if she should have swapped it for a more elegant purse.

"It has such atmosphere," Tristan continued while gazing upwards, "And the moulding is fabulous. Nobody puts that kind of craftsmanship into homes anymore."

"Yes, I think moulding is the last thing on anyone's mind when it comes to housing these days. Now it's all about having closets that are bigger than bathrooms."

"And who needs more bathrooms than bedrooms? So many bathrooms."

"That all need cleaning," Helene said while thinking woefully of her grubby sinks.

Watching Tristan unfold his napkin, Helene noted that he looked quite handsome. When she had previously encountered him at City Hall, he had been wearing a button-down shirt under a corduroy blazer, a look that reinforced his scholarly appearance. However, that evening he had on a finely knit cream and navy pullover reminiscent of a French après-ski outfit. Although her own wardrobe was mostly dominated by greys and blacks, Helene had picked out a cherry red cardigan for the dinner. Already enjoying their easy banter, Helene was glad to have made an effort with her appearance.

"Have you eaten here before?" inquired Tristan.

"Yes," replied Helene, "with my sister. But just for brunch not dinner. She's one of those brunch people.

Personally, the idea of lining up on a Sunday for an hour to be served a late breakfast is about as appealing as a church service."

"Except, church doesn't feed you."

"You clearly weren't raised a Mennonite," joked Helene.

"No, just plain old Unitarian. Accepting of everyone. But woefully lacking in pageantry. What's the point of religion without incense and statues? Where is the entertainment value?"

"Perhaps we could start a new religion that offers brunch in Gothic settings?" Helene conjectured. "At Craigdarroch Castle. They have enough dinner service to feed a congregation."

"I like that. I'm sure it would be a hit. The only deadly sin would be serving food that wasn't locally sourced."

Helene guffawed at Tristan's reference to the restaurant's menu—every item was grown or raised no farther away than the Cowichan Valley. It wasn't that she thought it was a bad idea for Vancouver Island to become more self-sufficient, but like all trends, the local food movement did seem to have become a religion. And as a journalist, she naturally resisted any dogma, even one relating to the provenance of potatoes.

"I think the sausages are quite good here," said Tristan as he reviewed the menu.

"And they do a fabulous rutabaga," suggested Helene.

"A rutabaga? I don't think I've eaten one of those since 1986."

"That's very specific of you."

"Not much else happened in 1986. Except for Wham releasing 'I'm Your Man,' obviously."

Helene only briefly grinned in response to Tristan's playful comment. She felt unsettled that he had mentioned one of her favourite bands. There was such a thing as getting along too well, too quickly. And after they had ordered drinks from a waitress who looked no more than a year older than Cleo, Helene excused herself to use the restroom. More pressing than the urge to pee, she needed a time out.

Ascending the wooden staircase to the toilet located on the second floor, Helene distracted herself from thoughts of her unnervingly enjoyable date by trying to picture the original occupants of the house: a stern yet loving mother tending to a noisy brood of a mere six children. The family wouldn't have moved in the same social circles as the Dunsmuirs who had built Craigdarroch Castle, but they must have been firmly middle-class to afford a two-storey home in James Bay. If any of their spirits still lingered in the hallways, Helene wondered what they would make of the chattering restaurant crowd. Might they be insulted to see their home turned into a place of commerce or would they appreciate the occasional riot of laughter filling the space with life? She hoped it was the latter.

By the time she had returned to the table, Helene had managed to refocus on the real purpose of the evening meeting—to discuss any developments in Tristan's investigation into the missing property records. At least she hoped that was the main reason they were spending time together. Or did she?

"How is the bread?" Helene asked with exaggerated brightness as she retook her seat. Tristan chewed and then swallowed before answering.

"Very wholesome. Like if it went to church it would have nothing to confess. No refined grains. No bleached flour."

"And delicious too?"

"Surprisingly so."

"Odd, usually only sin tastes good." An extended silence followed this slightly suggestive comment, so Helene took the opportunity to get down to business. "Have you come up with any new information on the signature? Any idea who faked it?" She helped herself to a slice of the virtuous bread while waiting for a reply.

"Not conclusively, but I do have one strong suspect. You remember that the signature on the property records release looked something like 'G. Longfellow' or 'Lindbergh.'"

"Yes, but you said no one with a similar name had worked at City Hall."

"That's true, but it got me thinking that when a person is under pressure, like when stealing a document, for example, their brain probably freezes up. And when they are trying to come up with a lie, they end up using something familiar, whether they realize it or not. Or they might purposely choose to leave a clue behind, as a sort of arrogance that they are too clever to be caught."

"I had no idea you took such interest in the workings of the devious mind," said Helene.

"I watch a lot of true crime documentaries. Helps with insomnia," explained Tristan.

Helene refrained from remarking that there were better ways to relax, like drinking chamomile tea, instead asking, "But how did your theory about the signature being a clue in itself help you?"

"I decided to focus on the city councillors, as they're the only ones who really have any power over housing policy. If you're gonna pay someone off, it would probably be one of them."

"That makes sense," said Helene, who could find no fault with his logic.

"Then I made a list of their interests or hobbies. Councillor Larker goes to dog shows. Therefore, I tried to think of a dog breed that looked like the fake last name, and 'Labradane' is a possibility or even 'Labradoodle'. I did the same thing for each councillor until I stopped at Davies."

"Davies?" Helene was taken aback. "Why Davies?"

"Well as you know, he likes to give off the impression of being an English gentleman. The cane. The way he pronounces 'schedule' with a 'sh' sound. But a few years ago he got quite drunk at a City Hall Celebration of Lights in December. And his accent started to slip from Gloucester to Gaspé."

"Like Gaspé, Quebec? But that's so strange. Why would he pretend to be British?"

Tristan raised his eyebrows. "Because he wanted to get elected in a place called 'Victoria?'"

"That's fair," agreed Helene.

"Anyway, for some reason, during this holiday celebration, he decided to start an argument about who was the greatest hockey player of all time. Something I'm woefully ill-equipped to offer an opinion on, I would add." The disdain in Tristan's voice indicated he enjoyed watching sports as much as Helene. "But what I happened to recall is that he kept on bringing up Guy Lafleur. You know the Montreal Canadiens player in the '70s. I believe he helped win five Stanley Cups."

"I thought you didn't know about hockey," challenged Helene.

Tristan smiled, "Guy Lafleur isn't so much sports history, as Canadian history."

"But how does a love for a French-Canadian hockey player connect councillor Davies to the property deal?" asked Helene, too distracted to notice the waitress approaching their table.

"Have you had a chance to look at the menu?" chirped the young woman, a pen poised over a pad ready to take their order.

"NO!" the pair declared in unison, which Helene attempted to soften with an apology and a request to come back in a few minutes. Once the waitress had retreated, Tristan picked up where they had left off.

"Guy Lafleur? The first initial is G, with a last name that starts with an 'L' and has some kind of flourish in the middle. Councillor Davies was writing the signature for his favourite hockey player. It's so obvious: G. Lafleur."

Helene leaned back against the tines of her wooden chair to consider Tristan's theory. In some ways it made a lot of sense that the councillor would use a name that was very familiar in a stressful moment. But this hardly qualified as evidence, not even circumstantial.

"How are we going to prove he did it?" Helene was putting the question to herself as much as Tristan.

"I've already thought of that. Again, thanks to too many late nights watching documentaries about American serial killers."

"Well, I'm glad you've had time to come up with a plan. I've been busy trying to find an actual killer who hunts people in the castle."

Tristan looked at Helene in confusion. "People? More than one? Did the police say the second death was a murder?"

Helene ignored his question, wanting to stay focused on the property records. "What do you suggest we do? Break into his office to look for papers linking him to Roddy Beck and the destruction of Mrs. Fernandez's home? I suppose you could get into City Hall after hours."

"That involves way too much risk with a very slim chance of success," Tristan said rather dismissively. "No, I propose we flush him out. Force him to make a move."

"How would we do that?" Helene could tell Tristan was enjoying taking the lead in the investigation.

"I will announce an audit of the property records. Might even add it's in response to some files going missing. Then we wait for the file to be returned. And poof, we check for fingerprints."

"Because you know how to check for fingerprints?"

195

Tristan simply shrugged. "How hard can it be? I'm sure there's a website we can get the gear from. Or even better, an app!"

The waitress returned once more to take their order and after their food had arrived Helene spent most of the meal playing devil's advocate to Tristan's plan. What if there were too many fingerprints on the file? What if there were none? What power did they have to hold an unethical municipal politician to account? However, none of her doubts were able to diminish Tristan's enthusiasm. In the end, she decided to go along with the scheme.

As Tristan indulged in an after-dinner coffee, Helene resisted pointing out that the beverage might be contributing to his insomnia, and they managed to talk about something other than badly behaving city councillors. On the topic of travel, Helene shared memories of living in Prague in her 20s and how she loved the architecture but could never quite get used to Czech dumplings. Tristan had taken a trip to Greece the previous year and his eyes lit up as he described plunging into the Mediterranean.

Waiting outside for Tristan's taxi to take him back to Esquimalt, the sky was mostly clear of clouds with a thin moon on the horizon. Helene had turned down Tristan's offer to drop her off on his way as she was looking forward to her short walk home as a chance to go over the evening's conversations.

Tapping his feet to a tune only he could hear, Tristan asked, "Do you normally go on dates?"

"Not really," replied Helene just as bluntly.

"Are you looking for a relationship?"

"I don't think so." Helene shrugged.

"But you would want to do this again?"

"Absolutely."

"Excellent." Tristan then leaned over and kissed Helene on the cheek before getting into the taxi that had just pulled up.

196

As she watched the car receding along the harbour road, Helene had no idea what had just happened. However, she also didn't really understand sunsets, but that didn't stop her from enjoying them.

.

.

Chapter 23

The launch of A.J. Beck's book was only one day away and Helene wanted to make sure she was prepared to quickly turn around radio and web stories. She had tracked down several archival photos of the *S.S. Clallam* from American historical societies and received their permission to use the pictures for her online article. The stark black and white images made the vessel appear substantial and inviolate, a tilting smokestack adding an air of leisurely confidence. It was difficult to imagine the steamship being tossed up and down like the waves were naughty children playing catch with other people's lives.

In the early afternoon, she reread a few of the more detailed reports that had been compiled of the maritime disaster. But they were all very clinical in their description, focused on the timeline of events rather than the unfolding human drama. The dry narratives made Helene even more eager to read the firsthand account by A.J. Beck. In her news stories, she was going to have to strike a balance between depicting the passengers' terror and factual information.

Recollections of her date with Tristan occasionally intruded on her thoughts and there was no denying that she had enjoyed his company: the way he leapt randomly from one topic of conversation to another was an entertaining diversion from the cares of work and parenting. Helene had even considered inviting him to the book launch but thought he might prove to be too much of a distraction while she was working. And although both the missing property records and the novel had connections to Roddy Beck, she wanted to keep the two investigations separate in her mind.

When the phone on her desk went off, Helene registered her disappointment that it was Lela's not Tristan's name on the screen. Answering the call on the third ring, she then walked into an unoccupied radio booth for privacy. She could never predict what her sister wanted to talk about, the latest boyfriend who was starting to bore her or the exciting trip she was planning to Mexico with girlfriends—in the end it was something much more unsettling.

"Mom's house has sold." Lela declared after a quick hello.

"It did? When?" Helene demanded, feeling a knot form in her stomach.

"The realtor just called to say the subjects have been removed."

"And when do they take possession?"

"January first."

Although the news of her mother's house selling was inevitable, it was no less shocking. At the time of their parent's death during the height of COVID, neither Lela nor Helene wanted to deal with dispensing of the home in Edmonton immediately. The thought of spending weeks sorting through mementos from a disordered childhood was utterly overwhelming, especially during a pandemic. Thankfully, there was enough money in the estate to keep paying the property tax and general upkeep, so they delayed putting it on the market. But a few months ago, a realtor had gotten in touch, saying they had interest from a buyer. The sisters accepted the initial offer since the financial windfall would be a welcome boost to them both. Helene could pay off her mortgage and Lela would enjoy many more trips to tropical climes.

"Now what do we do?" asked Lela. "With the stuff. In the house."

The realtor had hired someone to tidy the premises before showing it to the buyer, but nothing had been done to sort through the watercolours, vinyl recordings or rare musical instruments her mother had left behind.

Thinking about the timing, Helene quickly calculated that if the buyer was taking possession at the start of the New Year, it would mean they would have to clear the house through the Christmas break. And it was hard to imagine anything more vanquishing of holiday cheer.

As if reading her sister's mind, Lela suggested, "We could always hire someone to clear the lot out. Just put it all in a bin and be done with it."

At this suggestion Helene's stomach muscles tightened again—there was no right answer. She neither wanted to be submerged in the memories attached to the leftovers of her mother's complicated existence, nor did she want a stranger sorting through such intense souvenirs of private pain. Having been denied or freed from attending her mother's funeral due to the pandemic, she realized this was her last chance to process her mother's legacy.

"I need to think about it," she finally told her sister. "I've got a lot going on at work and I can't make up my mind right now."

"OK. But don't wait too long. It'll take time to find someone to clear it out if that's what you want to do. Especially over the holidays." After a short pause, Lela added, "I will support whatever you decide. If you want to go to Edmonton, I will go too. If you want to toss it all, that's fine by me."

Helene didn't know if it was the news that their home was going to be occupied by another family, permanently eradicating a museum to her difficult youth, or her sister's generous gesture to let her make the final decision in sorting out the house, but her vision grew blurry with tears. Lela and her sister had been through so much together: teenagers negotiating condescending conversations with police officers after their mother had called 911 about aliens, young women visiting their parent in a mental health ward reverberating with seismic screams. And because they didn't have a sane adult to depend on, the sisters took it in turns to play the grown-up when times were tough.

Before ending the call, Helene told Lela that she loved her and that she would make a decision in a week. Then she sunk into the studio chair usually occupied by the on-air technician and took several deep breaths.

Trying to recover a steady demeanor before returning to the busy newsroom, a particular phrase came to mind at the thought of visiting her mother's house: she was terrified of foundering. It was how the newspaper articles from 1904 described the fate of the *S.S. Clallam*. *The steamship had foundered.* Her fear was that the weight of the sorrow from the unresolved conflict with her dead mother would overwhelm her like an ocean's tempest, causing her to sink beyond hope of salvaging.

Helene's phone went off again, forcing her out of the melancholy stupor.

"Hello, Helene? It's Zofia. Zofia Bosko."

"Zofia, good to hear from you! I was going to give you a call ahead of the book launch. Clarify a few details for my story." As soon as Helene had said the words, she realized she may have gotten down to business a little too quickly. She proceeded more gently, "How are you feeling about tomorrow? Must be strange to be doing the launch without Roddy. Sharing his great-grandmother's legacy. I'm sure you never saw it playing out like this."

"You're right. I never imagined Roddy not being there. Or inheriting his fortune. And now his assistant has also died, but the police haven't said if it's an accident. Personally, I thought we should postpone the book launch. You know, out of respect. But I guess there would be legal ramifications if we did."

"Have you decided what you're going to do? About the money and the company?" asked Helene.

"To be honest, the money is a miracle, but as far as the company itself goes, I'm going to give it back. I mean, what business do I have running it?"

"Does anyone else know your plans?"

"Not yet, I wanted to get through the book launch first. Why?"

"I'm just thinking, both Roddy and Ameer were connected to the company and they both ended up dead. It might be a good idea to distance yourself from it."

"You think someone may try to kill me?" The alarm in Zofia's voice made Helene almost regret her blunt comment.

"Zofia, that company is worth millions, maybe even a billion. People have been murdered for much, much less."

"Can you get the word out? That I'm not keeping the company. I mean, you're a journalist. Would you publish something right away?"

The conversation had gone in an unexpected direction; however, Helene still owed her boss an article about the inheritance. She had put Riya off that morning, saying she wanted to wait for the police to publicly confirm that Ameer was murdered. But this latest development made the story too hot to delay writing it any longer. She was already coming up with possible headlines: Heiress Gives Back Beck Tech Fortune.

"I'd have to run it by my producer. But we should be able to put something together in the next couple of hours. Can I call you back after I check with her?"

"OK, sure. But now I'm really worried," said Zofia. "Please let me know as soon as you can."

"I will. Absolutely. But Zofia, if you didn't call to tell me about your plans for the company, why did you?"

"Oh, I almost forgot. I wanted to give you a sort of warning."

"Warn me? About what?"

"Or maybe it's that I mean to apologize, in advance. I will be sharing some news at the book launch tomorrow. Nothing to do with the company or my plans to give up the inheritance. But it's still something that will be quite shocking to everyone there, including you. I'm sorry I can't tell you ahead of time. Nobody knows this secret and its going to make some people very, very angry."

Helene immediately tried to imagine what Zofia was going to reveal the next day. Her only guess was that the academic had written the new book herself, not the celebrated A.J. Beck. But what could Zofia hope to gain by lying about it? And why would Roddy Beck have gone along with the scheme while he was alive? Not coming up with any plausible theories, Helene decided to instead focus on what she could actually accomplish: writing an article about Zofia's plans to walk away from a fortune.

As she expected, her producer was thrilled to hear that Helene was ready to write the article that would include exclusive information. However, Riya warned her that the piece would need to be vetted by lawyers overnight, just like all big financial stories that could impact shareholders. But since Helene had witnessed the will reading herself and her main interview was with a shocked heiress, not a disgruntled whistleblower, she didn't expect any problems.

Helene considered calling up Adrianna Beck, to get her reaction to the news that Zofia was giving up control of the company. But she didn't trust the almost-ex-wife not to share the news with another media outlet. She decided Adrianna's perspective would make a great follow up story for the morning, something to publish just ahead of the evening book launch.

The sun had long since set by the time Helene left the newsroom. Driving home along dark streets, she decided to pop into an upscale organic grocery store to pick up one of their free-range roasted chickens. Thankfully, Cleo had already made hotdogs and french fries in the air fryer for herself and Oscar. Helene couldn't face the prospect of cooking after the hours she had spent crafting the story about the future of Roddy Beck's fortune.

As it was evening, the grocery store wasn't very busy so Helene was able to make her way quickly through the aisles to the meat section in the back corner. She was relieved to spot one remaining chicken in the roaster, allowing her to momentarily believe in a benevolent universe.

Deciding to forgo vegetables, she was heading for the cash registers when the sight of familiar faces in the produce department sent her scurrying behind a stack of discounted cereal boxes. In the same way an off-duty schoolteacher didn't want to engage with students after work, Helene had reached a point in the day when she wanted to stop playing the part of a journalist. So she stayed well-hidden while watching as Mrs. Fernandez and her daughter carefully selected Roma tomatoes from an oversized bin. The elderly woman must have been released from the hospital earlier that week as she looked well, her cheeks were rosy and she laughed easily at a remark her daughter made. For her part, the younger Fernandez hardly spared a glance at the tomatoes, as she gazed at her mother with adoration and love. This unabashed display of filial affection obliterated Helene's sense of satisfaction from writing the article about Roddy Beck. She was once again reminded of the choice she had to make about whether or not to clear her mother's house.

As she made a detour through the chip aisle to avoid the two women, Helene could only fathom what it was like to possess such love for a parent. When her own mother was alive, she had avoided inviting her to Victoria. Somehow she was afraid that her parent's mental illness and narcissistic behaviour would poison her house or even her children, tainting the functional and caring family she had created. And after her mother's death, thoughts of their relationship were imbued with guilt and shame.

Passing her drooping bag of rapidly gelatinizing chicken to the cashier, Helene's heart clung to the one consolation for having such a problematic parent: the weight of love and grief was that much lighter. The news of her mother's death had not devastated Helene, if anything, it had brought relief—that Helene could stop trying to show affection to a mother who had spawned so much misery.

Recalling how Lucia Fernandez had gazed at her mother with almost primal devotion, Helene had to wonder what actions such love could inspire. Violence? Even murder?

But if Helene had been spared an intensely loving connection to her mother, the same could not be said for how she felt about Oscar and Cleo. Bringing to mind her cherished offspring while driving home from the supermarket, Helene knew she would kill to defend them with less compunction than ripping a well-seasoned wing from a roasted fowl.

Chapter 24

Like a pop concert for the literary set, the line-up for the Friday night book launch snaked down Government Street past bemused patrons lounging on pub patios. Helene's web story about Zofia Bosko renouncing her claim to Roddy Beck's company had obviously drummed up public interest in the event, especially considering the academic was the evening's main speaker. Thankfully, the staff at Munro's Books had been told to let Helene in through the back door, and she wondered if this was what it was like being a rock reporter covering a Rolling Stones concert in 1966, minus the drugs.

Even without her article going live that morning, Helene had no doubt the book launch would have attracted an enthusiastic crowd. A.J. Beck novels sold well, even more than half a century after her death. In addition, Greater Victoria was home to many book lovers, its library system was one of the busiest in the country. And as if public libraries weren't enough to satisfy the appetite of the book-craving public, the community also had an abundance of free little libraries. A few enthusiasts who were skilled in woodworking had even created outdoor cupboards for novels that were miniature replicas of their own homes. Once her children had outgrown them, Helene had deposited many picture books in her favourite little library on Parry Street in James Bay which had a peaked roof and burgundy staircase fit for a gnome.

Helene was glad to have arrived at the bookstore early to stake out a good seat. As was her usual manner, she chose a chair at the end of the aisle, facilitating an easy escape. Sadly, she had not beaten her rival, Gary Graham, to the event and it didn't take long before he made an approach.

"Nice article," Graham stated through gritted teeth and a rigid smile.

"Thank you," replied Helene, as though Graham was offering genuine praise.

Frustrated that his sarcasm had been misconstrued, the reporter continued, "Not entirely sure how you got early access to the details of Roddy Beck's will. Seems possibly unethical."

Helene had to choke back a guffaw. "This, coming from a man who followed the mayor to a restaurant to check whether her meal was 'sustainable?' Have you even heard of journalism standards?" Looking the disheveled reporter up and down, she added, "I must say, jealousy really isn't your best colour, Gary. You look a bit jaundiced. I would stick with insipid." Then, glancing at her phone, as if there was a message she needed to check, she said, "Now, if you'll excuse me, I must get ready. I understand there's going to be a big revelation about the book tonight." This comment had the intended effect of sending Gary Graham scurrying back to his seat to make a call to his office. Helene wasn't worried about tipping him off about Zofia's secret as everyone in the room would know it soon enough.

As it turned out, Helene did receive a text alert while the crowd continued to filter into the bookstore.

```
Flying home tomorrow
Woke up to pee
Saw your story about inheritance
Very cool
Almost makes me miss work
```

The message from Alex was followed by a laughing-face emoji.

Safe travels
At book launch
Gary says hello

A couple wanted to access the seats in Helene's row, so she turned to the side to allow them to pass before reading her friend's reply.

Why hasn't he been pushed out a window yet?
Just kidding
Must sleep
Check for news when I wake

Slipping her phone back into her pocket, Helene tried to imagine herself lying next to a lover in a Paris hotel room: negligee draped across an embroidered chair, the remains of room service on the floor outside the door. It seemed more like a scene from a predictable rom-com rather than something her future had in store.

And then, just as Helene was contemplating what it would be like to gaze across the breakfast table at another adult every morning, she spied Tristan waving from across the room. To make matters worse, she found herself waving back. However, to her surprise, after he stopped waving, he made no move to join her, perhaps surmising that she needed to focus on the proceedings, after all, she hadn't invited him to the event. She was both pleased and annoyed that he was being so thoughtful. Helene decided to distract herself from her duelling emotions by making a few notes about the interior of the shop in case she needed atmospheric details for her online story.

Above the crowd, the store's vaulted cream moulded ceilings and high ornate windows created an airy feeling conducive to bookish thoughts. The core of the establishment was dominated by a square wooden counter where staff waited to assist with searches or take payments. The substantial floor space was partitioned by lengthy shelves bearing the latest novels, picture books and nonfiction tomes, as well as a selection of leatherbound notepads and decorative bookmarks. The shop stopped short of offering the blankets and candles that some more modern bookstores flogged, blurring the line between literary pursuits and home decor.

The chairs, which had been set up behind the main desk, were now all claimed and people were also lined up along the bookshelves. Helene assumed the space had reached its maximum occupancy and there were A.J. Beck groupies outside, still vying to get in. Among those lucky enough to be inside the store, all discussion came to a halt as Zofia Bosko walked up to the microphone planted next to a table laden with books hidden under a cloth.

"Good evening everyone, and thank you for coming," Zofia began. "If Roddy was here tonight, he would be so thrilled to see his great-grandmother honoured in this way."

Recalling what Ameer had told her about Roddy Beck in fact feeling nothing but resentment toward his great-grandmother, and his family prioritizing her writing above everything and everyone, Helene wasn't sure he would have been gratified by the enthusiasm of these literary fans. However, the man liked to perform before a crowd, so the full house would have pleased him, nonetheless.

"I want to start by acknowledging that we are living on the traditional territories of the Lekwungen-speaking Peoples. And that the historical relationships to the land of the Songhees, Esquimalt and W̱SÁNEĆ Peoples continue to this day." As the academic offered the land acknowledgement, Helene recalled that Roddy Beck had failed to do the same when he started the press conference at Craigdarroch Castle. But perhaps this would have been too hypocritical, considering the Dunsmuir fortune was built on coal plundered from Indigenous lands.

"I want to first introduce myself. I'm Zofia Bosko, a professor of 20th century Canadian literature at the University of Victoria and one of the leading experts on the writings of A.J. Beck. Since you are here tonight, I assume you will agree that Alberta Josephine Beck is one of the most compelling and groundbreaking writers of her time." A murmur of assent passed through the older crowd, an expression of gratitude that for one night, and in one place, books would be venerated rather than a video on social media featuring a meal made of spaghetti and potato chips.

"Although Roddy Beck is no longer with us, I want to express my appreciation for his invitation to be a part of this remarkable project. I also want to take the opportunity to thank my mother, who worked so hard to give me a better life. Tonight's success would not have been possible without her." Zofia beamed as she spoke the words of recognition, but then there was a slightly uncomfortable shift in her tone when she added, "Unfortunately she wasn't able to make it to the book launch."

Helene couldn't help but be puzzled by the absence of Zofia's mother. Who would miss out on her daughter's big night? But there was no time to dwell on this question as the moment they were all waiting for finally arrived.

"Now, I am incredibly delighted to reveal the newly discovered work by the celebrated A.J. Beck: *A Grave Voyage*." A staccato of camera flashes went off as Zofia lifted the cloth from the books neatly arranged on the table. Helene knew there would be plenty of chances to photograph the novel before the evening ended, so she did not rush up to the table like the overly eager Gary Graham. She did, however, from a distance, examine a large poster of the book jacket which had been set up on the table, the design including a historic photo of the doomed *S.S. Clallam* in Pacific waters.

Zofia let the chaos continue for a few minutes as excited readers picked up the books and leafed through the pages—their delight not dissimilar to the glee of children discovering a stash of sea glass on the beach. For their part, the staff at the two cash registers were busy running through sales and passing out complimentary bookmarks, proving that the book trade was still a going concern, at least in Victoria.

About 15 minutes passed before Zofia returned to the microphone. "Thank you everyone. If you wouldn't mind taking a seat, I will read a few passages from the book."

As the crowd settled in, the academic shared the opening sentences from *A Grave Journey*. Helene was reminded of the first time she had heard Zofia speak at the castle—how the woman's plain and angular appearance was incongruous to her lyrical enunciation, her voice a melodious reprieve to ears used to enduring the cacophony of the modern digital soundscape.

Like many classic tales, the story began with a character embarking on a grand adventure. The protagonist, a young and intelligent woman, was fleeing an oppressive marriage at the dawn of the 20th century—perhaps a metaphor for the world trying to leave behind the conservative mores of the Victorian era. Helene quickly realized that the character must be A.J. Beck herself, taking the precaution of introducing herself to strangers on the ship as a man named Bert, a gender-shifting version of her real name: Alberta.

It was difficult to hear the narrator impart hope and anticipation for happier days, knowing the maritime disaster that lay in the hours ahead. Of course, the mystery remained as to how A.J. Beck had survived the foundering of the *S.S. Clallam*, which claimed the lives of all the other women, and their children, on board.

Whether it was due to A.J. Beck's elegant prose or Zofia's hypnotic delivery, Helene found herself drawn into

212

the storytelling in a way that made her forget she was there as a journalist. She held her breath as the woman came close to being discovered by one of the ship's crew. The kindness of the governess on board was a respite from isolation even as the deadly storm grew stronger. On occasion, Helene glanced at Tristan, who was leaning against one of the bookshelves, apparently also mesmerized by the story. She managed to catch his eye in a shared moment of delight at one of the pithier observations by the author about the divisions of the classes.

Zofia jumped ahead to a particularly terrifying passage describing the waves washing over the decks of the *S.S. Clallam* and the audience members were practically clutching their metal chairs like life buoys in anticipation of being swept away themselves. It was at the height of this chapter's action, when the tension in the room was as taught as a sail caught in a squall, that the stunning Adrianna Beck made an entrance. Like the sirens who lured sailors to their death, she immediately captured the attention of everyone in the room.

Faltering mid-sentence, Zofia sensed the shift in the room's focus. Closing the book in her hands, she too stared at Adrianna, the newly anointed author of how events would unfold in the room.

With this latest disruption, Helene realized she had attended two gatherings in the last three weeks which had gone off course, unable to reach their planned destination like the doomed *S.S. Clallam*.

Still standing at the back of the room, Adrianna appeared to be revelling in the awe her entrance had created, and in the manner of people in possession of exceptionally good looks, she was more than comfortable being gawped at. Then, as though a gun had gone off to signal the start of a race, half-a-dozen reporters leapt up from their chairs and clustered around Adrianna.

Although lacking in physical beauty, Gary Graham enjoyed the spotlight as much as the glamorous woman he was now standing next to. He announced his first question like an actor to an audience, projecting his voice while striking the pose of an intrepid reporter with his trusty microphone.

"How do you feel about having your husband's company returned to your control? What would he think of his wishes being ignored?"

Like probably every other reporter in the room, Helene had spent the day trying to get Adrianna to agree to an interview. However, her numerous phone calls had not been returned.

"I believe my husband was blinded by a fleeting association with one individual, not knowing that he would die so soon, obviously. And now the person responsible for this situation has merely put things right. At least partially."

Helene could hardly believe that Adrianna was all but accusing Zofia of seducing and manipulating her husband. Rather than expressing gratitude for regaining the company, she was using her moment in the spotlight to wreak some kind of public vengeance. The rich really did have an insatiable appetite to devour those around them.

Pivoting to look at Zofia, Helene observed the academic had turned as white as the pages of the book she was holding. Understanding that there was no hope of getting the book event back on track, Zofia spun on her heels and fled down the aisles of the bookstore, past the imperviously cheery covers of children's picture books.

Divided between the need to interview Adrianna as a follow up to her article, and the desire to talk with Zofia about the woman's accusations, Helene was frozen by inaction as Gary Graham asked another question.

"Are you insinuating that Zofia Bosko urged your husband to change his will, only to give the company back?"

For as much as Helene despised the unscrupulous reporter, she thought he had a point.

Not waiting for what was sure to be another vague and self-aggrandizing reply from Adrianna, Helene grabbed her bag and followed Zofia out the back of the bookstore. On her way, she passed a stunned staff member, who was wondering what had happened to the promise of a quiet bookish employment.

Thankfully, after exiting the building, her search for Zofia was brief. The academic was in the alley, one hand on the brick wall, as if to steady herself.

"Are you OK?" Helene heard herself uselessly asking when the answer was obvious. "Adrianna had no right to say those things."

"Oh, I don't care about that," said Zofia after catching her breath. "It just shows why Roddy didn't want to be with her."

Not sure if she was hearing a confession to an affair, Helene waited for Zofia to keep talking.

"I'm upset because I didn't get to share the secret, about the book," Zofia continued. "It's exhausting being the only one who knows the truth."

Considering the ethics of asking her next question, as the lines of friendship and journalism were becoming blurred, Helene's curiosity ultimately won out. "Do you want to tell me?"

Waiting on tenterhooks for Zofia to reply, Helene almost fell over when Tristan burst from the back door of the building next to where she was standing.

"Is everyone all right?" he asked Helene. "These book readings are really more exciting than I was led to believe."

"I think we could all use a drink," she replied with a sigh. "And I know just the place."

January 9, 1904
The Early Hours

In the small hours of the night, my mind and body had grown numb from shock and cold and it was a sort of desperate relief when I found myself ordered into action. A chain of men had formed from the engine room to the middle deck, each clasping a fire bucket, bailing out the water that was mercilessly filling up the vessel. As my sex had still not yet been revealed, I joined the effort, uncertain how long my strength would subsist. But death is a powerful motivator.

After what seemed like interminable hours of labouring, news went down the line that a tugboat had been spotted off starboard. In response, a weak cheer was shared among the exhausted men, and I believe I comprehended the camaraderie of the battlefield. We did, however, redouble our efforts in bailing as the water also seemed to be rising more quickly, as though the ocean was determined to thwart our possible escape from its clutches.

It seemed not an hour had passed, and my arms were numb with aching when we heard a calamitous shattering of glass. As the vessel groaned and twisted, it quickly became understood that the ocean was now pouring through the dining saloon windows. The call to abandon ship was heard and then the final harrowing scramble ensued.

The stairway had been transformed into a treacherous waterfall, and as I struggled to ascend, my eyes could perceive almost nothing, while my ears were assaulted by desperate cries for help. All at once I felt a hand behind me, and when I looked back, I could discern the outline of a tall gentleman.

"Stay on the vessel as long as possible," he shouted into my ear. "And we must find you something to which to cling once you are overboard."

The water had now reached my chest, and the man and I reached out to hold fast to anything wooden that might float. In the end we came upon a deck stool, which he pushed in my direction.

"Grasp onto this and do not let go. There is a chance yet you will survive." Something in the tenderness of these last words gave me the impression he knew I was a woman. But before I could thank him, he had moved on, perhaps to save another. His actions forced me to reconcile my difficult marriage with the truth that there were some good men in the world.

As the ship continued to founder and split apart, I became aware that a piece of flying timber could kill me as surely as the ocean, so I tried to avoid snapping debris by keeping myself on the very edge of the deck until the final moment. And then once level with the water, I dove out into the darkness, clutching my stool, like a doomed soul grasping onto the relic of the cross.

It is impossible to convey the violent intensity of the frigid waters. The icy waves immediately robbed me of breath and numbed my extremities in a sort of rehearsal for rigor mortis. I knew now that death did not come draped in a cloak and carrying a scythe, like the medieval texts portrayed, rather it washed over you with a consuming cold until all warmth and life had been vanquished. More like a rapidly depleting disease than a storybook assassin.

My last delirious thought was that since my body would be consumed by the ocean, I would have no grave. And although this was not the liberty of which I had dreamed, it was, in its way, still a sort of freedom. To sway amongst the flora and fauna of the sea forever, not to be condemned to a burial plot, like a perfectly preserved jewel *in a locked safe, a tomb not unlike the life from which I had escaped.*

Chapter 25

"I just have to text my mother. Tell her we went out. Even though she didn't come, she'll want to know how the book launch went. I'm not sure what to say."

Zofia was sitting across from Helene in the Barge and Whistle, rapidly typing on her cell phone. The building was older than Craigdarroch Castle but had only been turned into a drinking establishment in the late '60s. The walls were adorned with the banners of English football teams and adverts from local microbreweries. But Helene had chosen this pub not for its vaguely colonial atmosphere, but because she remembered it from the photos on Roddy Beck's desk from his university days. Seemed like a fitting choice for the evening and she had been wanting to check it out.

Helene had ordered a glass of chilled white wine whereas Tristan had chosen a dark Glaswegian beer that walked the line between liquid and solid. Zofia, not in a celebratory mood, asked the waitress for a ginger ale. This made Helene feel slightly guilty, since she didn't usually imbibe alcohol when she was driving, but one glass seemed allowable considering how the evening had unfolded.

"I'm surprised your mother wasn't at the launch," commented Helene after taking a refreshing sip of the Cowichan Valley Pinot Gris. "Knowing how proud of you she must be."

Zofia, in turn, lifted her glass and responded vaguely, "My mother is a woman of very strong opinions. And earlier today we had a bit of a clash."

Totally oblivious to the rapport Helene was trying to build up with Zofia, Tristan abruptly injected, "Sounds like most of the city councillors. They prefer talking to listening!"

Delivering a silencing glare, Helene let him know he was to play the role of observer. Admonished, Tristan focused on his beer's generous foam.

"You two must be so close, especially since she was a single mom. It changes the dynamic between parent and child," she mused. "Instead of being on opposing teams, you must fight together to survive. At least, that's how it is with my kids."

"You're a single mom too? Wow. I didn't know that. I think I'd rather not have kids than do all that work alone," observed Zofia. "Must be so hard."

Helene took another sip of her wine to quench her irritation at what felt like a flippant critique of her life. It didn't help that Tristan shot her a surprised glance; they had not yet had a conversation about the presence of children in their lives.

"I actually think it suits me quite well, outside of the endless exhaustion," she replied. "Not having to negotiate how I raise my kids or run my home with a man." At this point, Helene half-expected Tristan to make a dash for the door, but he remained in his seat, looking more amused than anything.

"Yes, but sometimes it can go too far," observed Zofia. "The parent starts to live through the child because they don't have their own life. It can be quite suffocating."

Realizing that Zofia was talking about her own relationship, rather than making a general statement about single parents, Helene decided not to take any further offence. "I think it can work the other way too when the child becomes too devoted to their parents. Losing sight of everything else." Helene was once again wondering what Lucia Fernandez was capable of when it came to avenging how Roddy Beck had tricked her parents.

Deciding that there had been enough philosophizing about parenting, Helene made a move to refocus on the evening's events. "What was it you wanted to share at the book launch? I know Adrianna interrupted your plans when she showed up like that."

"I thought she would be satisfied once I announced my intention to return ownership of the company to her, I assumed that be enough," Zofia shook her head in confusion.

"Adrianna probably also wants the bank accounts and control over what happens to the book," said Helene. "By the way, I love the title, *A Grave Journey.* A.J. Beck really does have a way with words."

"Except they aren't hers, the words," Zofia whispered while looking down at the table.

"Oh, did you and Roddy come up with the title?"

"Not just a new title. But a new book."

About to take another sip from her glass, Helene instead put it down and asked. "What do you mean, a new book?" She glanced over at Tristan to see if he had caught the significance of what Zofia was saying. Wiping a line of foam from his lip, he appeared equally bewildered.

"But A.J. Beck wrote the book, yes?" she asked tentatively.

Looking Helene directly in the eyes, like a sinner who is committed to finally making a confession, Zofia said, "She wrote short excerpts of the journey, describing getting on board the *S.S. Clallam*, meeting the governess, ultimately surviving the wreck. But there were only about 30 pages."

Letting this sink in, Helene then asked the next logical question. "So, who wrote the rest? Was it you?"

"That would have made it all right. 'Canadian scholar creates new classic based on writings of celebrated author.' The world would have been OK with that. Wouldn't have hurt my career any either."

"But if it wasn't you—and as talented as he was at everything in life, I can't believe it was Roddy—then who wrote *A Grave Journey*?"

"AI!" blurted out Tristan and then immediately appeared apologetic.

"Artificial intelligence?" Too confused to be annoyed by the interruption, Helene declared, "That's ridiculous!"

"No," responded Zofia. "He's right. It was Roddy's idea. He was working on a new AI writing app and he thought this was the perfect way to launch it. To let the world believe the book was the creation of A.J. Beck, and then a few months later, reveal the truth."

"And completely destroy his great-grandmother's reputation? To basically say that AI could write as well as her?"

"I didn't see that at first, but it's true. He had some drive to humiliate her that I never understood. Of course, he only told me it had been written by AI after I had committed to the project and I had no way out that wouldn't have ruined my own career. In the end, he promised to share the profits with me."

"And you went along with it?" Helene tried to keep the judgment out of her voice.

"I knew it was wrong, but is it horrible if I admit to being tempted by the money? I had been spending a lot of time with Roddy by then and I was coming to enjoy a certain kind of lifestyle. Being a university sessional doesn't exactly put you on the fast track for buying a house in this town. You know that better than anyone."

Did it all come down to the high price of housing in Victoria? Were people willing to trade their souls for three bedrooms with three baths? Then her brain latched onto another bit of information Zofia had shared. "I didn't realize you were a sessional and not a full professor. That really doesn't pay well, does it? But you always talk like you have this incredible career."

"It's all about branding, that's what Roddy would say," explained Zofia.

Branding—or lying, Helene wanted to rebut.

"And it's not just me I have to think about anymore, that's why I'm willing to take the money he left me," Zofia continued, placing one hand protectively on her belly. Suddenly, her nauseated reaction to french fries at their first meeting and the avoidance of alcohol made sense.

"You're pregnant?" Helene asked. "That's fabulous, congratulations!" Thinking a bit more about the situation, she added, "But it's so tragic that Roddy died before becoming a father."

Zofia all but choked on a mouthful of ginger ale. "Roddy? Roddy isn't the father! Why would you think that?"

Helene stalled as she tried to come up with a polite way to explain that this was what most people would assume. And if Adrianna had guessed Zofia was pregnant, that's probably why she was still hounding her—thinking that Roddy's child could be heir to everything, and one day may go to court to get it all back.

"Roddy was always just a good friend. A sort of mentor. No, I'm getting married to another academic. In the department of environmental literature. He's lovely, a wonderful poet, but he hasn't really made money a priority in his life either."

Helene's thoughts returned to Roddy, a man who had as many secrets as beach houses. But if he wasn't trying to hide Zofia's pregnancy and he planned to announce how AI was used to write the book, then what was the secret both the murderer and Ameer were holding against him?

Seeing that her wine glass was rapidly disappearing, Helene drank some water instead. Then, hoping to gauge Tristan's reaction to everything Zofia had disclosed, from a hidden pregnancy to literary fraud, she turned in his direction. However, before she could speak, he leapt up from the table, phone in hand.

"I've got an alert from my bat-cam!" he declared to the entire room. "I've got to go!" Without bothering to offer

225

any further explanation, Tristan grabbed his coat and headed toward the nearest exit. As the door swung closed behind him, Helene could not fathom how a video of a nocturnal creature might rival Zofia's shocking revelations.

Slightly saddened that Tristan was even more eccentric than she had first perceived, she could only give thanks that his true nature had been revealed before she had gotten in too deep. Trying to ignore the told-you-so voice in her head, Helene returned her attention to the woman across the table.

"So, you decided to go along with Roddy tricking the world into thinking the whole book was written by his great-grandmother. And then he was going to announce the co-author was his AI app?"

Zofia stared down at the table as she spoke. "He said it was the way of the future. And that I would never have to worry about money again."

"But wouldn't it have ruined your reputation as an academic?"

"Yes, but growing up in poverty with my mother, having to use food banks at the end of the month, financial security was hard to turn down. Not to mention, a house. Holidays in Europe, even."

As much as Helene was tempted to condemn Zofia for her decision to go along with the fraud, she knew what it was like to be raised by a mother who couldn't or wouldn't keep the fridge stocked. The deprivations of childhood left a chasm that couldn't be filled by decades of middle-class stability.

"What changed your mind? Why did you decide to reveal the secret tonight? Before Adrianna interrupted your plans, that is."

"I'm not sure exactly," Zofia looked up from the table. "I think it was the closer I got to motherhood. I didn't want to bring a new life into this world with the lie hanging over my head. What kind of example would that be to my daughter?"

Helene couldn't help but grin, "It's a girl? That's wonderful."

"Thank you," Zofia beamed back. "And who knows, I may still be able to find a path through the mess. Maybe write a book about it all. There certainly seems to be no shortage of interest from the media. That's what Arnold thinks I should do—the father of my child."

"Arnold's probably right. As my old journalism professor used to say, a scoundrel will make headlines as easily as a saint. Not that I'm calling you a scoundrel," Helene clarified. "But Roddy might just have been one."

"That's something my mother would probably have agreed with. She never said anything outright, but I always had the sense she didn't want me spending so much time with him. Also, she is totally against me revealing the truth about the book. That's why she wasn't at the book launch. We had a big blowout just before."

Helene could only imagine a mother's concern about her daughter getting too close to the likes of Roddy Beck. The tech guru wouldn't let anyone stand in his path to success, not since creating his first website at university, at a time when he frequented the very same pub Helene and Zofia were currently drinking in.

Taking in the environment once more, wondering how much it had changed in 30 years, Helene looked behind Zofia at the wall decor. Between an antique horseshoe and a poster of a mirthless royal Beefeater in red and gold, a few photos were hanging. On closer inspection, Helene realized they were of the same era that Roddy Beck had kept on his desk. In fact, there was a copy of the exact picture she had spied in his office, of him raising a glass with his university friends—perhaps the pub was trying to trade on the fame of their former clientele.

Next to the familiar photo, there was another that was almost identical, save for the addition of a waitress standing behind the group, serving tray in hand. For an instant, Helene thought she was seeing double, as the woman in the photo looked exactly the same as the woman sitting across the table from her. Then, like a pair of binoculars coming into focus, the double vision allowed her to see clearly for the first time since Helene had beheld Roddy Beck's broken body on the ground outside Craigdarroch Castle.

"Where did that photo come from?"

"What photo?" The academic asked while glancing around the pub, trying to identify what Helene was talking about.

"Never mind. My mistake," said Helene, realizing it was better if Zofia was kept in the dark for now.

Taking a last sip of wine, Helene made distracted apologies and left the pub with only slightly more grace than Tristan had managed a few minutes earlier. Meanwhile, one headline was being broadcast in her mind: it all came down to motherhood and murder. Giving life. And snatching it away.

Chapter 26

Lounging on the daybed in the living room, Helene chewed on toast while her son energetically explained how he had used a low-ranking weapon to defeat a player who had more life-force in his game. As he was gesticulating wildly with his thin arms, she was doing her best not to sprinkle crumbs on the cushions.

"The magma sword can usually melt the crystal mace, but because I used the last of my shadow blocker, I gained strength through surprise!"

When it came to comprehending the rules and strategies of video games, Helene was hopeless and Oscar knew it. However, if she occasionally nodded and grunted in interest, he was happy enough. Having his parent's attention for a few minutes during a day crowded with errands and chores was all he wanted.

"I made it to level three and then the doom trackers got me. But I had two lives left, so I didn't die."

On that first Saturday in November, it took extra effort to focus on her son's virtual universe and not to be distracted by the real-world goal which had dominated her mind since exiting the pub the night before: returning to the Dunsmuir mansion.

Helene now believed she had identified who was responsible for the murder of Roddy Beck and Ameer Anderson, although she was still uncertain how and exactly why the murderer had struck. She hoped that returning to the scene of Roddy Beck's press conference three weeks ago might trigger a helpful memory.

Helene needed extra sustenance that morning as her sleep had been broken and restless. She had repeated dreams about the moments leading up to Roddy Beck falling to his death, waking abruptly just before his body hit the ground.

In the early hours she had given up on slumber altogether, reaching for the copy of *A Grave Journey* that she had bought at the book launch. The poetic prose from the perspective of a woman trying to escape from a domineering husband was captivating and relatable even 100 years later. However, Helene couldn't help but scrutinize the passages as she was reading, trying to guess if they were written by A.J. Beck or AI. In the end, her analysis kept pulling her out of the story, and she wondered, once the truth was revealed, whether this mix of human and artificial authorship would make the book a success or failure.

As sleep continued to evade her, Helene had searched on her phone for further details of the sinking of the *S.S. Clallam*. Apparently, a damaged deadlight—a sort of porthole—allowed water to pour into the ship despite the crew's best efforts to plug it with blankets and wood. The engine room became flooded and the boiler fires went out, leaving the boat adrift in the midst of a powerful storm. The captain then ordered all women and children into three lifeboats, hoping they would be able to reach the coast of Vancouver Island which was just a few miles away. However, these small vessels were utterly ill-equipped to be released in a storm, leading to the deaths of all the terrified occupants. In the following hours, other vessels arrived to offer assistance, but the captain delayed abandoning ship until the *S.S. Clallam* was almost underwater. In the end, 56 people died in the disaster with three dozen surviving. And it now appeared there had been one who had escaped death and the attention of authorities: the author A.J. Beck.

It was just after 7 a.m. when Helene clicked on one last web link. A photo of the Trial Island lighthouse materialized, followed by an article describing how, in the wake of the devastating *S.S. Clallam* shipwreck and the tremendous loss of life, the decision had been made to build the beacon for sailors. Recalling how she had been kayaking in the area a couple of weeks ago, it now felt like she been paddling through a graveyard. As though the nearby Ross Bay Cemetery had expanded its boundaries into the ocean, to include these sunken souls.

A few hours later, after she had finished a second piece of toast and kissed Oscar on the crown of his head, Helene heaved herself off the daybed. She was keen to get on with her investigation and wanted to be at Craigdarroch Castle when it opened at 10:00. Thankfully, the sky was overcast, which might keep people at home—she hoped to have the tourist attraction to herself if she went early enough.

Even though Helene believed the killer was unaware that she was closing in, she still felt it might be prudent to let someone know where she was headed—the last time she had been hot on the trail of a murderer it had landed her in very cold water. Not having yet heard from Detective Bloom since several officers had come to inspect her damaged kayak, she assumed he had dismissed her concerns. She supposed it was possible that the vessel's hull could have cracked on some rocks and a piece of tape had inadvertently gotten stuck to the bottom. Perhaps investigating the death of Roddy Beck was making her overly suspicious. Either way, she didn't want to contact the police officer again until she had more concrete evidence.

She decided instead to send a short text to both Alex and Detective Kalinowski, wishing them well on their journey home from Europe and casually mentioning she was planning to visit the castle.

Closing the front door behind her, Helene's goodbyes went unanswered; Oscar was engrossed in his video game while his sister was enjoying the gluttonous sleep of a teenager. To prevent them from worrying, she left a note on the kitchen table telling her children she may not be back until late. Struggling with exhaustion after her wakeful night, she smothered a yawn as she started the car and backed out of the driveway.

Helene was pleased to discover that her effort to be one of the first visitors to the castle on the gloomy weekend morning had paid off. After purchasing her ticket from a bespectacled docent and crossing over the driveway to the main entrance, she entered the ostentatious Dunsmuir mansion to be greeted by a hushed silence. Oddly, the air seemed to possess an echo of whispers, like when a schoolmarm enters a classroom and the children fall quiet lest their secrets be overheard. Taking in the ornate grandeur of the previous century once more, Helene shook off a sense of trepidation, blaming it on the morbid events connected with the building, both historic and very recent.

The wooden railing was cool to the touch as she climbed up the broad stairway. Wearing jeans and a pale grey pullover, she could only imagine what it would have been like to ascend the steps in a stiff corset and floor-length gown. Helene thought the landings between the four floors would have provided women with a place to catch their breath, lungs heaving against the strictures of their elegant clothing. By the time she had reached the top level, Helene was inhaling the heirloom-scented air deeply, like a wealthy 19th century woman for whom exercise was considered immodest.

Surveying a space that had once been a Victorian ballroom, a university library and a place of respite for wounded soldiers, Helene had a strong sense that she was not alone. Perhaps too much history and too many conversations had reverberated against these walls for the rooms ever to be truly empty again. Voices and stories clung to the worn surfaces like dust that could never be entirely banished. Helene was uncertain whether this intangible company was a comfort or not.

The purpose of her visit recalled, Helene moved into the eastern section of the fourth floor, retaking her general position at the press conference from three weeks ago. The chairs were no longer set up, so she simply stood in an approximate spot and tried to remember the placement of everyone else in attendance.

Roddy Beck and Zofia Bosko were at the microphone.

Mrs. Fernandez and Ameer lingered near the staircase to the upper landing.

Most of the journalists had kept to the chairs, although some photographers bordered the room for a better shot.

Growing frustrated with a memory tickling the corner of her mind like a shy student who refused to come forward, Helene closed her eyes to envision the details.

Three mannequins in Victorian dresses remained frozen in time, debutantes waiting an eternity for their turn on the floor.

A black grand piano was a soundless but substantial reminder that the original purpose of the room was music and dancing.

And then, in the same way the mannequins and the piano were taken for granted, Helene suddenly recollected a group of staff members gathered at the back of the room. Easily overlooked in their anonymous uniforms, some were even wearing masks as a COVID precaution. Helene was now certain that one face, with only glinting and purposeful eyes revealed, was familiar. The hair was greyer and the forehead had been creased by time, but the countenance was a match to the woman she had spotted in the photo in the pub of Roddy Beck and Harold Webb from their university days.

Standing in the middle of the empty space, Helene was momentarily pleased she had managed to confirm, through her own memories if not hard evidence, that Zofia's mother had been at the press conference in the guise of a cleaner. This exercise had further cemented her theory that the elder Bosko was responsible for the murders.

And then, as if her recollections had suddenly come to life, Ludmilla Bosko materialized at the top of the stairs, her maskless face now twisted with determined hate.

Out of shock and an instinct to protect herself, Helene took one step backwards, deeper into the ballroom. However, the distance she had retreated was easily overcome by the length of the antique billiard cue Ludmilla heftily swung in her direction.

A stunning crack followed by a riot of pain caused Helene to crumple onto the floor, gravity and the blow to her head offering irrefutable arguments against remaining upright. Before giving way to the darkness entirely, Helene was momentarily entranced at the sight of the three debutante gowns on mannequins mercilessly spinning in space, their chance to waltz arriving after a century of waiting.

Late January, 1904

My dreams ebbed and flowed like tides. Sometimes I was submerged in suffocating visions of women and children gasping for their last breath before a wave unremorsefully claimed them. At other moments, I had flashes of being tossed onto a pebbled beach as if no more than a lump of flotsam. The ocean's numbing cold seemed to have followed me onto land, only relenting when I was seized by a raging fever. In my most delirious state, I recall begging my father to damp down the fire from which I could make no escape.

While existing in a state somewhere between sleep and wakeful delirium, I could not comprehend the words which gently buzzed around me like bees, possessing only a honeyed kindness in their tone. At first, I thought the women must be speaking Spanish or French, of which I knew a smattering of words, but I came to realize the syllables and cadence were entirely unfamiliar. Coming more fully to my senses, it dawned on me that these women, with long plaited hair and woven tunics, were not European in ancestry at all. They were the occupants on this land from the time before white people arrived in boats. And now they had rescued me from that same ocean which had given passage to the invader.

Once I was able to sit up in the nest of wool blankets and take some food by my own hand, my most pressing concern was that the authorities would be alerted to my presence. I was in no fit state to explain my arrival on these shores and feared I would be hastily returned to my husband like an errant mule. However, I soon perceived these sympathetic people, with their own language and ways of living, wanted the attention of officials no more than I did.

We carried on for what seemed like weeks in a ritual of communication by hand gestures and perplexed smiles, as I recovered from the nautical catastrophe.

Although I did in earnest attempt to not overly ruminate upon the dark night of the doomed journey, for fear it would bring on the symptoms of melancholia, the discovery of discarded newspapers reawakened the horrors. The first article I surveyed was from the January 12th edition of The Daily Colonist newspaper.

When the fleet of small tugs, launches, and search parties were engaged in the search, which resulted in the two lifeboats and eight bodies of victims of the wreck being recovered, No. 1 lifeboat of the starboard side was found drifting off Beacon Hill by the tug Albion, which had been dispatched by J.H. Greer, and an examination of this boat has since shown that it did not capsize but filled as a result of the plug hole being left open. The cap, lying in the little dust-marked place which shows that it must have lain there for some time, was ten inches or more from the open hole. In this boat was the body of Miss Harris, of Spokane. Seated in the boat, with a lifebelt around her, the dead woman's hands clutched the sides firmly and her clenched teeth are evident of the grim despair that filled her. She had clenched her teeth so firmly that her lower lip had been pierced.

Reading over the passage, I concluded that the incompetence of men was as boundless as the ocean. Forcing terrified women and children into lifeboats that were nothing short of death traps. Despite my growing despair, I could not resist reading a subsequent article which made evident the captain's continued poor judgment.

At the coroner's inquest yesterday some remarkable details regarding the disaster were brought to light. Edward Lannen of Seattle, a survivor, swore that the steamer Clallam did not display any distress signals, nor was any attempt made on the part of those on board to attract the attention of a steamer which passéd the foundering steamer about 4 o'clock on Friday, an hour after the women and children had been drowned. Capt. Roberts would not accede to the request of a number of passengers to put them on the tug Holyoke after the sinking steamer was picked up. During the terrible night the only light on the vessel was a lantern hung about halfway up the foremast. The only other lights onboard were our lanterns used by the bailers. In view of these facts and the fact that it is shown that Capt. Roberts could have had the tug tow the Clallam around Cattle point into the lee of San Juan and in the comparatively calm waters in forty-five minutes at the most instead of allowing the tug to proceed on into the heavy seas on a three hours' tow to Port Townsend, the criticism of Capt. Roberts grows apace.

As if I had been returned bodily to the suffocating ocean, I could scarcely draw breath as I read further. A few paragraphs following, the article contained the most damning details of all.

It is certain that the captain did not want to give up the ship. While the Alaska Steamship Company owns many boats, the Clallam was the only one built by them out of the money they had earned in the steamship business. The staunch little craft was the pet and pride of the entire fleet. Capt. Roberts himself is a large stockholder in the concern and was interested in more ways than one in the vessel.

After learning how self-interest must have guided the captain's decisions on that fateful night, I was overcome with waves of nausea as though I were on the decks of that wretched ship once more. Grabbing the entire stack of newspapers, I carried them to the fire and watched them fiercely burned to ash.

The women who cared for me could sense my renewed agitation even as I took to my bed. An elder in the group placed her seat in close proximity and took up her knitting. Over the hours, the steady clicking of the needles evoked memories of my grandmother, their hypnotic rhythm lulling me into sleep. And perhaps because I had endured enough torment in the daylight hours, for that night at least, I slept without disturbance.

Over the passing weeks, the only real unease that ever arose between my hosts and myself was entirely of my own making. I had come to realize that maintaining my copious blonde tresses was an indulgence I could no longer afford. If I was to make my way in the world as a man, I must not put myself at risk of discovery whenever a strong wind tugged at my cap like a schoolyard bully. Indicating to one of the women with whom I had become comfortable that I wished to prune my locks, her initial reaction was one of horror. It took several days of repeating a pantomime of cutting my hair before the women gathered near my bedside for what appeared to be a heated discussion about my request. Eventually the woman I had come to think of as a friend, despite the barriers of background and language, came forward with a knife to perform the task. She plaited my hair in a single long braid before removing it with a skillful and painless cut. Wordlessly she took away the slim twist of hair, as if caring for a corpse which required proper and respectful disposal.

Perhaps if my tresses had been dark in colour, I could have contemplated remaining in this new community which was free from stultifying dictates of society. But I *instinctively knew that my fair complexion and flaxen hair, even when shorn, would attract unwanted and even injurious interest. It would be an act of utter selfishness to put my generous hosts in the way of danger.*

When I was well enough to walk without trembling, the women brought me a second-hand blazer and trousers. They now seemed to intuitively understand my need for male costume. Every day I would take walks to regain my strength, each time a little farther, until I knew I was well enough to say farewell to those who had brought me back to life.

As I was making my final preparations to take my leave, the woman who had come to be my friend came forward, passing an object from her clutched hands to my own. Opening my palm to investigate the gift, I saw that it was the rubber ball which had belonged to the young boy who had perished on the S.S. Clallam. I have no recollection of how the toy of a dead child ended up in my possession, but I perceived it as a talisman which had bestowed protection upon me.

In late January, under a clear but cold sky, I bid the women farewell, expressing gratitude in the smatterings of the language I had come to master. It was with much regret that I returned to the world of carriages and corsets, if in a rougher island setting.

Yet before I did make my first new acquaintance, I resolved to adopt a moniker. I shortened my first and middle name, Alberta-Josephine, to the initials A.J., so my sex would remain obscured. My invented last name, Beck, would honour the governess, Miss Beck, a woman on the cusp of embracing a great island adventure, who was instead murdered at sea by the actions and ignorance of men. I would never abandon the memory of her bravely comforting a child, as though she were his mother, before they both met an appalling and unnecessary death.

In becoming A.J. Beck, I was shedding my former name like a Lazarus rising from a watery grave. For if, in my new life, I was to be a writer of stories, the first one I would craft would be my own.

Chapter 27

Helene was awakened by a burning, urgent thirst. A searing dryness in her throat. Like she had been consuming sand for days. Inhaling bowls of beach.

Then the act of swallowing made her aware of the pressure across her mouth: a cloth running between her lips and teeth which was secured at the back of her neck. To prevent her from talking or calling for help, presumably.

Her limbs were equally unhelpful, her hands tied in front and her legs secured to a pipe or maybe a beam. It was impossible to tell because it was impossible to see. Helene had awoken to a world abandoned by light, and the darkness was hostile. Almost hungry. The sensation of having arms, but the visible proof had been consumed by blackness—like phantom limbs lost to war.

Ensconced in a false night, Helene could sense that the walls were close; perhaps it was the way sound carried when she tried to shift her body, the dull echo of a cloistered space. A very large closet or a tiny room. And it smelled even more powerfully of antiquity than the rest of the castle: the scent of dust seasoned over time and moldering paper. Helene thought she might be in a place used to store items not fit to put on display for visitors. Like chipped chamber pots or dented journalists.

Her efforts to loosen her wrist bindings brought no relief, so Helene rested for a moment and thought about why Ludmilla Bosko would have left her tied up in the cramped space. The woman may have been worried about being spotted dragging a body from the fourth floor since there was no elevator in the building and the mansion would have gotten busy very quickly that morning. Was she waiting until the castle closed to dispose of Helene? Or was she hoping

Helene would simply die of thirst and become another museum relic? Crafting a modern trilogy of murder in the Dunsmuir mansion, like a prolific author.

The thought of her untimely death being included in an updated castle brochure to the delight of ghoulish visitors made Helene even more determined to escape her bonds. Clumsily laying herself on the ground, legs still fastened to the upright structure, Helene stretched herself out to make a tactile survey of everything she could reach in the room. Carefully feeling her way across the space in an arc, she resembled the compasses children used to draw perfect circles for their lessons in geometry.

Helene's grasping search immediately bore fruit when she struck a wooden box with her bound hands. Dragging the container closer so she could sit upright again, she set about trying to identify the objects inside, using the limited freedom of her fingers. The process brought back memories of a game played at a work retreat, when colleagues were blindfolded and instructed to determine what they were holding by touch. The challenge was supposed to heighten the senses beyond sight. However, as she desperately scrabbled through the box for a useful item, growing dizzy from the scent of mildew and disturbed dust while keenly listening for the sound of her attacker returning, Helene's senses could not have been more keyed up.

The first article she retrieved from the box had a smooth disk at the centre and a pointy bottom. Something that would spin perhaps. Like a wooden toy. Possessing no sharp edges with which to cut ropes, Helene set it aside. She next pulled out a bottle that was smooth and felt as though it could be made of glass. Her raging thirst had not abated and the urge to check for water was instinctive. But Helene recalled that the Victorians were known for their toxic tinctures that included everything from strychnine to cocaine. It might even be a small bottle of Paris green paint famously containing arsenic.

After briefly considering smashing the glass to create a cutting edge, but deciding she would probably end up slicing her hands or getting blood poisoning, Helene tucked the bottle safely back into the corner of the box. As she searched by touch once more, desperate to discover a more useful object, Helene's hands got caught in a tangle of chains. Pulling the whole rattling mess out, she laid it on the floor to better determine its purpose. Using the tips of her fingers, she ascertained that the contraption had a central metal disk from which the thin chains radiated like sunbeams. At the end of each tether, an item was attached, all varied in shape and texture. Helene enjoyed a small if empty victory when she quickly identified the first article as a watch. She accidentally pressed the button to release the device's circular cover, bringing to mind the tardy rabbit in *Alice in Wonderland.* For a moment, Helene considered that her circumstances were not entirely unlike the perilous adventures of the intrepid girl in the surreal children's story.

The next two items were easily recognizable as a hefty old-fashioned key and a small case that popped open to disgorge a thimble—the sewing implement finally triggering the memory of the encounter with a museum docent from three Saturdays ago. Cleo had asked about a curious object on a dresser that appeared to be a combination of a toolbox and a bracelet. The staff member had called the contraption a "chatelaine" and explained that it held all the devices a Victorian woman might need. And then the first flicker of hope lit up the suffocating darkness of Helene's impromptu prison: the docent had mentioned that in addition to perfumes and sewing tools, the chatelaine sometimes included a knife.

Taking care not to scatter the device's tentacles in her excitement, Helene continued to trace the paths of the remaining chains with her fingers. The next item she groped had pages like a miniature notebook, likely used for writing down the names of suitors. After that was a crucifix which Helene thought was unhelpfully morbid. Her frustration escalating, Helene clasped the next object in desperation, her fingertips getting stuck in two circular rings. Exhaling in relief through her moist gag, Helene knew that she had failed to find a knife, but she had discovered a pair of scissors.

Rewarding herself with a brief rest in the gloom, Helene considered that the chatelaine was a sort of smart phone for the Victorian woman. Instead of having a camera, music streaming and virtual maps, it held miniature tools to make 19th century life easier. And in a convoluted way, if these antiquated apps helped her escape the clutches of Roddy Beck's killer, then it was somehow a tribute to the inventors of handy tech through the ages. She only hoped the late owner of this particular chatelaine liked to keep her apps well sharpened.

A scuttling sound in the walls reminded Helene that, since there was no way to know how long she had been knocked out, it could be near to closing time and Ludmilla's possible return. She also wasn't eager to encounter any resident rodents of Craigdarroch Castle, as she had had her fill of Victorian Gothic ambience for one lifetime.

Unable to use the scissors in the traditional manner due to her constrained hands, Helene pushed the blades open to create a continuous angled cutting surface. She then carefully pushed the pointy end of the instrument between her skin and the bonds. Despite repeatedly pricking herself, Helene's determination paid off and the straps soon fell away.

Once her hands were free, Helene stretched and rubbed them to get the circulation going. Her fingers felt slightly numb as she ripped away the gag from her mouth but she was desperate to take a deep breath of the admittedly musty air.

With the prospect of escape becoming more tangible, Helene then tugged at the ropes which bound her legs to a fixed structure. The restraint was more substantial than the cloth used on her hands, and she had to redouble her efforts to make any progress. At one point her fingers became slippery with a warm liquid, and she realized the scissors must have sliced her skin. Wiping the blood on her jeans, she was momentarily grateful that she couldn't see the state of her clothes.

A few minutes later, her limbs and jaw sore but unfettered, Helene still faced one substantial challenge: the absolute darkness gave no hint as to where a door or exit might be. Overwhelmed by exhaustion, thirst, hunger and a throbbing head, Helene drew her legs up into her chest and wrapped her arms around them.

In an effort to replenish her energy, Helene tried to picture her children's faces. However, what instead came to mind was a vision of their backyard lilac tree. Four years ago, the sapling had been a Mother's Day gift from Oscar and Cleo which Alex had helped to purchase and transport. On many previous occasions, Helene had fondly described the lilac trees that had grown in the front yard of her childhood home in Edmonton. The lavender and white spring blossoms were one of the few delights she could share with her own mother, a pleasure even mental illness could not blemish. And the scent was so sweet and heady, it was best enjoyed with closed eyes, allowing the one sense to overwhelm the soul. It was a fragrance so unlike the bouquet of antique detritus that threatened to choke her now.

At the thought of her affectionate children and their lilac tree gift, Helene's determination to escape was renewed, which is when she heard a thumping to her right. Like someone or something hitting a wall. A tennis player practicing alone. Or a child who lacked a friend with whom to play catch.

Listening for several seconds longer, to correctly ascertain the precise direction the noise was coming from, Helene scrambled across the floor, pushing the wooden box of objects out of her way. Once she reached the wall, she put her ear up against it and was rewarded by a reverberating thwack from the other side. Knowing she didn't have the time to consider who or what was guiding her, Helene desperately searched the surface for some kind of doorknob or handle. She soon discovered a square outline of a hatch, slightly larger than a coal chute, but with no obvious way to gain purchase. Blood once more making her fingers sticky, she managed to claw a gap between the metal cover and the wooden wall, the sound of the bouncing ball continuing all the while as a sort of maddening encouragement.

Marshalling her strength, Helene desperately tugged on the edge of the hatch and although the gap wasn't getting any bigger, she could faintly feel that some kind of mechanism was shifting. Several more minutes of strenuous effort passed, and Helene was again on the verge of despair, when the ball struck the wall with a final great thud and the rectangular metal door swung open in her hands. The release of the handle caused Helene to fall back into the suffocating space, but once she had recovered from the shock, she quickly clambered forwards, squeezing through the small opening in the wall, and falling into the ballroom.

Lying motionless on the floor, dazed and overcome with gratitude, an entire minute must have passed before Helene thought to glance around the room to see who had been tossing the ball against the wall. The space though was empty, save the three gowned mannequins who appeared to be judging her disheveled condition. However, when Helene looked down to examine the injury to her hands, she saw that she was in fact clutching an antique rubber ball. She didn't recall grabbing it as she came through the hatch, but there was no other explanation.

Using considerable effort, Helene pulled herself into a sitting position to better examine the prison from which she had made her escape. It appeared to be a secret storage room, built behind the east wall of the ballroom. She was surprised that Ludmilla Bosko had known the room existed.

Not wanting to get any closer to the gloomy chamber, she did see that the hatch handle lay in pieces on the floor, Helene's jerking having broken off the aged lock.

"Well, at least I don't have to bother dragging you out of there."

Helene turned around quickly to discover that she now had company. She had not heard Ludmilla's approaching footsteps, but that could have been due to the pounding of her throbbing head. Her eyes, however, had adapted to the light in the room after the pitch black of her prison and could clearly discern the outline of the gun Ludmilla was pointing in her direction. Helene had to restrain a nervous laugh at the fact that her arduous escape had been in vain.

Chapter 28

"I should have taken down that damn photo years ago, only I hated going into that pub," Ludmilla explained. "Reminded me of having to put up with all those lewd comments in hopes of getting a tip. But when Zofia said you were asking about the photographs last night, I knew you had guessed—that I had killed Roddy. I suppose it was only a matter of time before you made the connection. Journalists can't help but cause trouble."

Even though her life was in immediate danger, Helene still bristled at this criticism of the media. Not to mention, she thought Ludmilla had fled Poland to enjoy the freedoms of a democratic country, including an independent press. However, with a gun aimed at her chest, Helene realized it was probably not the right time to point out the woman's hypocrisy.

"I realized you and Roddy knew each other when you were young. That's true. But I still don't know exactly why you had to kill him." As Helene made the accusation of murder, Ludmilla did not flinch.

"There were so many reasons he needed to die. It's hard to choose just one. His arrogance? His greed?"

Wishing to postpone Ludmilla's plans for her own untimely death, Helene led the conversation in a different direction. "But you also didn't want him to reveal that the book was partly written by AI, did you?"

Ludmilla's voice rose an octave. "It would have ruined Zofia's career! Lost her the university position! She's so close to becoming a tenured professor. All that work, for nothing!"

"And your sacrifices too. Coming to a new country. Starting over. Having to work as a waitress in a pub. Serving drinks to the likes of Roddy Beck and his friends. Arrogant young men who had the world handed to them."

"But you have to understand. He was so charming when we first met. Interested in my life and struggles. I had never met anyone like that in Poland. No one had ever paid attention to me in that way. Even buying me kwiaty, flowers."

"What happened?"

"What always happens in a story like mine, I got pregnant. And I was terrified. A new country? No family? I hoped Roddy would do the right thing, but I couldn't have been more wrong. When I eventually worked up the courage to tell him, it was like he became a different person. He accused me of sleeping with his friends. Claiming he wasn't the father. It was disgusting." A look of shame passed over Ludmilla's face, like she was reliving the humiliation of decades ago. "So I raised her on my own. I quit waitressing and became a house cleaner. No one bothered me with flowers then."

"Zofia was his daughter." Helene was confirming what she had guessed the night before.

"She was not his daughter in any real way," Ludmilla scornfully stated. "He did not help raise her or feed her or hold her when she cried."

"But how did he track her down so many years later? Was it just coincidence?"

"Is there such a thing as coincidence? I don't know. She'd always loved the stories of A.J. Beck, maybe because I'm an immigrant and she really wanted to understand this island. And then last year, out of the blue he contacted her, asking for help with the book he found."

"When did you decide to tell him the truth about Zofia?"

"After she told me about the AI and I knew it would ruin her career. But when I tried to explain to Roddy who I was, he was just the same as before—calling me a liar, saying I wanted to blackmail him. Then I told him stories of our time together, all those years ago, when he was a student and I was a pretty waitress. In the end, he had to believe me. Then he was the one trying to offer me cash to not tell Zofia. Afraid she would be angry with him. But I didn't want money, what I wanted was for the world to keep believing his great-grandmother had written the whole book."

"Because Zofia had authenticated it."

"And then he promised to 'set her up in life.' As though the years I did all those dreary jobs to put her through school were worth nothing!" Having grown quite agitated, Ludmilla took several slow breaths and continued her story in a more matter-of-fact tone.

"So I threatened him, said I would tell Zofia he had abandoned her. Abandoned us. Leaving me to raise her—a single mother in a one-room apartment while he bought houses in L.A. and London." An icy look of satisfaction settled on the woman's face. "And that scared him. I mean, really made him afraid. Of ugly, old me. That I had something to hold over such a rich and powerful man. Because he liked Zofia a lot. And once he knew she was his daughter, he didn't want to lose her."

The fact that this woman, without wealth or status, had gotten a hold over Roddy Beck reminded Helene of her son's video game, when a weaker player overpowered a stronger one by using a weapon in an unexpected way.

"But why did you end up killing him like that, pushing him out the castle window?"

"It's called 'defenestration,' a method favoured by Communists to eliminate those who become a problem, like Roddy Beck. You see, I had given him a note to meet me on the landing, and I still thought I could stop him from revealing the secret about the book. But there I was, looking at this rich man, who had everything in life, and I realized he would end up stealing Zofia. Like he stole my youth. And my freedom. My chance to build a good life after coming to

251

Canada so full of hope. In the end, it wouldn't matter if she found out he had abandoned us, he would use his charm and his money and she would eventually forgive him. Powerful men like that, they get away with everything. Even in the book, this story about the ship that sank. I read it, and it's the same. All those women and children dying so horribly at sea. And the captain, the man who was responsible, he just went on with his life. This never changes. In Poland. In Canada. 100 years ago. Today. The men, they always win."

Although what Ludmilla was saying sparked uncomfortable thoughts about how her own father had abandoned his children, Helene knew this was hardly the time to applaud the woman's analysis of men's impunity. Instead, perceiving that Ludmilla was in a confessional mood, Helene took her chance to learn the whole story. "Did Ameer guess that Roddy was Zofia's father? Did he threaten to tell her unless you urged her to give back control over the company? Is that why he had to die?"

"Even though Roddy abandoned her, Zofia was his daughter and the company and the money should be hers. Not some cloying apparatchik who suddenly got greedy."

"But then she gave the company back and she also plans to tell the world about the book being co-authored by AI."

"I know!" Ludmilla burst into hysterical laughter. "Children! You do everything for them. And they throw it all back in your face. But you can't help it when you're a mother. You will do anything. That's why you must also die. Zofia must never know I murdered her father. She wouldn't forgive me."

Recognizing that her chances of escaping the deeply disturbed woman were fading like the sun outside the ballroom window, Helene fixed her mind to a singular purpose. Squeezing the antique rubber ball still clasped in her right hand, she pulled back her arm and propelled the child's toy at the gun Ludmilla was holding.

The weapon went off, but in a wild direction, hitting one of the elegant mannequins square in the chest, causing it to tumble to the floor. While Ludmilla was momentarily distracted by the commotion, Helene dove at the woman and knocked the gun from her hand. The weapon clattered to the floor and flew under the belly of the grand piano.

Scrambling back on their feet, the two women stood face-to-face in a ballroom which had borne witness to so much history, Helene had a fleeting thought of the tragic irony that they must fight each other rather than the men who had oppressed their sex for centuries.

When the older woman lunged in her direction, Helene tried to move out of the way, but strong hands managed to seize her by the throat. In an attempt to free herself, she struggled backwards, eventually ending up with her spine pressed against the stairway railing causing Helene to briefly consider why she had possessed a fear of water for so many years when heights were obviously the greater threat.

Unable to resist any longer, Helene's body began to tumble over the banister, but, at the last moment, she managed to grab hold of a wooden spindle. Hanging over a four-story void, she resisted looking down, refusing to accept she was about to become Ludmilla's third victim.

Thankfully, she did not have to discover the limits of her own adrenaline—a chorus of swearing echoing against the ballroom walls let her know help had arrived. Her rescuers had come up the servant's stairway at the back of the ballroom to avoid detection. After Ludmilla was yanked backwards in a rage, Detective Kalinowski and Detective Bloom materialized above the railing, each grabbing hold of one of Helene's arms, pulling her to safety.

Her own body finally being given permission to collapse, Helene's vision was briefly eclipsed by darkness. When she opened her eyes, it was to the sight of Alex staring down at her from above.

"I can't leave town for a few weeks without you getting into trouble. I guess there'll be no more honeymoons in Berlin for us."

"Berlin? Never again," vowed Detective Kalinowski, now back on her feet. "Not if I have something to say about it." After affectionately kissing her bride on the lips, she added, "The next trip is to Bermuda."

In the corner of the ballroom, Helene spied Ludmilla slumped against the wall, all the fight had gone out of her. There were no promises of travel in the murderer's future except to an all-inclusive with bars across the windows and doors.

Chapter 29

A cool breeze on a Sunday morning in November was hardly an overwhelming enticement to drink coffee in the backyard, but Helene had grown weary of the view from her bed and was not yet ready for the clang of cups and competing conversations symptomatic of a coffee shop. Overhead, moody clouds threatened but did not deliver rain, so lace-up boots and a thick blanket kept her warm enough. Sitting opposite her on a faded plastic lawn chair, Tristan appeared decidedly chilly in a stylish but thin overcoat and jeans. She resisted the urge to offer him a fleece blanket, not having finished punishing him for abandoning her at the pub.

"How is your head?" Tristan inquired for the third time since he had arrived.

"Still hurts. And the world tilts if I get up too quickly."

"But the doctors think you only have a minor concussion?"

"It's so hard to know," said Helene, not about to let him off that easily. "Head injuries can be tricky."

"I guess it's a good thing you were hit with a billiard cue and not a fire poker."

"I'm not sure the museum staff would agree. The pole was an antique and now it's kindling. At least the cricket bat used to kill Ameer survived."

Shifting his body slightly, attempting and failing to find a more comfortable position in the stiff backyard furniture, Tristan then asked, "But how did Zofia's mother …?"

"Ludmilla."

"… Ludmilla, how did she know you would be at the castle?"

"I suppose after she discovered I was asking about the photographs in the pub, she must have waited outside my house all night and followed me in the morning. I think it was pretty spontaneous. Otherwise she wouldn't have had to lock me up all day in the castle like a character in a Brontë novel."

"How did she even know about that closet in the back of the ballroom?"

"She had been a cleaner at the castle for years. And that's why she could get easy access to the place. She knew about the space behind the ballroom and the old laundry chute where Ameer died. It had been boarded up for decades before she prised it open."

"But when she came to Roddy's press conference, wasn't she worried someone would recognize her?"

"Ludmilla knew all too well that no one looks at the hired help. Not when someone like Roddy Beck is in the room. And she wore a COVID mask just in case Zofia looked her way."

"Clever woman. She almost got away with killing you too. Good thing your friends showed up when they did."

"Yes, it's only too bad it took them so long to see my text message. But Alex and Karolina had their phones switched to airplane mode for the flight home from Europe. They tried to reach Detective Bloom while disembarking, to see if he could get there immediately, but it was Saturday, and he was off duty. Fishing, obviously. Although strange time of year for it."

"Halibut."

"Halibut?"

"It's the season for halibut."

"Right. Well, he didn't catch any fish yesterday, but he was pleased to discover an oil can in Ludmilla's car after they took her away. I suspect it will match what they found on the window hinges of the landing Roddy fell from. It could prove his killing was premeditated despite Ludmilla's claims it was unplanned. Bloom also found a roll of tape that looked like the piece clinging to my kayak."

"Kayak? How does your kayak come into all this?"

Not wanting to alarm Tristan without cause, Helene had previously avoided telling him about the cut in the bottom of her boat, the one which could have led to her drowning in the ocean. So she ignored his question and focused on delivering another wave of guilt. "Unfortunate, wasn't it, that I didn't have someone to come along with me to the castle?"

"You didn't ask or let me know what you were doing!" protested Tristan while slapping his hands together to generate warmth.

"That is hardly the point. And after you ran out of the pub like some madman yelling about bats, what was I supposed to think?"

"Yes, sorry about that. You were busy talking with Zofia and I was eager to catch the mayor in the act."

"The mayor?" Curiosity made Helene forget her sore head. "I thought it was a bat-cam."

"It is a camera for bats. *My* camera for bats. I usually have it set up to watch them on the eaves of a nearby church. Fascinating creatures. Beautiful and much maligned." Starting to wax prosaic about the fanged mammal, an impatient look from Helene got Tristan back on track. "I decided to set the camera up in the City Hall office. It's very small and clipped onto a shelf. And then I announced there would be an inventory of all the property records. I knew it was only a matter of time before I caught someone trying to return the file unnoticed after hours. The one with the record of Mrs. Fernandez's house."

"And you caught the mayor?"

"Video doesn't lie."

Helene didn't want to ruin Tristan's triumph by pointing out that due to advances in AI, lying was exactly what videos did. Instead, she asked, "How did she react, when you confronted her?"

"At first she tried to deny everything, saying she had found the file lying around the office. But when I threatened to put the video on YouTube, she admitted to altering the records, claiming it was for a good cause. She knew that if the Fernandez house was demolished, more condos could be built. She seemed pretty sincere, at least to me."

"But what did she do to make sure the home got torn down?"

"She made a fake house inspector's report, stating the place was riddled with asbestos, old wiring and lead pipes. Then, after Mrs. Fernandez started making accusations of wrongdoing, she removed the file."

Helene toyed with a leaf that had fallen onto her lap while considering what Tristan had told her. "That would have devastated Mr. Fernandez. He spent his whole life making improvements to his home while maintaining its original design. At least he never saw that report," Helene mused before her thoughts became pragmatic. "What are you going to do with the mayor? Force her to resign? Expose her fraud?"

It was Tristan's turn to be contemplative. "I'm not sure. If I force her to resign, then someone like Councillor Davies will end up as mayor. And he would never get any housing built. He's too busy pandering to the folks who want to keep their neighbourhoods the same. If you think about it, Strauss committed fraud for a good cause."

Helene was impressed by Tristan's mutable morality. Strictly speaking, the mayor should lose her job. But perhaps he was right, that it would only slow down much needed housing.

"For now, I've asked her to name the whole housing project after him."

"After whom?" asked Helene, wondering if confusion from her head injury was kicking in.

"Carlito. Carlito Fernandez. Lucia's father. She's agreed to call the place Carlito Court. I thought that would be a good way to honour him."

"Wow," responded Helene. "That is a really good idea."

"Don't sound so surprised," retorted Tristan.

"Not surprised. More pleased. But wait, if it was Mayor Strauss and not Councillor Davies, then the fake signature on the paper to release the file, it wasn't Guy Lafleur?"

"No, it was Gordon Lightfoot. The mayor is a huge folk music fan. It makes sense. And the two names look quite similar when scrawled across a page.

Helene recalled seeing the concert posters from the 1970s hanging on the walls of the mayor's office on her recent visit. "Well, at least she stayed true to something. If only Canadian culture. But speaking of staying true, as a journalist, I really should expose what the mayor has done."

"And if that does more harm than good?"

"What's the alternative? You holding this secret over her? Like a sort of blackmail—to make her do what you think is right?" Having lately borne witness to the violence that could erupt from the fear of secrets being revealed, she was a bit alarmed at this proposition.

Tristan gave her a roguish grin. "I think it's an option worth considering. It might be for the greater good."

Helene wondered if this was the beginning of a benevolent dictatorship, with Tristan having the real decision-making power behind the mayor's office. Sadly, history was clear that despite any good intentions, dictatorships never stayed benevolent for very long.

As the wind picked up, Helene pulled the blanket around her a little more tightly. Her head was starting to ache in earnest, partly from Saturday's encounter with a very hard billiard cue but also in trying to follow Tristan's questionable ethics.

"I think you need to ask his daughter," said Helene. "Lucia Fernandez?"

"Yes," she confirmed. "First of all, the family needs to know the truth. That they were tricked into having their home destroyed. So they don't have that hanging over them for years to come. Then, they should be the ones to decide what happens to the mayor. You can lay out both sides for them; how keeping Strauss in office might lead to people getting much needed homes. But it's not up to you to dispense justice. You weren't the one who was wronged."

Tristan looked like he was going to protest, but Helene simply stared him down, making it evident that she would brook no argument.

"I guess that's fair," he said in a resigned tone. "I suppose justice is more important than anything else."

Although pleased that Tristan was going along with her plan, Helene wasn't sure justice was that simple. Ludmilla had killed Roddy because she thought that, after years of ignoring Zofia's existence, he had no right to her affections—especially if he planned to destroy her academic career by revealing the use of AI in *A Grave Journey*. But the murder of Ameer was not justice, it was done to protect a secret. An entirely indefensible action.

Tristan's proposal to name the housing project after Carlito Fernandez caused her to consider whether there was any kind of plaque or memorial to the victims of the *S.S. Clallam*. All those women and children being sent to a watery grave by the arrogance of men and then having their stories erased by the sexism of history. At the time of the tragedy, she knew their families had been denied any form of justice. The captain never faced charges and another subordinate crew member was offered up as a scapegoat for not checking the seal on the deadlight.

"Mom, have you seen my ..." Like an actor bursting onto the stage to provide some light relief at an intense point in a drama, Oscar had thrown open the porch door.

However, he was shocked into silence to discover his mother was not alone.

"Hello!" Tristan greeted Oscar loudly and cheerfully, in the way adults without their own children are known to do, like they are meeting someone from a different planet and want to make clear their intentions are friendly.

"Hi," Oscar responded suspiciously, after all, his mother rarely invited anyone to the house besides Alex.

While enjoying Tristan and Oscar sizing each other up, Helene finally broke the tension by asking, "What do you want sweetheart? Are you hungry?"

Looking away from the backyard intruder, Oscar then made a solicitous appeal. "I was wondering if, you know, it would be OK, because it's been almost a week since …"

"How much is it?" Helene guessed her son was hoping to buy a new weapons system or character for his game.

"11.99 plus tax."

"Canadian?"

"American."

"OK," she replied, the cost of a video game upgrade seemingly inconsequential after coming close to dying. However, as Oscar stepped back into the house, pulling the porch door inward, Helene caught the edge with her hand to prevent it from closing.

"I have something for you," she said to her son. "I found it at the castle."

Reaching under her blanket and into her bathrobe pocket, Helene was mystified to find it empty. She was certain she had brought the antique rubber ball into the backyard, having kept it close since her battle with Ludmilla.

Oscar looked at her in a matter-of-fact way. "Mom, I don't want another kid's toy. Especially 'cause he's got no friends to play with. Not since he went into the cold water such a long time ago." Offering no further explanation, Helene's son pulled the glass door closed behind him.

"What was that about?" asked Tristan.

"I'm not sure," mumbled Helene, wondering how Oscar had guessed she was planning to give him the ball she had found at the castle. Was he implying the toy had belonged to the child who had died on the *S.S. Clallam*? Was this the boy he talked about seeing after their visit to the castle?

Knowing her skills as a journalist were all but useless in understanding her son's ability to sense what other people could not, Helene instead decided to concentrate on the parts of her life she could control. Like whether to continue spending time with a clerk who had revealed a penchant for meddling in municipal politics.

Closing her eyes to soak up a brief appearance by the November sun, Helene resolved to keep Tristan around for a while. Despite the fact that Alex would always be her closest confidant, being married was inevitably going to make her less available. So, just like the city was adding more housing stock, maybe it was time for Helene to add to her roster of friends. Like a home, a good companion was a safe harbour for the soul.

As the silence stretched out between the pair, Helene was pleased that Tristan made no attempt to break it. Her thoughts had turned to another choice that lay ahead—what to do about her mother's house in Edmonton and the debris from her neglected childhood.

If the recent encounter with a murderer had taught her anything, it was to be wary of disturbing the past. Ludmilla's attempts to seek vengeance for being abandoned as a single mother ultimately hurt her own daughter more than the actions of any other. A loving mother was now behind bars. A father Zofia knew only as a friend was dead.

Old wounds were like dark clouds that lingered harmlessly on the ocean horizon for decades, but once unleashed, a sorrow's storm would drown the innocent as surely as the guilty. And an act of retribution was a lifeboat that promised escape from a soul's tempest but could instead founder in the tides of despair and death.

Resolving that her own friend's punishment had gone on long enough, Helene gingerly stood up and retrieved a second blanket from the house. After passing a grateful Tristan the fleecy covering, the two sat side-by-side in sympathetic appreciation for the warmth of polyester and pleasing company.

Acknowledgments

This book would not possess the precise details of the foundering of the *S.S. Clallam* without the incredible input of Pacific Northwest historian Erik Kosick. A regular contributor to the Washington State Historical Society's *Columbia* magazine, he has studied the *Clallam* foundering for over a decade. Details such as the vessel decks having stools instead of chairs were contributed by Kosick.

The newspaper passages included in this novel are from the archives of the *The Daily Colonist*.

Some of the passengers who died on the *S.S. Clallam* are buried in Ross Bay Cemetery but there is no memorial to the lives lost.

Gratitude to my editor Audrey McKinnon and proofreaders Rayna Corner, Andrea Fajrajsl and Laura Paetkau.

Special thanks to my cousin Cally Pouliot and friend Jennifer Duggan for supporting my writing.

Credit to Dave Lackmanec for his fabulous cover design.

And love always to my first draft reader and tireless companion in my battle with ovarian cancer, Jason Sokoloski.

If you enjoyed this book, please leave a review on Amazon or Goodreads. Reviews are critical to the success of indie authors.

I love hearing from readers: jeanworks@yahoo.ca

To see photos of the places described in this book you can visit my instagram: @snufflewort_
                twitter: @snufflewort

Manufactured by Amazon.ca
Bolton, ON